Black *Butterflies*

Thanks to my brother Graeme for his belief and support, and to my mother Isabel, for supporting me even when she didn't quite believe in me.

Black
Butterflies

John R Gordon

First published in September 1993
by GMP Publishers Ltd
P O Box 247, London N17 9QR, England

A CIP catalogue record for this book
is available from the British Library

ISBN 0 85449 199 6

Distributed in North America by InBook
P O Box 120470, East Haven, CT 06512, USA

Distributed in Australia by Bulldog Books
P O Box 155, Broadway, NSW 2007, Australia

Printed and bound in the EC
by Firmin-Didot (France)
Groupe Hérissey (24659)

To Rikki
Lover
Brother
&
Friend

Prologue

THE PALL-BEARERS were white. Even in that, Floyd's mother had betrayed him, and outraged those who knew and loved him, one final time. *He wouldn't have wanted white pall-bearers,* Wesley thought. *It should've been my shoulder under the coffin. Mine and Tony's and Mikey's. And the coffin would've been light as a bird because we would've been bearing the weight of the wood alone, Floyd's body being borne up by other powers.* And the mourners should not have been dry beneath their black umbrellas watching as the sky's tears soaked the white men and stained their suits. That realisation made Wesley close his umbrella and let the rain become his tears as it covered his face, and the spasming air his grief. *They shouldn't have been white men*, he thought. *At least that.*

He put his arm around Sharon's waist, gathering the folds of her white coat under his fingers, and stared at the slice of polished granite at the head of the grave. It wasn't Floyd's gravestone. Not to Wesley, not yet. And it wouldn't be even when he came back there a year and a half later, drunk, in the navy-blue suit he had worn for the wedding. The gravel had hissed like the sea under his dragging feet, he remembered, and the full moon had cast his shadow blue among the shadows of the railings, caging it there. And he had knelt beside the grave, not praying. Not witnessing. Just acknowledging: that he was as trapped by the earth that lay between them as the coffin that could not rise and soar on the night winds. He had lain there waiting for some denial of that earth; for some tiny movement or sound, his heart pounding against his chest and against the earth he lay sprawled upon, wishing that like the rainwater he could soak into the warm and throbbing soil and sink down. And later and only just before the dawn he had come home with wet patches on his knees, leaving behind not the dead but an empty bottle of Bourbon, and taking away not the fact of the death, but a pocketful of green marble chips. And when Sharon had asked him where he had been, he had told her the first lie of their marriage, less than four months in.

He looked down at the dark, wet, glittering earth. Soon his turn would come around and he would have to bend and take a handful of that earth and let it fall with a dull thud onto the lid of the coffin below, the dead noise symbolic of the lack of resonance in the body beneath it, unable to accept the fact of the death then, just as he would be unable to accept it a year and a half later. And after Sharon had let the earth fall from her palm (she believing totally in the fact of the death, stronger than Wesley in that, and more certain), he had taken her arm and led her away from under the black and staring eyes of Floyd's mother. Floyd's mother, who had not let them come to the service. Floyd's mother who did not want them to come even to the burial because she saw only shame in it.

When Sharon had phoned Mrs Philips from the hospital that night, to tell her that Floyd was in intensive care *(needles in his arms and tubes in his face up his ass and in his dick, his chest rising and falling but not breathing the machine breathing the pain falling from his face like overcooked fish from the bone)* she told Wesley that Mrs Philips had just said, (even though she who always went to bed at ten o'clock had been woken at one in the morning), "I'll be there," and put the phone down. But she never came, and Floyd died without regaining consciousness, leaving Wesley to believe that what she had really said was, "Time is fair," meaning fair to her; that it had brought her what she had been waiting for. And he knew when she did not come that she was sitting at home, next to the telephone but not waiting for it, her Bible open on her lap, saying to herself over and over, he believed, "The Lord giveth and the Lord taketh away," saying it not with humility but with pride; that her shame was finally to be cleansed. And at the funeral she saw only herself, the oak in the fury of the storm, unyielding and unbroken. "I, like Job," he believed she said, "tested beyond endurance, I endure."

Wesley twists on the settee, one arm dead and bent up behind his back, whirling dizzily in the suspirating darkness, his staleness oozing into the close air, beery breath filling the room, inside still stumbling blindly, the pub door hitting his shoulder, drinking with friends and then alone, stained glass doors banging and echoing, trailing feet then jacket along the floor and going not to the bedroom but to the settee, which says everything about his life right now, and hunching to his chin a blanket that he didn't find himself, which says the rest.

He wakes suddenly in the small hours, his heart torn in the dark and airlessness, knowing that the woman he had so much wanted to make love to last night is sleeping by herself in the next room, her head resting so lightly on the pillow as to barely crease it, much less leave stains on the clean, scented linen or pollute the scented air with stale body-smells. *The shorts and the lager, the lager and beer and the Thunderbird,* he thinks. *I wish I could throw up.* His stomach, his aching stomach, is spreading bloated outwards and floating unsteadily a foot above where it ought to be. *Just me and Floyd, going out drinking, just like we did.* He is crying now, and he says out loud, "it's the drink man, just the drink," knowing as he says it, knowing because he says it, that the drink is nothing to do with it. "Floyd," he whispers, thinking, *I am the thief on the cross, the one that turned Christ down, the one who saw but couldn't believe. And Sharon, lying in the other room not awake now, and if she's lucky not dreaming either, she's the right thief, the one who took the violence and even the death as what was to be, who faced it and married me so she could keep hold of what was left behind of him. And Floyd James Philips is Christ and like Christ he is dead and like Christ he died by violence and maybe that was his destiny. And maybe we knew that all the time. Maybe we knew it all the time but couldn't accept it.*

In the other room Sharon lies wide awake in the dark, staring up at the empty ceiling, listening to Wesley shifting about on the settee, asking herself not why he beat her up the day before, but why not sooner? Or later? She can't sleep for trying to think of something that is an answer to that and not just an excuse. She struggles ineffectually for ordinary words when it is poetry she needs. But she is too tired for the poetry she is thinking of, and not yet and hopefully never tired enough for the rhythms of the blues: It is only the frustration of a relationship gone sour. And she knows it is strange and possibly even perverse, but it is only now that Wesley is back that she feels she can go to sleep.

Chapter One

WESLEY CROSSES THE factory floor and it seems to him that the endless rows of stacked paint-tins and the forklifts part like in all the movies, like in all the Westerns, so that the line he is walking is straight. And the rage that has been clenched inside him for days, months, for five years maybe, is opening, curling back tensile and strong and talonned. It is no longer under his control. He has reached the edge now; he is walking along the very edge. A violent shudder runs up his body but he keeps on walking.

Ron Gates isn't facing him, is turned away. He doesn't even notice Wesley until Wesley grips his shoulder and spins him round, and even then he is smiling, like it's all a big joke to call a man a boy a thief and a liar and abuse the colour of his skin. And Wesley hits him hard, five years of waiting in his twisting wrist and arm, and for a second the smile looks stitched on and then it falls. Wesley's nostrils flare like a dragon's as he hits Ron Gates in the gut, the fat of Ron's gut surprisingly hard against his fist, and he is well over the edge now.

Ron Gates falls back, hits the floor, scrabbling and cursing, too fat and too winded to jump up straightaway. And for a moment the black men and the white men watch him where he's fallen, and Wesley standing over him is all black men now just as Ron Gates is all white men, and the black men and the white men are paralyzed by the stretch of history that that entails.

Then the moment is over, and some of the white men hurry

forward to help the fallen shop steward. Although they don't dare to touch Wesley they don't want the fight, so as they help Ron Gates up they hold him back also. But in holding him back they open him up too, letting Wesley get a second punch in, and a third, the five years wild now and tearing through his blood. And then his black mates are grabbing him, pulling him back from Ron and trying to pull him away from the edge, his mate Stan's voice hoarse in his ear, flecks of saliva in his ear, Stan's lips brushing his ear:

"Chill out, man. Chill out, for Chrissakes."

And below him Ron Gates is shouting, screaming almost, convulsing against the arms gripping him, his hate burst into flames and shapeless and out of control. And Wesley doesn't hear what he's saying but he knows anyway because he's heard it all a thousand times before; and his anger keeps on floating out of his eyes, shining and endless.

And the brothers hold him tight like they feel the wildness in themselves, like they know that if they let him go he will try and kill Ron Gates because right now that's all he can do, even though Ron Gates' racist shit same old shit anyway only a little worse today is not what's made him angry, nor is it the job even, the forklift: "About as challenging as going for a crap," he had once said, and then realised he had spent six years going for one long crap; not anger at that though all these things have always made him angry: It is anger at his life. And today he is going to change it.

The wildness in him slows as he is held there, and sinks back down. He stops struggling, goes limp, as if it has gone. But it is still there, under pressure: The wildness, the anger and the chaos.

He fakes calmness.

Gradually the brothers let him go, their hands staying close to stop him falling, like a child, but into violence, not onto the floor. Ron is still trying to get free, kicking out at Wesley, but his legs are too short and the white men are holding him too tight. Wesley stands in front of him, hands hanging loose, palms open, at his sides. He says nothing. Then he turns away. His black mates part to let him through and for a moment he is a hero. Someone pats him on the back.

"We be'ind you all de way, man. 'E shouldn'ta call you tief, man. Motherfucker shouldn'ta call you tief."

And then they are all behind him. He crosses the factory floor, passing forklifts like dinosaurs, walking out on his job, walking out on his life. On a stack of pallets a radio is playing. It is Billie Holiday singing:

"I'm travelling light
Because my man has gone
So from now on
I'm travelling light. . . ."

* * * * *

Fourth of November 1981

"Hey, Wes, man, you goin' to Carol's party?"

"I thought it was Claire's, man."

"Well it was, yeah, but they gonna 'ave it round Carol's yard cos 'er old man wouldn't let 'er 'ave it at 'is place, innit."

"Yeah man, I'll be there. You goin'?"

Floyd nodded, gazing out through the wire-mesh around the playground over the dual carriageways, into the blue-grey haze beyond them. Wesley stuck his fingers through the mesh and leaned into it so that it pressed against his face and moulded to the shape of his thighs and crotch and the palms of his hands, and touched the wire with the tip of his tongue. It tingled. He looked round at Floyd.

"Carol still goin' out with that John geezer?" he asked.

"Na, man, that's old news."

A week old, Wesley thought, wondering like he wondered every time any of his mates wanted to lay her, and even though he felt an electrical current tingling at the base of his balls when they said it, Why her? Because to him her natural blonde hair,

13

her solarium tan and her cheeks (sculpted by dragging so stylishly on so many cigarettes), even her breasts and buttocks and even her brains (Business Studies at college), just showed him how cold and hard and joyless she was, taking her warmth from the black boys who lost it gaining something worth far less. Taking it from Floyd. Wesley called her a hard-to-get slag, which meant she'd go down on anyone if it made her look good enough. Or dump them. He knew Floyd had the look she'd like: He was only fifteen but he had a great body from running for the school and working out, and his skin was smooth and aubergine-dark. Wesley knew Carol liked black on blonde and he knew Floyd would like it too. *Go down on him and dump him*, Wesley thought, and the thought made him burn with guilt and bitterness.

He watched Floyd shaking his curls in the yellow autumn sunlight, the highlights flashing gold in his wet-perm, the sun behind his head like a halo, dazzling.

"You comin' round to my place after school, man?" Wesley asked. "I got to fix me sister's tea anyway, yeah."

"Dunno, man," Floyd replied. "Maybe." Then he smiled. "Yeah, I'll come, man. Sweet."

Wesley knew he had sounded unwilling because he never wanted to go home and felt guilty about it. He had to pretend that he would've wanted to normally and today was just an exception. Really he came around to Wesley's most evenings after school. Wesley's mother was an SRN working a lot of nights, and because his sister Trisha wasn't old enough to be allowed to use the deep-fat frier, Wesley had to cook her tea anyway, so it wasn't awkward for Floyd to be there. That morning his mother had peeled some potatoes and left them in a bowl to be chipped. There was a packet lasagne in the fridge too, so he didn't have to think about what to eat, which was good: He knew he wouldn't feel hungry when it was ready anyway. He never did before a party.

As Wesley and Floyd were leaving school that afternoon they saw Alan Baxter, the sports teacher, standing by the gate.

Floyd ignored him as they passed by, but after they had gone just a little way down the road Baxter called,

"Are you going to sprint practice, Philips?"

"No sir, I got exams this term. I gotta revise. Come on, man," he breathed to Wesley, "before he starts up."

They hurried off. Once they were round the corner, Floyd looked back.

"Fuck the bastard," he spat.

"Don't you want to be a sprinter, then, man?"

"Yeah, man. I just don't want to be a moron is all."

They walked on in silence, kicking through piles of rotting brown and purple leaves as they crossed the park, soaking the bottoms of their trousers. A group of skinheads were playing football on one of the pitches. Their shouts were muffled by the cold, damp air.

"D'you reckon you'll do it then?" Floyd asked, out of the empty air.

"What, get off with someone? Dunno. Yeah." Wesley's sports bag started to dig into his back so he shifted the weight of it onto his right shoulder, and wondered if he could be bothered to do his homework before going out that evening. It was a history essay on the causes of the First World War, which he didn't understand and didn't care about anyway.

When he had said that to Mikey, whose baby dreads were just beginning to sprout long enough to need a tam, that he didn't care, Mikey had replied,

"Who di fuck waan fi know 'bout some white-man war, man. De more a dem dead di better. Chuh." He spat on the ground. "Don't do it, man. I-man tell you, is just imperialist shit."

In Mikey's eyes Wesley could see the reflections of visions in the sky, blue and shining and vast.

He knew Mikey was right, but he did the essay anyway. It turned out that the war was all about the Europeans getting land, mostly in Africa. From the way it was written in the blue history book, *Europe 1830-1945*, you wouldn't think the land

15

belonged to anybody before that. So Mikey had really been right. But Wesley felt no desire to breath fire from Jah's nostrils and dream strange dreams of gold and dressing like kings, or mask bitterness with the fervour of a new church, finding Christ's face in that of an Ethiopian despot, a man who hid in fear in his private jet when he saw his loyal followers massed on the hot tarmac at Kingston airport, who gave Bob Marley a ring which (he said, and why shouldn't it have been true) burnt him sometimes. No. He just wanted to get some qualifications and start earning. That was his vision.

He pulled himself out of the bath. His school tie, white shirt, charcoal-grey trousers and underwear lay in a crumpled heap on the bathroom floor. He dried himself quickly and carelessly, and sprayed himself all over with Right Guard. He didn't have to shave really, but he slapped on the Brut anyway. He looked in the steamy bathroom mirror, wincing at a couple of spots on his forehead. After scrubbing his face with soap and a flannel the spots stood out much more brightly than they had before. He swore and gave up. Then he pulled on a pair of very brief neon-orange underpants and flexed in front of the mirror doubtfully. He carried on dressing; white tee-shirt, cut away under the arms but not around the neck, gold chain, skin-tight denims, white socks, low-cut black Italian shoes, black leather bomber jacket, fingerless black leather gloves, and wraparound fifties sunshades (if he had the nerve to wear them). He looked in the mirror one final time, adjusted his belt, then hurried out of the house, pausing at the front door to shout, "Bye, Trish," to his twelve-year-old sister, who was watching the TV in the front room. "Go to bed at ten, you hear?"

"See ya," she called back, not looking away from the screen.

Wesley had said he'd meet Floyd at the bus stop at eight. He looked at his watch. *Shit*. Five to eight. He ran all the way to the stop, getting there just as the bus was pulling in. Floyd was leaning there, cool and tough and sexy and lean, waiting for him. Wesley touched Floyd's hand and shook it. His crotch stirred slightly. Floyd smelt of bitter oil and cocoa butter. Wesley wanted to press his warm, smooth cheek to Floyd's and smell and feel his skin, so he hugged him, just for a moment. Floyd staggered and laughed, the gold flashing in his mouth making Wesley's heart cramp for a second, then relax.

"Let's get on the bus, man," Floyd said. Wesley bought the tickets and they climbed to the top floor. Floyd led the way, leaving Wesley gazing at his muscular ass as they climbed. Once Wesley almost stumbled and buried his face in it. He steadied himself, then wished he hadn't. But they were upstairs before he'd thought about it, and the thought was gone.

"What'd you bring to drink, man?" Wesley asked, pointing at the carrier-bag sitting between Floyd's feet.

"Southern Comfort," Floyd replied. They were sitting right at the front of the upstairs of the bus. Behind them was empty except for an old wino in a trench-coat who sat at the back muttering to himself, oblivious to everything except its lurch and judder. Floyd dragged on a long white filterless cigarette, staring out into the bleary night. Wesley shoved his hands deep into the pockets of his leather jacket, fingering his keys, paper hankies and a small square packet. His face burned with embarassment as he remembered going into the pub and slipping into the Gents, walking up to the machine, washing his hands as the door banged open and a fat man went up to the urinals, trying not to meet the man's eyes as he wasted time waiting for him to go. Finally he inserted the money and pocketed the packet. His heart was hammering as he strolled out. Of course no one turned to look at him or anything. But that was why he'd had to hurry to meet Floyd: He hadn't really allowed himself time because he had been nervous about having to go into the Royal Park. It was one of the rough pubs on the corner of the Estate, where they came down heavily on underage drinkers, and Wesley had been afraid of being thrown out by one of the barmen the moment he opened the door. But it was Friday night and they were already busy serving and he hadn't needed to go up to the bar.

He looked up at his reflection in the bus's windscreen. His eyes were black smears on a weeping face. Behind it the sky was a polluted orange, lit dully by the synthetic glare of the city.

"This is it," said Floyd. Wesley had never been to Carol's before. It was near Clapham Junction, one of those three-storied blocks of flats put up in the shadows of the towerblocks. "Number 53." They bounced nervously up the concrete stairwell, Floyd leading the way. Just faintly they could hear rhythms in the air. Floyd stopped at one of the doors and pushed the bell.

"Come on," he muttered to himself, pressing the doorbell again. He was dressed all in white, his pleated trousers buckled at the waist. The door opened before he had taken his finger off the button and music flooded out into the night. It was Claire who answered it. She smiled brightly, running a hand through her spiky, tinted hair.

"Hallo, Wesley." She kissed him coyly on the cheek. "Hi Floyd." He held up the carrier bag for her to take. There was the sound of a plate breaking somewhere behind her and she sighed and turned and disappeared into the dimly-lit interior. They followed her inside. Floyd closed the door behind them and unzipped his jacket. The pulsating music, its rhythm insisting and hypnotic, drew the two youths into the crowded, heaving living-room.

Time moved like a worm crawling: Each minute, each track, was long, each hour was short. The atmosphere became airless and charged as the crowd heaved rythmically together. A million minor social fluctuations had taken place by then, and Wesley was dancing slowly with a girl who had been in the year above him at school called Liz. She was doing a secretarial course now at the Tec and drank sweet white wine with orange juice in it. She had just dropped her boyfriend because (at least this was how she told it) he never washed and he was a real wally, a real prat. Wesley wanted her to stop talking. She had a deep tan and straggly bleached-blonde hair, and a thinness that made her look like models do, at least to his eyes then. Their bodies were sealed together, arms encircling each other, she not reacting as his hands moved down to her buttocks. They were alone there, just like all the others were alone, sealed in their little groups, a unified crowd to the eyes only. The music went on and on, a drug coursing through their systems, a big space in a tiny room, and Wesley, forgetting himself, began to become heavily aroused. He felt the pressure against the line of his underpants and realised that she would feel it too. Embarrassed, he tried to move his hips away, but hers remained in place. He stopped dancing.

"D'you want to go, then?" she asked. She seemed so self-assured, seemed to know everything. He felt awed. He swallowed.

"We could go to my place, yeah?" He spoke with assumed calmness, and the even deepness of his voice was shocking to him. "Me mum's working nights."

"Alright."

She fetched her own coat. They slipped out without saying goodbye, unnoticed he thought, but of course it was all round school the next day. His desire dwindled on the bus and panic rose up in him. His hand kept touching the packet of condoms in his jacket pocket. *This is it*, he thought, his stomach knotting, thinking back to all those porn movies he had seen that suddenly seemed very vague and distant now; the distance from the voyeur to the viewed.

The bus doors opened pneumatically and Wesley and Liz stepped out onto the harsh and brittle street. Wesley felt the driver looking at him as he got off, saying to himself, *you're about to score, son, your first time isn't it, isn't it. Hope you know what to do, son, it's really obvious you've never done it before, really obvious, really obvious that tonight's the big night. Let's hope she doesn't know you don't know, that she knows enough to know how to make you look like you know, make you look good, cos it she doesn't t all the magazines and books won't help you get it up and keep it up.*

The air was cold and still. Inbetween one state of mind and

another, they said nothing as they walked up Wesley's street. As he slid his key into the lock he put a finger to his lips and whispered, "Me sister'll be asleep." Liz giggled noisily. "She's only twelve," he hissed. The door shuddered open, and they crept in, making all the surreptitious noises that drunk people always make when they try to sneak into a house without waking anyone up. Wesley snicked on the light in the lounge.

"D'you want a coffee?" he asked after a moment of embarrassed silence.

"Yeah," she replied. "Why not?" Tiredness had erased her glamorous surface and she seemed quite plain now as she stood behind him, her hands on his shoulders, swaying.

"I don't really want a coffee, Wesley." She ran her hands down the outsides of his thighs. He felt excited, but he didn't want her. He didn't know what he did want, but she was *there*, wanting him, or something she thought he had. They kissed in a tonguing, dilatory way.

"Shall we go to your room?"

"No, man. Let's do it here."

He was suddenly ashamed of his small room, the crumpled school-clothes, the posters of pop-stars and an old painting he had done when he was a kid, the dusty model aeroplanes hanging on threads from the ceiling. He couldn't do it there.

They began to undress, slowly and clumsily, exposing themselves under the harsh ceiling light. When they were down to their underwear Wesley said, "I got a rubber." He hoped that she'd come up with some reason for not using it because he might mess up putting it on, might mess up both of them like he had a few weeks ago, when he had bought a packet just to try them on. He'd totally wasted one and had to pull and stretch the other one a lot before he could look at his sheathed dick black under the latex, too sexual to look stupid at that moment, but stupid later, stupid now. *Some of the lads use clingfilm*, he thought. *I'll have to do that if I can't get the rubbers on..* Then: *But I can't walk to the kitchen bollock-naked, with a hard-on, and tear a piece of cling-film off that I watched me mum wrap food with, ripping it off along the serrated edge.*

Liz's eyes met his. "That's really considerate, Wesley," she said, and he wondered if she screwed around a lot and most of the other guys weren't, her voice was so matter of fact, as if he had just helped her on with her coat or something, and why that should matter. He started fumbling with the packet, slipping out the foil rectangles inside, only taking down his underpants when she looked down at her own, wondering as he rolled the rubber down over his half-erection where Floyd was and what he was doing, wondering if he was doing this too, stretched out on top of some girl, lean and hard, taking her up and up, and for a moment it all meant something. But every move Wesley made made what was happening mean less and less. Like how he couldn't reach out to undress her the way he knew he should; like being too unsure of her body to do much foreplay except squeezing her breasts, too shocked somehow to suck or bite them, and looking into her face, suddenly so unknowable, wondering if he was doing the right thing, kissing her so he wouldn't have to see her face, and shutting his eyes as if he hoped that, unimpeded by sight, his body would know what to do. But one of his heels pressed against the armchair where Trisha had been sitting when he went out, so he had to keep that leg bent at the knee, and keep the other one straight so it wouldn't bump against the coffee-table, and cramp kept touching him along the length of his thighs. *What am I doing here?* he wondered, knowing it was a stupid question, feeling stupid for thinking it even. But perhaps it wasn't really such a stupid question after all, seeing as it was the one all religions tried to answer, even right down to *this room* and *this girl*.. And as he moved his hips against hers and began to pump them in response to her chipped red nails biting into his buttocks, he felt relieved that he wasn't going to come immediately and wondered if he would come at all, because if he could, then all that relentless pounding would pass him off as a good screw if nothing more, and although nothing could be more real than the body heaving against his, the lie and the rumour were eventually more important.

Maybe she'd had an orgasm too, although she hadn't screamed. He didn't ask; he just pretended he'd fallen asleep straight away and held her loosely for a while with his eyes closed. After what seemed like hours, she gently lifted his arm off her and got to her feet. He peeped as she dressed, listening to her small sounds that sounded large in the night. She sighed, another small sound, but large in meaning and not because of the darkness. She said goodbye quietly and left without kissing him. After he heard the front door click shut he went up to his bedroom, pulling his briefs on at the foot of the stairs, and lay on his bed with the light off, his mind troubled.

And he remembered now what he had remembered then, lying there in the dark, stories Floyd had told him; about how Floyd came from Haiti a long time back, his family did: how he had a grandfather whose name was Dellacre which was Delacroix which was the name of the man who had owned his grandfather's father from back when they still had slavery. And his grandfather Eugene who he had met only once in his whole life when he was very young, who had told him stories about Gede and Legbe and about zombies in the rustling canefields, and the story of the man he had given salt to in a goat curry who had run screaming through the cane to a churchyard and started clawing down into the green earth with his bare hands. *And the loa like snakes with the faces of Catholic saints that he told me (Floyd told me) were his loa, and how he was a scientist like his grandfather, who could look at the sun without blinking and whistle and call them out (the loa) to dig his fields. And I dream them now: They stay unseen but I know they're chained there in the dark, whispering canefields, serpents with the faces of saints. And I run and I run but however far I go I can hear the whispering of the cane or is it the loa all around me.*

Other thoughts began to float around Wesley's head like flies around the lampshade on a hot day: *Five years. Five years even more meaningless now, that leave me only older, he was think-*

22

ing, and it's Monday morning and I have been taken down and Sharon has been taken down from our crosses (that cast their long black shadows even over our graves) that are not the true Cross but themselves only shadows of it, and we have been buried. We look across at each other in the dark with our spirit eyes that can see through anything, and wish that our hands were not bound to our sides, so that we could pray for resurrection and not lie for eternity in cramped, airless boxes under the ground like the others whose voices filter through the rain-soaked earth that surrounds us.

It was five years since Floyd James Philips had died and Wesley had been crucified. *Without even being religious*, he thought, *without even believing, I have borne the pain.*

He thought about Sharon that morning, looking in her long white dressing-gown and with her hair piled up in a geometrically-arranged white towel, like some African noblewoman or priestess. He had watched her move gracefully through the kitchen, an alienating vision of beauty, though it was not her beauty that had alienated him. It was the way the whole flat and everything in it seemed to flow out of the whiteness of that fabric which wrapped her as lightning wraps the storm. He knew he no longer belonged there, and every movement she made in the air that was hers since yesterday, when they had been shouting at each other over nothing, over the stupid medicine cabinet with the broken hinge. When she hadn't said, "If Floyd was here," but had got very near to it, asking him why he couldn't lift a finger for her in that way that made the unsaid said, him saying, "I don't need this shit, man, fuck this shit," and staring into her eyes for the last time although he didn't know it then.

Even after he had mended the door she wouldn't leave off, standing there so full of the pride and grace that came from certainty, almost screaming, saying, "I work all day too you know, and clean the whole flat and do all the washing and cooking. Did you know that? Did you know?" and he was shouting back, "you should have married some fucking Jeffrey Archer. You should've married some fucking millionaire," until her voice and his voice filled the room with words and he had to hit her just to make some space in the crowded air.

He had slapped her round the face.

Not hard — even as the flat of his hand touched her face he slung it away in shock — but he had never hit her before. Unlike a lot of the men he knew, he had never felt he had that right. And now like recast bronze her face was new and burning hot and shone, and his hand was burnt and throbbing, and he knew that the reasons a lot of men give for hitting their wives were nothing to do with it, were only lies.

She had sat down heavily on the floor, shocked, her caramel-coloured skirt pushed up around her thighs, and then there was silence. She had stayed where she was then, very quiet and very still, watching him moving around the room, waiting for him to get out. And as soon as he could, he had gone.

He knew she would never forgive him and that he had no right to expect her to, anymore than he had had the right to take out everything that was wrong in his life on her. But it wasn't forgiveness he needed anyway but understanding: *She has always understood me,* he thought, *something about me, better than anyone, so she knows I didn't hit her even though my hand is still tingling.* And he knew it wasn't the pain that made the difference to her because she was strong and bore pain without flinching; it was the breaking of the promise they had made to each other the night Floyd died, which was unspoken and without words, and which Wesley only understood now because it had been broken.

And then he was at the funeral again, watching the rain like glass veins covering the skin of the broken brown earth risen over the body, thinking, *it could be me. By rope or needle or plastic tube and running engine. It could be me.*

Chapter Two

WESLEY'S HEART POUNDED as he looked down on the dual carriageway and his breath was ragged. He had run all the way here, to be here, on this arching footbridge beneath a wide flyover, saying to himself even as he left the factory, *it has to be this one place and nowhere else but here,* as if he was already here and this bridge was the beginning of all his thoughts. He leaned heavily against the railing, bracing himself with his hands and looking down, leaning so heavily that maybe he would slip and fall if he was only careless enough, the rail was only as high as his crotch. And his breathing was still tearing his throat not because of the running (which was nothing to him who trained every day), but because of the wild beauty of the spiralling descent below him. The wind was blowing strong here, strong enough to maybe tip a man over if he was standing near enough to the edge. Wesley gripped the handrail tight, watching the cars like beetles glittering on the curve of the road below, and under the flyover the roar of their passing echoed around him like the whispering of spirits. He closed his eyes and listened to their voices floating above his head, tempting him, but he wouldn't and couldn't let go of the handrail whatever they promised, only grip it more tightly still.

Slowly he opened his eyes, squinting in the glare of the new moment, looking down as from a mountain, perhaps, over the kingdoms of the air, seeing them all, all at once. He watched the cars flowing in opposite directions for a while and then, indecisively, let go of the handrail and stepped back from the edge. And then there was only the rumble of cars and the sound of the wind.

Unlocked, his arms began to tremble uncontrollably, and the cold wind blew a deep chill into him. It was making his ears ache, so he turned his face into it and let it beat tears from his slitted eyes as he looked acoss the rumbling dual carriageway, across the city, and into the blue haze beyond it all. And then he crossed the bridge and started to head towards it.

The streets he was walking through now were masked with memories, and each step he took took him further into the past. He remembered waiting on that corner, waiting for Floyd.

He reached up and fingered the gold stud in his left earlobe. He and Floyd had got their ears pierced at the same time, for a laugh, for a dare, and for a self-conscious coming of age, the pain the initiation and the sleeper the tattoo. He remembered Floyd's cousin Tony's girlfriend, with her tattooed parrakeet and punk make-up, chilling his ear with ice and alcohol before pushing the needle into the squeaking cork and it hurt like hell. And Wesley flinched but didn't say a thing, and Floyd said "Fuck" when it went through but didn't move at all and his (Floyd's) ear bled for days and Wesley's didn't bleed at all. Wesley's mum hadn't minded but Floyd's mother was a Jehovah's Witness and upright in the ways of the Lord, and for her wearing gold was whorish or like a sailor and sailors were whores to her too. The whole street had heard word-for-word the argument they had had over that, she and Floyd, Floyd saying *Bitch, Motherfucking bitch, I hope you die cos then I won't kill you, won't fucking kill you*, she saying *Bad and Lazy and Good-for-nothing* and things like that. And, *You should have died. You should be dead* (and Floyd never said but someone said she had the carving knife out then, like Isaac she would have thought, or just a madwoman. But maybe no one saw it really. But maybe it was true just the same).

After that, Floyd had stayed at Wesley's house for three days, acting all the time as if nothing had happened. And then he had gone back to his mother's house still wearing the earring, and there was no argument. But all the same, that bitterness remained between them that was not, and never would be, cast out. *And maybe*, Wesley thought, *that was why he became a boxer.*

The streets were narrow with the past here, and the air was close with petrol fumes. Everything was smaller, closer together than he remembered it. He wondered what it would feel like to stand on top of a mountain.

When he was just a kid they had lived in a two-room flat with a toilet and a bathroom at the end of the corridor, him and his mother. He couldn't remember much about it except that you could never get away from the smell of the cooking, and so for him poverty was the smell of food in the living-room. His mother would shout at him when she was tired, which was mostly, and she cried a lot: He used to listen to her crying to herself softly after she thought he was asleep. Then she would rub her eyes and get up and heat a pan of milk, and sometimes she would know he was awake and they would share a cup (always a cup, never a mug, because that was why she came to England; that *education*) and she would tell him stories about JA and about their family there. He couldn't remember them now, not the words or most of the names; only that they were a little pool of blue and green that pushed the shadows apart. And she would sleep in that light and beneath those green leaves.

It's strange, he thought. She looks much younger now. But she hadn't been much more than a child herself then, and her age had only now grown up to her experience and wisdom. Pressure: Those two shitty little rooms, with carpets with mould on their undersides, and the settee still marked from where the flea-powder couldn't be brushed out, the fleas not from cat or dog, his mother asking herself, "Don't no one 'ave pride inna dis 'ere country at all?" as she puffed the powder down the cracks. "Lord 'ave mercy." She hated it, the grey and the dirt and the black tidemarks on the concrete every time it rained.

Ruffs on the city's shoulders, she had said once. Lord 'ave mercy.

The flat was in an old run-down Victorian terrace in Streatham, and the walls were partitions so thin that you could hear someone cough in the next-door flat, and the creak of their bed-springs.

If anyone ever asked him what was his lucky number, Wesley would always say eight, because they left that place on the eighth of the month, of whatever month it had been. Uncle Marcus, with his wide smile and always smelling of cigars, had got them up the Council housing list somehow. Perhaps that was why he had always hated Uncle Marcus; because he owed him a debt that he couldn't repay. Or perhaps it was the way Uncle Marcus would accept a glass of sherry from the bottle his mother always kept in the sideboard, never drinking it except with guests, and watch his mother's buttocks as she bent to pour the sickly amber liquid. Once, Uncle Marcus had caught Wesley watching him watching her, and he had smiled a smile that was not quite a leer and, twinkling his eyes, had said, "Come here Wesley." His voice was deep and rich, a preacher's voice: "You're going to be a man soon, my boy. What do you want to be?" He had hated Uncle Marcus for asking that, too. He couldn't remember what he had replied, but he knew what he had wanted to say: *Not you.*

Before him stretched a long, uneven line of yellow planks fencing off a building site where some houses used to be, and then a low multi-storey car-park. Beyond that his eye was caught by a worn neon sign on iron rods that spelt out

P
L
A
Z
A

The cinema was showing *Terminator II* and there was a fat blonde girl sitting behind the glass. Everything was like it was when he was last here, when he and Floyd were fourteen, sneaking into Xs, trying to look tall and broad or being bold as brass to get in. Even the girl was the same. Somehow he had expected, after all, that it would have been closed down and sealed up, made into a monument to Floyd James Philips. Like all of it: All his past was flowers picked for the wreath and his present the wake which was now almost over. And he was holding white orchids in his hands but there was no monument to scatter them in front of so he crushed them, and the dew on their leaves was the tears on his upturned face as he stared up at the neon sign black against the grey sky.

But the cinema was open just like it always was, the same girl at the cashdesk and really the same film, it didn't, had never mattered, and he was fourteen again, waiting in the rain by the side-door just before the film started, hoping to slip in unnoticed, into the warmth. But he didn't remember the films, not one of them. What he remembered was the waiting, the uncertainty, and then the fear of being spotted and getting thrown out; sitting low in the red velvet seats with broken hinges and looking straight ahead, waiting for Pearl & Dean and wishing you'd gone for a piss beforehand. And Score, tall and dark and glowering-handsome in his tuxedo and bow-tie, who'd sometimes leave the firedoor off its latch for them to sneak in through. They'd know they were in luck, him and Floyd, if there were a couple of girls hanging round outside too, although the girls always squealed and giggled as Score ushered them in, careless of being caught by the other usher, a pinch-faced bitch who'd throw you out just for talking. But then she had been too embarrassed to stop Floyd from screwing some girl in the back row one Saturday night. ("She can't have *not* noticed, man," he'd said afterwards, laughing. "She *can't* have. Like, there was this box of popcorn jammed under the seat, so every time we move it makes like a crunching sound, and the chair squeaked like shit too. Man." And he had stopped laughing and rubbed his eyes, then taken another swig from the can that sat between his thighs, while Wesley looked at his crotch to see if he had a hard-on and thought that he did, while he, Wesley, shifted around on the seat to try and get his own wedged less uncomfortably down his trouser-leg.)

Score didn't care what they got up to, except for slashing the seats and stuff like that. He was a boxer too, which would've been how Floyd got to know him, from hanging around the gym after school. He might have been a relative of Floyd's too, Wesley couldn't remember, but then he hadn't been at the funeral.

10th February 1986

Sharon is talking and Wesley is sitting on the sofa watching her and listening, and she is strong and beautiful and full of fire and even anger. She has been going out with Floyd for just over a year now, feeling the storm in him that she doesn't know will break tonight (but not over her head but over Wesley's, who is a changeling, because Floyd is a changeling too, which is what it will all be about when all the words are over, something that Wesley will have known from the very beginning was trapped in the air between them). But she doesn't know and of course he doesn't, so she is just more restless than she usually is before going out for the night. She is wearing a tight black pencil skirt, white blouse and jacket and soft white boots. There is gold in her swept-up hair and her piercing eyes have been made up into mocking cats' eyes.

"I've got to chuck it in," she is saying.

"But the money's good, ain't it?" he asks.

She sighs, pricking her hair with a comb.

"That's not the point," she says, looking out of the tops of her eyes, trying to make double chins in the mirror.

"It's like, there's got to be something better than shuffling paper and watching the boss looking at your tits, there's got to be."

Wesley shrugs. "Yeah," he says.

"I mean I might as well be dead as carry on doing that. I want something with a future, anything with a bit of training, I suppose. I mean —" she turns away from the glass and looks straight into Wesley's eyes "— a trained chimpanzee could do what I'm doing. Most of it, anyway.

"People are so wasted."

She is staring into the mirror again, beyond the reflection this time, gold eyeshadow put on by reflex alone, and Wesley knows she is thinking of Floyd. They fight, she and Floyd, and argue, but they always make it up, always come back to each other. Perhaps it had to be that way because they were so alike: It was fire and fire, flames inseparable like in a furnace. "Cat an' dog," Wesley's mother would say, but really they were cat and cat.

That evening the three of them had been invited to a party by a girlfriend of Sharon's. Floyd had promised to pick Wesley and Sharon up at half-eight (in the rust-scabbed green Ford Capri he had bought off his cousin that he spent more time under than running), and Wesley had gone round to Sharon's to wait. She was ready when he got there at quarter past really, even though she was still fiddling with her make-up and touching her hair. She was one of those people who are always ready. Or that was how she seemed to him although he knew it wasn't really true; so confident and poised, like nothing in the world could make her blink. Sometimes she frightened him with that. Even six years on, she frightened him.

Floyd was late and Sharon hated to be late. By the time it turned quarter to nine she was angry; though looking still on the outside, she was burning inside. At five to nine there was a melodramatic screech of rubber on tarmac as a Ford Capri, colourless under the yellow streetlights, tore to a halt outside the house. The horn beeped twice, the long blasts making Sharon draw breath sharply.

"The bastard," she snapped. Wesley, embarrassed, made a sympathetic noise as he turned away from the window he had been watching from and let the curtain fall back into place. He hoped Floyd wouldn't beep the horn again but he did, playing an unmusical tune on it. Behind Wesley Sharon was stuffing a few essentials into her white clutch bag, each movement violent, biting her lip, saying "alright, alright," under her breath. A moment later and they were banging out of the house, the steel-tipped heels of her boots ringing on the concrete steps. Wesley's snow-white trainers made no sound as he moved up level with her. She pulled the car-door open and wrenched the seat forward for Wesley to get in. He slid inside and she slammed the seat back and sat down heavily on it, tugging the door shut behind her. Then she turned to Floyd, but instead of swearing or shouting she just looked at him intently.

"What's wrong?" she asked, her voice soft.

He threw the car into gear.

"Nothing."

The word was barely audible, strangled in his throat and muted by the roar of the engine. He pulled out from the kerb and they sped off. She touched his cheek but he jerked his head away, just like a child.

Wesley hadn't even said hello to Floyd and now there seemed to be no space for it, so he just sat quietly in the back, watching the headlights of cars in the night like fallen stars drowning in the gutter. The bleaching neon lights slid over the car's interior in shrinking, swelling planes. Beneath them Floyd's face looked smooth and carved, but his eyes like knives were full of shining pain. And he had shrugged Sharon's hand off because he couldn't take her touch, or any touch, right now, because he was a man. So he hid himself behind a man's mask where his flinching away from her was his only confession. Wesley watched his grip on the gear stick, his heavily-veined hand large and dark and tense and strong, the plain gold of the ring flashing out against the darkness in the glare of the neon, a grip tight with despair. And unlike the rhythm of a movie, but like the beat of an anguished heart, they did not plunge into the night but jerked uneasily from red light to red light and from gear to gear, in forced response to the surrounding, demanding traffic. And Sharon beside Floyd, wanting to take his pain with her touch, a pain that was too bared to bear the slightest touch, and Wesley wanting to take the pain too, like he would later wish he could when Floyd was in the ring; the pain and the hurt that were the price of the pride he felt when this man his brother Floyd fought.

Tears of rain squeezed down the glass under the pressure of horsepower and spread like veins. Fragments of their faces were all caught up in the fragmented light, then lost as yellow opened into black. And no one spoke because each of their minds was too full for words. Wesley rubbed his hands on his skin-tight denims to try to warm them up, and then buried them deep in the pockets of his white padded jacket. In front of him, Sharon rolled down her window, and the cold, fumey night air replaced the taint of vomit and plastic and cigarettes.

Wesley stared at the back of Floyd's head. His hair was short and slightly boxed, now gone kinky, and creeping down the back of his neck in two lines, following the muscles. He was moving his head in time to the George Benson tape they all knew so well that they stopped hearing anything but the rhythm of the moment the first note was played.

Watching Floyd lost in that rhythm, and watching Sharon, Wesley felt so strongly that it was all here; that in the three of them was the answer to all the questions, and that that answer wasn't deep and it wasn't supericial, it only was.

The motor died and Floyd flicked off the lights. The three of them got out of the car empty, waiting to be filled, feeling nothing. Floyd pushed the bell and someone opened the door and they filed into the coloured light and wall of compelling sound. Immediately the beat enfolded them they all felt lighter; words were not necessary or even desirable here. Sharon passed Wesley a can of Crucial Brew. He peeled the ring-pull back and took a swallow before offering it to Floyd, even though he knew Floyd was driving and training and wouldn't drink. Instead he was dancing, the rhythm coursing through him, pulling his hips like he was on wires. For three hours, every time Wesley saw him through the crowd, Floyd was pumping his body hard, his rich brown skin glistening under a black mesh vest, sweat making diamonds in his armpits. And he wore mirror-shades which like his eyes were empty, his mind like his body caught by the beat, the pull on each muscle forcing his pain from him and twisting it into a spiral of sound. Sharon moved round the room fluidly, a glass of white wine in her hand, dancing with old boyfriends and talking to girl-friends with excited, exaggerated gestures and popping her large brown eyes.

The room was getting slowly more and more crowded and Wesley got chatting to some old friends so he lost sight of both of them. The next time he saw Sharon, she was plunging out of the sea of bodies, her face set, and he knew that she and Floyd must have had a fight. He walked up behind her as she bent over a heap of coats, rummaging around for her jacket, watching her full buttocks as she thrust them out, unconsciously erotic, or perhaps deliberately tauntingly sexual to wind Floyd up, for he emerged from the swaying mass of sweaty bodies at that moment, his eyes wooden, the mirror-shades on his chest glinting with more life than his eyes did.

Sharon turned to Wesley. Her eyes were full.

"Let's go," she said. He was drunk on white wine and lager and charged with music so he smiled and said, "Sure," and threw Floyd his leather jacket and Floyd caught it and they floated out of the door on a goodnight.

Rhythms were still running through Wesley's head as they walked to the car, and within that swirl of music Sharon's heels rang on the pavement like the street was an echo-chamber. And the click of the car-lock and the slam of the door seemed as loud and shocking to his ears as gunshots in the night.

Wesley's sodden tee-shirt clung to him, now unpleasantly cold. "Good party," he said.

"Yeah," Floyd grunted. Sharon, her face unreadable in the smeared reflection on the windscreen, moved her head slightly, nodding in agreement.

Ten minutes later they drew up in front of Sharon's house. Floyd left the motor running while she opened her door to get out.

"I'll drop you home, Wes," he said, half-turning his head, his profile with its straight forehead, broken nose and large lips so arrogant and savage and noble and full of pain that night. Sharon turned back at the sound of his voice and looked at him quickly, doubtingly. Their eyes met and he breathed in, his adam's apple rising as he swallowed. Suddenly she bent over and kissed him on the cheek.

"Goodnight Floyd. Night, Wes." She smiled, wrinkling her nose. Then she slipped out of the car, closed the door with a firm click and hurried up the steps to her house without a backward glance. For a moment she was a silhouette against a rectangle of light, and then she was gone.

All that time Floyd had been watching her. He wrinkled his brow.

"She's beautiful," he said, bleakly. Wesley nodded. Floyd looked away from the closed door and threw the car into gear, pulling out to the dull, slow click of the indicator. His movements were casual now, or weary, dripping with the style of despair; but as he drove on Wesley could see the tension that was still in him, and feel the violence that was in his neck and tangled round his head. He played with the radio for a bit, jabbing at the buttons, then left it silent.

"Christ," he said, "Christ," his voice cracking it was so near to the edge, like a singer pushing at the extremity of his range. Wesley caught his breath and waited for something more, but nothing came, and they pulled up outside Wesley's house without saying another word. Wesley's chest felt tight as he turned to Floyd to say goodnight. Floyd was still looking straight ahead. Wesley wanted to touch him but he was afraid to.

"Come in for a coffee or something, man?"

The words fell without emphasis and the affirmation "Yeah"

hung in the still air. They walked up the steps side by side in the silent, roaring night. It was past three a.m. so they stole through the familiar darkness of the flat as like cats as they could.

Once Floyd had pulled the door of the small kitchen safely to behind him, Wesley snapped on the light. He lifted the lid of the kettle to check there was enough water in it before flicking the flat white switch on the wall. Turning to rinse some cups, he wondered what shift his mother was on, when she would be back. As he put them down he felt Floyd's breath warm on the back of his neck, and Floyd's arms wrapping themselves around his waist. For a moment Floyd rested his chin on Wesley's shoulder so their cheeks were touching. Wesley's neck prickled and the spot behind his balls clenched. Then he twisted round in Floyd's arms and faced him. The pit of his stomach fluttered. Floyd looked like a frightened child, his eyes wide, staring straight into Wesley's, his mouth trembling, trying still to bite back the terrible scream that was always near for him. He seemed so totally alone, and Wesley gripped his hot, bare shoulders, needing to end his desolation. Floyd held Wesley's sides gently in his hands, just below the shoulderblades, still staring into his eyes. They pulled closer, arms wrapped around each other, their bodies sealed together by their sweat, the scent of soap and sweat and hair-oil mingling. Wesley held Floyd's trembling muscular body tight, taking the convulsions into his own body. He felt Floyd's arms, strong and warm, tight around his back. The kettle began to boil and thick white steam silhouetted them as they stood there.

"Kettle's boiling." Wesley spoke gently.

"Yeah," Floyd replied, his voice a whisper.

They released each other slowly, smoothly, anxious to avoid any rejection. Wesley turned to make the coffee. Floyd squeezed his shoulder, really tired now, and shook it with his large hand before letting it fall to his side.

"Wes, look man, can I tell you something?" he asked. Wesley looked round at him.

"You don't have to tell me anything, man."

"Yeah, I know that, but. But I want to, man. It's important to me."

Wesley dumped sugar in the coffee.

"You looked pretty out of it tonight, man," he said. But Floyd didn't hear the words, only the tone of his voice saying, *Tell me.*

"Me and me old lady had a fight this evenin'," he said quietly. "It's why I was late. Jesus, that bitch. Sometimes I hate her so much, you know, man, I could just. . . But then I guess I must love her or I'da split her skull long time, yeah? Cos she only hates me, man. She don't feel nothing for me except hate. You think that's bullshit, yeah?

He looked straight at Wesley then down, shaking his head in denial.

"Yeah, well it's the truth. I don't know why, man. I ain't never done nothin' to her except I got me old man's name. Oh yeah, and I got a dick between me legs. So she reckons I betrayed her twice, yeah. Once by bein' a man, and once by bein' me old man's son. Just for bein' me old man's son." He shook his head, caught Wesley's gaze with his own.

"You remember when I was eight and I chucked her Bible out the window, and she beat me so I couldn't sit down for days? And everyone said it was a cruel shame to whip a child like that? I still got the scars on me butt, man. The social services came round and all that shit, yeah?"

Wesley thought back to that time in his childhood when there had always been trouble, and when he hadn't gone to see Floyd for three whole weeks because each time he had wanted to go his mother had put him off for some reason or other. Even as a child he had seen she was covering up something she wasn't able or prepared to talk about.

"Yeah? You remember? Well, no one really knew why she was so hard, man, only she was a God-fearing woman." He laughed a short, coughing laugh. "She was God-fearing then, man, so afraid God had cursed her she almost pissed herself."

His voice fell. "I did. I wasn't brave then, not as a kid. Not now either, I reckon."

He looked at Wesley again, then looked away.

"No-one knew the real reason, you know. Man, she shoulda beatin' her own backside you know, not mine. Not mine. The neighbours said it was because me dad had left like a few months before, and she was takin' out her revenge on his bastard. They said he was a fine-lookin' geezer, me old man, and her cunt was too tight and dry to keep him and that that was the curse she was so fuckin' frightened of, even though her womb was fruitful. They said. Maybe that had somethin' to do with it — it didn't make her hold back any, I know that. But that weren't the real reason. The real reason was she knew exactly why I threw that fuckin' Bible outta the house, man. *Exactly* why."

Listening to Floyd speak, Wesley felt he was hearing a confession, listening to a confession.

"The Bible. The fuckin' Good Book. The way she touched it up made me skin crawl. It was one a them old King James ones with all gold writing on it, but the gold was mostly worn away from bein' rubbed and touched up by generations of sick, cold hands. Does that sound crazy, man? She once told me it was bound in Our Lord's skin you know? And then she beat me cos I wouldn't kiss it to swear I weren't lyin' about somethin', I don't remember what. It was like — " He stopped, groping for words — "Like everything to do with that book, everything that touched her soul, was to do with death or dying, you know what I'm sayin', man? I *hated* all that stuff, man — I still do — even though bits of it are probably down there in me soul, burnin' and rotting there. If I got a soul, which I probably ain't by now. And one day when she was shouting and hating me and blaming me I just grabbed that Bible and threw it out the window and onto the street. She stared and stared like she was going to pass out with rage, man! I could feel her veins throbbing right the way across the room. What was really weird, I dunno, maybe the final sick thing, was, she started beatin' me before she'd even gone out to pick the Bible up from off the street. But that's not why there's all this shit between us, man, that's not why at all. Maybe she hated me even then and I just didn't know it. But she was my mother and I didn't hate her — not yet."

"You don't have to come out with all this, man," Wesley said softly. But he was wrong, and he knew it.

"The shit comes from way back when I was a kid," Floyd began, as if Wesley hadn't spoken. "I was seven years old, I reckon. She had been walking me home from school like she did every day back then. She always hated the traffic, didn't ever want to let me out, you know? It was cold, man, very cold, and clear. I was wearing these red mittens and a crappy blue anorak she got cheap from the Matma discount. I was happy, man, like kids are, you know? Lookin' at cars goin' past and shit, her pulling me out of the way of people walking on pavements. You know, the kinda people who look at their feet not the sky, and still knee you in the face cos they don't see nothin', and I didn't see 'em anyway cos kids never pay attention to what's goin' on, yeah? Me nose streamin' in the cold. She was carryin' a heavy shopping-bag in one hand while her other was holding mine tight, like. We was walking through sort of broken ground, you know, bits of concrete and steel girders and twisted up junk and broken walls you wonder what they were. It was just some multistorey or somethin' they had pulled down, but it was like castles to me or shit, and everyone said it was dangerous and you shouldn't go there, but I didn't see the danger, only the turn-on of goin' where you ain't supposed to be. Anyway, me old lady got gassin' with this old woman she knew from long time back and they labrish so much they weren't payin' no mind to me or what I was gettin' up to. I sneaked off and hid behind a leanin' concrete wall, waiting to hear them callin' me back. When I didn't hear nothin', I went scramblin' off across a heap of rubble and I was in there, you know what I'm sayin'? In the magic castle." He stopped abruptly, looked at Wesley. "You know the place.

Now there's that playground where the sniffers hang out."

Wesley nodded.

"Anyway, I was runnin' about, fooling, not thinking what me mum was gonna say when I got back, just turned on by bein' free cos that's the biggest turn-on of all, man. And then I was climbin' along this narrow ledge covered with barbed wire and crap, twenty feet up and I got frightened cos it really was dangerous. I tried to turn and I caught me ankle in the wire and fell off. I was too surprised to make a sound. I don't remember hittin' the ground or shit, but I remember lying there, feeling all bruised and scraped, me fingertips raw sose I couldn't stand to touch nothin'. I just lay there. After a bit I knew I had to move, man, but when I tried to, I felt this pain in me leg. It was so sharp I screamed like a fuckin' guinea-pig, man. Or like a little girl. Then I looked down, yeah. Man, it was disgustin'! There was this long cut and me leg hanging open and the glass that did it was all dusty and the shape of a shark's fin still stuck in the cut. Maybe I threw up, I don't remember. The pain was like a big black cloud, and I couldn't see properly. I was screaming me head off by then and even through the pain I felt me throat burning. I haven't ever been that afraid again, man, or only the once. Only the once, yeah. I don't know when I passed out, like, through loss of blood, or how long I was layin' there. I suppose I'da been dead if it'd been more than a coupla minutes. I saw things, you know, hallucinations. Some of them was just like a swarm of black speckles moving about in front a me eyes, but there was other things with teeth and claws like dogs, and for a moment I felt I was floating above myself and in the tall blades of green grass under a blue sky, like Africa maybe, feeling things without knowing what they were. Then I was drifting like into the white light with a man in white with a thin pale face in it standing over me. I must've looked terrified, because he smiled and said, 'You'll be alright, sonny.' Then he turned to someone I couldn't turn me head to see. 'This cut's pretty bad. He'll need twenty stitches and a transfusion.'

"The next thing I heard was me mother's voice sayin', 'I'm sorry, doctor, I can't allow it.' His head turned so I couldn't see his face. 'It's my religion,' she said, with like smugness or contempt for this heathen doctor who was just trying to save me life, like it was a explanation, like that made it alright. The doctor's voice was dead-pan, like careful not to sound like he despised her.

"'He will die if he doesn't get a transfusion, Mrs Philips,' he said, 'your son will die.' Man, I *panicked* on that operating table, man, but I couldn't move. I wanted to just run away from the both of them. He couldn't't've believed the fuckin' bullshit he was hearin', man. I don't know if he thought black peasant but I wouldn't blamed him, yeah, cos what else was it if it weren't ignorance and superstition? Not fuckin' piety. Not fuckin' sanctity. Just ignorant shit. And she was so proud of it that she could say, 'I let my child, my first-born and only son, die. To do God's will, I let my son die, I chose it just as Abraham picked up the knife to cut Isaac's throat with, because it was God's will.' Then she could mourn and wear black and wear a face of radiant serenity and grief. That's what she wanted, man. I swear that's what she wanted. But we weren't on the right mountain, we were in hospital where the doctor would probably do it anyway. Tell her to take him to court cos he knew no one in their right mind would pay any attention to a mumbling peasant woman wearing a large silver cross. So after a long pause she muttered 'alright' and then I reckon she left. So it weren't the pain or nothin', it was that she said *alright* like it was the order for a execution. So I knew, even then as a little kid, that I had died to her on that table. Man, I was in hospital for seven days and she never came to see me except on the seventh day to take me home. I don't know how she could've done that either. And she ended up hating me because she hated herself, and I was like the symbol of how she'd betrayed everything she believed in, and I ended up hating her for that. That's why she's nice to you, man, cos you're more like she wanted me to turn out, and she wants to save you from being corrupted. Jesus, she's so fucked up and she's always taken it out on me, man. And she ain't got the right."

His eyes were wet and shiny. He looked straight into Wesley's eyes, searching for something. Finding it, he looked away. He pulled out a cigarette jerkily and lit up. After a moment he looked at his gold Rolex.

"Shit, man, is that the time? I gotta be goin'."

He stood up slowly. Then:

"Thanks for listening, guy."

Another pause.

"I would've told Sharon, man, only she's too strong. You know, I don't want her to think I ain't under control."

Wesley nodded.

"Goodnight, man."

They shook hands firmly and the physical contact lingered. Then Floyd turned and slipped out of the house. Wesley watched him get into his car. The engine stuttered into life and the lights snapped on, then Floyd was gone. Wesley closed the front door gently and sneaked quietly upstairs to bed. The next morning he got up early and emptied the two undrunk cups of coffee down the sink.

Chapter Three

IN THE POCKET of one of his jackets were the stubs of two tickets for Fight Night at the Park Lane. One was for the fifth of November, 1986. The other was for 18th February, 1987. It was a jacket he didn't wear anymore.

5th November 1986

Wesley was fumbling with the laces of his trainers when the doorbell rang. He jumped up and looked around him, his mind still clouded by dreams, trying to concentrate. In a moment of guilt he shook out his blue-and-white striped duvet and flopped it over the unstraightened bed-sheet, not because it bothered him, the bed being like that, but to stop his mother from doing it when she got in, which he knew she would if he left it. She didn't rest enough as it was, he reckoned, without having to clean up his mess.

Out of the window the sky was blue and hazy and the sun was bright, though it was too early in the day for there to be warmth in it yet. The brittle light drew yellow bars across the carpet from between partly-opened curtains and Wesley's wristwatch flashed white gold as he snatched it up and tugged it onto his wrist. He hurried down the hall, past his sister Trisha's bed-room, trying to be quiet because she didn't have to be up for school for another hour. The bell had probably woken her anyway, but still he made the effort. Normally he was on the doorstep before Floyd even turned the corner at the top of the street, but this morning he just hadn't been able to get out of bed. He got the door open just before Floyd pressed the bell again. Floyd froze his hand in the air and grinned, the expanse of slightly gap-teeth saying 'lazy sod.' His teeth were like that because his mother had thought it was vain for a boy to wear a brace. They touched hands.

"Warm, ain't it," Floyd said.

"Could be the heart of the Caribbean, man," Wesley replied with a shiver. Floyd was wearing his poseurish black shorts, white socks and brand-new Nikes, a black tee-shirt and finger-less grey gloves. He hopped from one foot to the other and rubbed his bare, muscular arms while Wesley closed the front door. Wesley had a grey tracksuit top on, orange shorts and black Filas. His legs prickled with goosebumps as he pushed his keys deep into his tracksuit pocket, and the two of them set off, jogging gently down to the corner, then looking for a pace as they started up the high street.

Soon they came to the edge of the reservoir. Small trees with broken branches overhung its streaked concrete banks, and the water was a grey-green, dimpling slick. Another runner crossed their path, a girl in a pink jump-suit, her long blonde hair streaming out behind her, bouncing with every step. She looked neither to left nor right, and her hair was pinned back by the headphones of a Walkman, a funky rhythm floating round her head. There was no one else around, and she suddenly picked up speed, accelerating out of sight down a high-walled alley.

They jogged halfway round the reservoir, Floyd a little ahead of Wesley. Every so often he would look round and catch Wesley's eye. Suddenly he turned his head and shouted: "C'mon, man, catch me!" and sprinted off, gathering speed with every stride. Wesley pelted along after him, his feet pound-ing on the uneven concrete, echoes bouncing back at him like slaps. His heart was racing, not from the exertion but from the wildness that Floyd charged in him, that made him feel he could run until his feet caught fire and never notice, if Floyd was only there in front of him. He caught him up at the end of

44

the reservoir where it met an industrial estate, still going at full speed, and grabbed at his waist, almost stumbling as he caught a fistful of fabric. They pulled up in a windscreen-wiper sweep in front of a blackened brick wall daubed with white anarchy signs around a large NF logo, its letters eight feet high. Someone had drawn a thin A in front of it. They laughed, breathless, bending over and touching their toes, gulping in air, Wesley keeping hold of Floyd's tee-shirt, his knuckles against Floyd's stomach. Their chests rose and fell in unison. Feeling the warmth of Floyd's belly against his hand, Wesley felt awkward, and let go of the fabric. Floyd hawked and spat while Wesley touched his toes again.

"Let's go," Floyd said.

The army-green swing-doors of the gym flapped open-shut, open-shut, and the two young men's trainers squeaked on the shiny lino, their reflections shivering along beneath them. A way off, they heard the dull clinking of metal being moved. Spots of black light drifted across their retinas from being out in the bright sunlight. They turned down a flight of stairs and into the locker-room. Wesley opened his dented tin locker with one of the keys on his crowded key-ring.

There were a few others in the weights room, even this early: a large red-faced man who neither Floyd nor Wesley had seen before, and a thin, wiry Rastafarian who waved his hand in acknowledgement to Wesley.

"Ow ya doin', man?" he called, flicking his shoulder-length dreads back from his face.

"Not bad, man. And you?"

Mikey shrugged his narrow shoulders and laughed.

"I&I still a lion inna disya Babylon," he intoned, before resuming his seat at the pec deck, sending the black iron plates slithering up and down the greased metal shaft.

Wesley carried on limbering up. He tested his right calf, which he had damaged two weeks ago on the multigym, and it felt fine. A little weak, he thought, but not crippled. In his head he modified his exercise routine accordingly.

He was proud of his routine. It was a good system, he knew, because Floyd copied a lot of it. He had mostly devised it himself, not drawing too heavily on any one school of thought, using his own experience to shape articles he had read about the techniques of Bertil Fox, Frank Zane and Bill Richardson. He liked the science of body-building, the method. It made him feel intelligent and professional in a way nothing else did: master of his own body and of his mind. It was the same reason he loved kung fu films — the road to perfection and mastery that anyone could follow if they had the discipline, and anyone could understand if they had the rightness of mind. And that was what the weights were really about -- discipline, determination, and mastering the physical, the body, realising what it's like to know and feel the shape and structure of every muscle you have: the two parts of the shoulder muscle, the posterior and anterior deltoid, the latissimus dorsi. Their very names were in a language of ancient wisdom. And learning and feeling it was a transformation from ignorance to knowledge, from inert flesh to delicately etched veins and sharply-defined muscles. He knew some people thought big muscles were just lumps of fat, but those people were stupid and blind. When he flexed his arm and ran a finger down the groove in his bicep, he knew that he had created within himself something rare and precious.

He had read a karate book once that said, "When you change yourself by sheer discipline, the spirit flourishes like a bound tree." What that meant was you grew strong and healthy, all dead wood cut away, and perfectly symmetrical. What looked like a sport to others was an act of faith for Wesley. He still felt an aura of reverence every time he picked up a barbell, a sensation appropriate for an object which made him stronger in body and spirit, more like himself and more beautiful. Now like in a ritual he was lying there, the leather rim of the couch biting into his back, holding up but barely the barbell with its cartwheel weights. And like angels or priests Mikey and Floyd stood either side of him, their fingertips touching the circles of cold iron. Wesley grunted as he looked up at their crotches and shadowed faces, every muscle tensed and hard, struggling to complete the set.

C'mon, man. You can do it. C'mon.

Trembling and dripping sweat he finished, and his arms and legs felt like water. But he was smiling as he loosened up afterwards, because he knew he had taken another step along the path.

"Man, that felt good," Wesley called out, as shampoo and scalding hot water gushed over his upturned face. He handed the Timotei back to Mikey.

"I thought you was goin' to bust a blood-vessel, man," Mikey shouted back, lathering up his dreads a second time. "You lookin' good though."

"Hey, Floyd, man, you fightin' tonight, right?" he called to Floyd.

"Yeah, man, tonight's the night."

"I&I no believe in violence man, but if a man stan' in ya way, mosh it up, me say. Jah send you victory, man. For righteousness."

"Thanks, man. Hey, Wesley, you comin' tonight, man?"

"Course I am, man, ain't nothin' could stop me from being there."

Floyd got out of the shower and walked over to the lockers. Wesley knew he was embarrassed; he knew Floyd wanted him to be there very much that night because he needed someone who really believed in him. Not like Sharon, who had once said when he asked her, "If you're ready, you'll win," as if her hope made no difference to his readiness.

Coming back from the blues a year ago, him and Floyd, stumbling into Floyd's living-room at two in the morning wild drunk, Floyd trailing a bottle of wine from his sleeve and slamming it on the table, scattering playing cards from his pocket. "C'mon, man, c'mon," he had said, throwing his homburg onto a chair, rolling back the cuff of

47

his shirt and setting his elbow on the table, his hand ready to grip. Wesley slipped clumsily out of his jacket, letting it fall to the floor. "Okay, okay," he said, sitting down opposite him, "okay." He swept bills and letters onto the floor with a drunk's elegance and placed his elbow on the table. The moment their hands interlocked they sobered up. They joked as they flexed and strained against each other under the yellow lamplight, their hands still slippery with sweat from the heat of the packed blues and too much Red Stripe, but they weren't joking. The sound of their breathing filled the air as the minutes passed. Then Wesley felt Floyd's arm waver. He slowly pushed it down, Floyd refusing to give up and break the hold until his knuckles touched the polished wood. His face was set. "Again," he said, swigging from the bottle of wine. Slowly Wesley took up his position and met Floyd's hand a second time.

Wesley won all four bouts they had. After the fourth Floyd just swore bitterly and sat slumped on the floor with the music turned up so loud the neighbours banged on the walls. Then he sat there in silence and drank Thunderbird until he collapsed unconscious on the carpet. Wesley picked him up and carried him into his bedroom and laid him on his bed. Then he unlaced Floyd's shoes and slipped them off, so when he woke up the next morning with a splitting headache, he would know that Wesley still believed in him. And for someone who beat him to still believe in him was worth more than adoration or blind faith to Floyd.

Mikey, Floyd and Wesley got dressed quickly after showering, leaving behind their sweat and cramp and anger and foot-prints in talcum powder. Outside the gym they split up. Mikey waved as he cycled off and shouted, "Good luck, Floyd, man. See you Sunday." He had some job in a garage back then. Floyd was going off to see Sharon and maybe walk to work with her. Wesley had to go to work too, the same job he was to be doing five years later (*until today, he thinks, until today*). And even then he had thought, it's not work for a young man, someone with a future, or at least time to spend ahead of him. It should be an old man doing it, someone who'd tried it and failed, or who didn't want to do it anymore; didn't want to live. Someone whose spirit was already dead and who had no songs to sing.

The sky had been clear for the city, and between the buzzing orange haloes of neon he could see stars like diamonds on blue velvet. The fight was happening at the old Park Lane Theatre, a Victorian-fronted building on the opposite side of the common to Sharon's parents' house. It was Friday night, FIGHT NIGHT in silent-movie script, framed by rows of flashing light-bulbs.

He joined the short queue outside the double doors. Inside, ornately carved and painted wood was lit by raw yellow bulbs. On the walls hung photographs of former boxing champions, some discoloured with age: Joe Frazier, Larry Holmes, Johnny Owen, a signed photograph of Marvin Hagler, and several local fighters who hadn't made it big but hadn't failed either; they were still waiting on the clock for the big break maybe, or maybe by now they were resigned to oblivion and a dead-end job. Wesley stared through the glass at the manager, Joe Freeze, a heavily-built man in his fifties who looked every inch the local villain he was meant to be. He ran a heavy, gold-ringed hand through his slicked-back silver hair and smiled a lipless smile as he talked to a stooped little man in a ruffled lilac shirt (not the regular referee at the Park Lane, Floyd told Wesley later). The lights of a turning car changed the glass into opaque, flaring yellow. When it moved off, they had both disappeared.

Behind Wesley a short queue had already built up. It was a big night for the Park Lane because both the top-lining contestants were up-and-coming local names who drew a big crowd. There were going to be three bouts that evening. Floyd's was the first. Wesley remembered that several managers were supposed to be there tonight. That was why it was such an important fight for Floyd. He looked back over the queue, half-expecting to see Sharon. Maybe she's already inside, he thought. She had said she wasn't going to come; that she couldn't bear it. But she knew how much it meant to Floyd, so he thought she might have changed her mind.

He scanned the crowded interior but still couldn't see her. Some friends of his waved but he didn't join them because they looked set up to make trouble, and he didn't feel like trouble tonight. Instead he sat in a single seat three rows back from the ring, treading on the toes of a complaining old couple on his way to get there. He looked at his watch. The bout was meant to have already started, but no one was in the ring; it stood empty under the harsh white lights. He stared at the glistening plastic slit by red ropes, its outlines sharp against a muddy background pricked out with eager eyes and faces. The hall was packed now, and it was already hot and close. Wesley slipped out of his black leather jacket and stuffed it under his chair. A feeling of anticipation was beginning to build; the chatter got louder, reached a peak, then fell again. As it rose a second time, peppered with yells, the MC walked quickly down the aisle and swung himself nimbly into the ring. He flicked the flex of the mike to free it from the rope it had caught on. The MC's hair was short and white, and his face seemed permanently red. There was slight rowdy applause as he clambered up. He rotated in the middle of the ring, appealing for quiet.

"Ladies and gentlemen," he began in a slightly flustered way, "we've got three bouts this evening. Six courageous young men. I'm sure you'll like 'em. Sorry we're a bit late, but one of them's only just this minute turned up."

He stepped out of the ring and disappeared. A thrill ran through Wesley. Was that Floyd? Several more minutes passed, with the crowd growing more and more restless.

"Yorkie, Yorkie, we want Yorkie," the chanting began. The MC was a professional Yorkshireman who layed it on thick. People began to stamp their feet. Then out of nowhere it seemed, he was back in the ring, this time followed by the withered little referee and an attractive, knock-kneed girl wearing a gold lamé bikini and tottering uncertainly on six-inch heels. Wesley watched her awkward progress, fascinated.

". . . Your referee for the night, Jackie Peers!" (thunderous applause) "And counting the rounds, the lovely Suzanna Sue. Give her a big hand!" (more thunderous applause and cat-calls). Suzanna smiled in best dumb-blonde tradition, coyly bending one leg in front of the other, showing herself off to best advantage. Wesley was suddenly glad that Sharon wasn't there. It was like how he imagined a slave-market would have been: over-eager punters' cocks being teased before the hard sell. He felt profoundly disturbed. But at that moment he became aware that the two contestants were walking towards the ring, proud men after all, not slaves, and everything seemed suddenly recast. Tension flared up in him again.

Remembering it now it seemed to him that he had been as close to the two fighters as the referee, and every minute detail stayed sharp in his mind: the crease in a glove, and the shadow of a nipple.

"In the blue corner . . . 'Fighting' Floyd Philips!"

The crowd heaved and cheered and shouted.

"And in the red corner. . . . Mark 'The Mangler' Brenner!"

There was more applause and cheering, from different sections of the crowd this time. Wesley was still cringing from the title the MC had coined for Floyd. He was in great form tonight, flourishing like a circus ringmaster, his patent-leather shoes glistening like spinning jet. Brenner was a skinhead and the NF had a strong following round there, so Wesley knew the bout was set up to heat the crowd. Forgetting for a moment why the others were there, he wondered what they had done it for. But looking around the crowded hall he already knew the answer: Faces tight and glinting like coiled springs, bodies and minds wound always too tight too, tightened by all the hours of frustration they endured five days a week and every week. And they needed the violence to loosen their tight skin and tight bones, and the blood to wash themselves clean in. It didn't matter who was up there, as long as they knew he was up there for them. So they pitched Floyd's black-and-white designer shorts against the Union Jack that covered Brenner's crotch thinly and not decently. And the MC like a flag floated above it all saying, 'This is you up here, this is your fight, and it is as great and terrible as war.'

By now Wesley had blanked out the people around him. He was alone: just him and the ring, all gleaming white and waiting, and the referee no more than a smear of lilac and black part of that waiting too. In that moment before the bell when time was straining like a taut bow, he watched the two men in the ring. They were both tense, sizing each other up, eyes meeting momentarily then flicking around the hall. Seen from below they seemed like giants, and the event itself made them both colossal despite each being stripped bare to his pride and his terror and less, because even those things had been left behind them in their tiny dressing-rooms. And even their anger was hanging on the bell.

Floyd stood with his arms loose at his sides, assuming cool, his muscles gleaming a rich dull brown under the bare light. His tall head seemed to touch the roof, his eyes blocked black by his brow, his face unreadable. He shook his arms out and then rubbed the shining red gloves together. A length of white cord coiled out at the point where his slim, sinewed forearm entered the glistening plastic. His black silk shorts had a broad white waist-band, and his boots were black-and-white too. The skinhead was jumping up and down on the spot, sparring at the air, and making a show of confidence. He was more lightly built than Floyd, and under the lights his skin seemed lard-white, but laced with blue veins under the shadows, and touched with red. His large ears made his cropped head look chimpan-zee-like. But even with the blue tatoos faded on both his arms he was something more than he had been when he was out drinking with his mates the night before, now that he was up there in the ring. At the very moment the bell rang, Wesley looked at Floyd and realised what he hadn't realised until that moment; just how beautiful Floyd was.

The two fighters came forward. The referee bowed his head

between them and with his hand on Floyd's neck repeated the formula of unheard words. Then he stepped back and the fighting began, though the actual fight had started before the two men got into the ring, before they had walked as powerfully as possible across the hall even, right back to when they were sitting right where all the people were sitting now, looking up and feeling tight.

At that strange moment of anticlimax when the sparring had begun, but before it had evolved into the excitement of the real fight, Wesley's eyes ran round the front rows of the ranks of seats either side of him. Sitting on his right were the trainers and maybe some managers, he couldn't tell. They were just another sort of pimp, Wesley thought, white and middle-aged in toning pastel suits and ties, feeding off the youth. One of them wore mirror-shades. Wesley looked back at the ring again. It was always larger than he expected, but never large enough for the vanquished to escape the victor. In the end anyway it was the crowd and not the ropes that held him there, wanting blood for its money. Anyone's blood would have done, but tonight it was Floyd's blood they all wanted, his blood and his sweat and his pain: Floyd like a carnival Christ with a bullfighter's spear in his side. Shocked by that realisation, Wesley watched the fight with unblinking eyes.

It was all so personal now, a private thing his hard eyes saw as his shoulders hunched against the greedy gaze of the crowd, the pit of his stomach clenching so hard that he forgot to breathe. He didn't know which punches caused the real pain, but he wished he could take some of it into his body and against his skin. Perhaps he did, just by being there. Perhaps that was why Floyd had wanted him to be there. Where was Sharon? The bell rang. Floyd's older brother Tony was acting as his second. He was talking very quickly, and Floyd was listening. He gargled and spat just as the bell rang again. The fight had a terrible, remorseless quality to it: no one could leave now. The crowd were shouting and cheering — it was a "good fight", fast-paced and aggressive, a mirror held up to their anger and bitterness. Floyd's tragedy was that he was here, and his glory also. Neck muscles tensed and strained and veins roared. Both men glistened with sweat and their eyes were locked together always. The skinhead's face was as red as his gloves and boots. Wesley was crushed in the tension of it: the duck and weave, the perpetual searching for an entry, the lightning strike, seeking and denying that conclusive moment, the moment the whole crowd waited for. And within that waiting the shrugging off of ribs that might be broken not bruised and kidneys that could be slowly haemorrhaging. The fight ebbed and surged, and suddenly the skinhead was bounced to the floor by a volley of blows. He sat on the canvas looking dazed, with Floyd over him as nearly astride him as the referee would allow. The skinhead tried to stand up, urged on by yelling voices, but halfway to rising he stopped and sat down abruptly. The referee counted him out, his florid gestures made for the benefit of the crowd and unseen by the purple-eyed youth whose downcast face was a patch of blue shadow. There was rowdy clapping, and jeering as the skins deserted their ten-minute hero. Floyd stood tawny and magnificent in the middle of the ring, apparently oblivious to his surroundings, looking up at some space at the back of the hall, his eyes hooded by the light above him. The MC stepped into the ring beside him, clicked on his microphone, and announced:

"Ladies and gentlemen, the winner by a knockout" (cheers), "Fighting Floyd Philips!"

He held up Floyd's gloved right hand and it seemed as tall as a mountain to Wesley. At that moment Floyd finally smiled a broad band of white, soaking up the adulation of the crowd, transformed by victory. He looked over to see if his opponent was alright. He seemed to be; he was sitting on his stool and talking. Several of his skinhead mates were clustered round his corner.

Wesley left his seat just before the next bout was introduced and made his way to Floyd's tiny dressing-room, which was now crammed with people. Some of them he knew, like Tony,

Floyd's brother, and Mikey from the gym. He wormed his way through to where Floyd was leaning against a wall, a white towel draped round his bare shoulders. He had removed his gloves but his hands were still taped. He was always very careful about his hands, ever since he had broken one punching a wall when he was a kid. They hugged.

"You were beautiful, man, really beautiful."

"Thanks for being there, man. I love you."

He smiled and looked into Wesley's eyes, his gaze unfathomable. Suddenly he turned his head and shouted, "Yo, Sharon!"

She had appeared, framed in white by the black space of the doorway. She was smiling and she looked radiant that night. People parted as she made her way nervously across the room to where Floyd was. He drew her to him with one arm, (the other still hung round Wesley's shoulders), and kissed her smooth brown-satin cheek. Their eyes met. Could she read what she saw there any more than Wesley had tried to do? Suddenly they both laughed, Wesley and Sharon, and Floyd hugged them to him.

Out of the crush Tony appeared, a tall barrel-chested man with close-shaved hair and a heavy moustache. He was the colour of an aubergine and still shiny from the excitement of the fight. He was carrying a bottle of champagne and a couple of glasses.

"I thought we should celebrate in style," he said, smiling. They popped the cork and poured the excited, guttering liquid into the round, flat glasses. There weren't enough glasses to go around, so Tony gallantly offered his to Sharon, who accepted gracefully. Floyd took a small sip from his glass and handed it to Wesley. A small drop of blood slid from his lip into the clear liquid and was unfurling like a skein of crimson silk. Wesley raised the glass to his lips and drank.

18th February 1987

That night he had a dream among the empty beer-cans, an unremembered dream, and when he awoke he felt maybe just cramped and hung-over, but later he made those feelings and the not-remembering a premonition; how he had been twisted in his sheets like a corpse in its winding-sheet, then opening his eyes in the early morning with the sun so bright on his face that it felt like a stone had been rolled away from the window in the night. And he had felt a terror then for Floyd, because there was a price for that that had to be paid: for the wideness of the sky and for the eyes to see it with. For Floyd to pay because each time he stretched his arms out Wesley saw the shadow of the Cross upon him, and every hill he climbed was only one hill after all.

Wesley had looked out at the white sun, dazzled.

Floyd was sitting in the kitchen in his tracksuit, guzzling a pint of milk, his head tilted back, stretching his long throat, his adam's apple rising and falling. To Wesley he seemed large that day, filling the room with his presence like a picture fills its frame, and everything, the chairs, the table, the newspaper on the red-and-white checked tablecloth, the walls and ceiling even, were only there because he was there, like he was the reason for it all. He put down the half-empty bottle and wiped his hand across his mouth, belching and leaning back on the red-emulsion chair. Idly looking down at the newspaper headline, he saw it was a multiple sex-murder, and creased his brow.

"What a crock of shit, man," he said angrily, flicking at the paper. "Shit and lies. I don't wanna know, man; it's not real, just lies. I got me own life to lead. I can do without this shit. I just want to live, get on with it. Jesus."

He snatched up the paper and folded it over so only the sport and the cartoons were showing before throwing it back down on the table. Then he was silent again. Wesley watched him as he exhaled, his chest sinking as he stared into space. Floyd glanced up at the kitchen clock.

"It's right, yeah, man?" His voice was dry and quiet, and he had to clear his throat to get the words out. Wesley glanced at his watch.

"Bout five minutes slow."

"I'd better get off, Wes, man," Floyd said, rolling to his feet. He was wired through with nervous tension that morning, sparks making him twitch as he stood there, rubbing his hands together, making a sound like the sea in a shell.

"See you tonight then, man."

He tapped Wesley playfully on the chin, the ghost of a punch, gazing intently into his eyes and not smiling. Wesley couldn't help but grab his wrist and try to wrestle him off-balance. Floyd laughed and fought back, his eyes staying on Wesley's, tickling Wesley's belly with his free hand, making him laugh and lose his grip. He tried to fight off Floyd's eager hands but he wasn't quick enough to catch his wrists again. They struggled round the room laughing, bumping into chairs, the table, sending the bottle of milk rolling onto the floor. It smashed wetly over the lino, white spreading across the red in a broadening pool.

At the sound of the bottle breaking Wesley put up his hands to stop the game and looked round behind him. Floyd gripped his waist, and his stomach shivered under the firm, sure touch.

"Gerroff, man," he said without turning to look at him. But Floyd's hand stayed where it was. Wesley turned his head then and met Floyd's eyes and suddenly he couldn't catch his breath at all. Floyd opened his mouth, about to speak, but now he couldn't even whisper.

They stood like that for maybe half a minute. Then Floyd looked down at the spilt milk and sighed.

"Shit man, we better get this mess cleared up, yeah?" His voice was trembling and he kept on having to clear his throat.

Wesley nodded, breathing again. Floyd squatted down and started fishing out the bigger pieces of glass. Wesley carried the bin over and held the flap open for him to throw them in. When he had got them all out, Floyd sopped up the milk with a dish-cloth.

"Better throw it away, man," he said, looking up at Wesley, "there might be splinters in it." He stood up. "It might be dangerous." His voice was even now, but he was glancing at the clock anxiously.

"Get going, man. See you later," Wesley said gently.

"Later, man."

They touched hands lightly, the ghost of a touch, and Floyd was gone. He left the kitchen empty and meaningless.

Wesley knew that part of the reason Floyd was so nervous was that Sharon had agreed to come to the fight that night. Floyd had been happy and very surprised when she had said that she would turn up for it, as casually as if it was something she was always doing. Wesley picked her up half an hour before the fight was due to start, and they walked slowly across the common together. It was only Floyd's second big local fight, but he had fought in Coventry once since his win there before. He had won in Coventry too, on points.

It was less crowded that evening, the Park Lane, and Wesley and Sharon managed to get second-row seats. Sharon gathered her coat around her like everything there was dirty, and put the bunch of red rosebuds she had brought with her down gently under her chair. "Why shouldn't a girl give a bloke flowers?" she had said to him when he had asked who they were for, and he had shrugged and thought, *Yeah, why not?* wishing he could do something like that too. Sharon looked at the ring, as yet unlit, nervous and expectant. Wesley squeezed her clenched hands.

"Don't worry," he said. "He'll be fine. Just fine."

"Yeah," she replied. "I know." But she couldn't look at Wesley.

The crowd wasn't as rowdy as it had been the other time, but still a tension was building in the smokey air, an anticipation of something almost forbidden. The fight was later in starting than usual too. Maybe they were deliberately stirring the more passive crowd up because they waited until a chorus of "Why are we waiting?" before the ring was lit up and the MC came bouncing down the aisle.

Floyd was on first again. It was all the same; the MC, the embarrassing, wobbly blonde with her coyly bended knee, music- hall corn, and time arced and tense and tight, everyone waiting for the moment of release. Floyd's opponent this evening was a tall, lanky black boy called Paul Green. (Even the MC couldn't conjure up a pugilistic title for him. Wesley had thought up "Paul the Mauler".) He had a tall, cylindrical head, his hair was wet-curled and styled back from his forehead. He looked nervous, his eyes scanning the auditorium, resting only momentarily on his opponent. He clapped his gloves together noiselessly. Floyd was loosening up on the other side of the ring. He looked calm as he sized his opponent up with a level gaze. The referee brought them together, muttered the vows, then the bell rang. They touched gloves lightly, then fell slightly apart before coming together, guards up, to fight.

Then it was the eighth round. Wesley was aching with frustration, every muscle in his body cramped with tension as he sat on the edge of the narrow, thinly padded seat. He turned every now and then to look at Sharon. She stared ahead unblinking, her lips slightly parted. He wondered why she had come tonight, although if he had looked into himself he would have understood the necessity that drew her there without the words that would fail to describe it anyway. Needing a word, he decided she was brave.

The fight had been fast to start with, but Paul Green had turned out to be more of a dancer than a puncher. By now both of them had slowed down and found a pace, taking breathers where they could. They glistened like lovers as they hugged in the middle of the floor and in that moment it seemed to Wesley that they were two stars hanging stilly in a void of night. He hid within a heartbeat, waiting, not hearing the jeers of the crowd as it called for the referee to separate them. The referee stepped forward and pulled them apart. And it was then that it came: Paul Green got a loose, slow punch past Floyd's guard, a weak punch, but it clipped Floyd's head at an odd angle, against the weight and flow of his body. For a fraction of a second Floyd absorbed it, but then he collapsed and hit the canvas with a rapidity and violence that seemed unnatural. He lay there twitching and convulsing, his muscles locked, and taut as whipcord and knotty as seamed rope, his neck a mass of tree-roots, his face torn in agony by the red-and-white gash of his mouth. His eyes were clamped shut, the lids violently creased, his forehead twitching with veins in spasm and twisted into heavy black lines. Everyone was on their feet. Sharon screamed. Wesley stood too, gaping as the doctor, referee and seconds clambered into the ring and crowded round Floyd. For a moment he was hidden by them, and Wesley caught Paul Green's face, a picture of stupified shock and fear and uselessness. He was struggling desperately to remove his gloves and there was no one to help him. Wesley ran forward and plunged into the crowd washing around the ring. He scrambled up, grabbing the ropes. He would have fallen back from the ring, it was so crowded, if Tony hadn't grabbed him by the armpit and hauled him in. But there was nothing he could do when he got there except wait for the ambulance. He couldn't even see Floyd for the other people, and he had no reason to shove them out of the way just to look at him. His mouth tasted like burnt rubber. He watched Tony's head bobbing up and down like a bird; like a chicken. Then the siren was outside, and the crowd was grudgingly parting for the stretcher-bearers. It was only through the mesh of red and blue-tipped ropes and steel cord that he found himself looking on Floyd's profile, beaded with sweat, but now quite relaxed. The doctor was putting his pencil torch back into the breast pocket of his navy-blue suit. The two white-clad stretcher-bearers had lifted his body carefully but clinically onto the battered green stretcher and then strapped it firmly into place. Wesley watched the way the muscles hung off the bone, the absence of tension, the way the whole body wobbled with each jolt of the stretcher, and how the head lolled as the bearers slid it between the ropes. Then they began the long, slow march to the double doors with the unlit EXIT sign above them. The first few ranks of the crowd were silent, the noise rising the further away people were from the procession of the stretcher. Paul Green, now degloved, was holding his second by the shoulders, his deep brown eyes white with tears, talking very quickly, giving a thousand excuses or apologies to someone to whom he owed no apologies and who could thus not grant him absolution either. Where was Sharon? Wesley looked around the hall wildly and couldn't see her. It wasn't until later that he found out she had gone in the ambulance with Floyd. He realised now how alone he was in the crowd, and the realisation made it unbearable to be there anymore. He pushed and shoved his way through, ignoring shouts and abuse, wading through shit not people, until finally he was outside in the empty air. His lungs and heart and guts torn out, the cold wind ragging the hole inside, the ring of raw nerves shrinking from it, mind closed against the terror of the violation, he stood there beneath the empty, terrible sky. He knew Floyd was dead. Floyd James Philips was dead. Dead On Arrival. He wanted to scream, even knowing that no scream could be loud enough, and even if his voice could shatter glass, knowing the note would not be pure enough. In his head a storm was raging, and meaningless words fell from his lips as though he was drunk on death.

He knew he had to be there, though, despite all that; he had to go and be there. In front of him there was a taxi-rank, and a taxi waiting for hire. He went up to the window and peered in. The driver, a large black guy with tied-back dreadlocks, turned and looked back at him. Wesley stared into his eyes and couldn't speak because he knew that if he tried to, he would start to cry and not be able to stop. His eyes felt hard, and dead as wood.

"Where to, my friend?" The driver's voice was smooth and easy.

"The hospital," Wesley whispered, his voice like his body a shell now, without feeling, so when he spoke he didn't cry after all. He got in the back of the cab and pulled the door shut.

"Wife 'avin' a baby?" the driver asked, laughing softly to himself. Wesley didn't answer and the man fell silent, thinking perhaps about his own three children and leaving Wesley to stare out of the window and let the orange city light wash over him as the taxi wallowed through tired but restless streets. It was much bigger than Wesley remembered from when he had ridden in one as a kid, and rounder too. He sat back in a corner of the swelling seat, one hand stroking the smooth brown leather, the other hanging loosely between his sprawled thighs, breathing the suspended air imperceptibly, maybe in shock now, not thinking at all.

"Dis de 'Ospital, man."

The taxi pulled up and Wesley's gorge rose again, forced up by panic. He saw Floyd fall like a gunshot and writhe and thrash in a frenzy, everything over before anyone knew what had happened; no build-up, no slow-motion descent with sweat floating and shining like crystal from a chandelier, and no sad music as he drifted down (that character) not smashed on the canvas hard and broken like Floyd was broken.

"Where's Casualty, man?" he asked, looking up at the black mass of the infirmary. His voice was high and urgent.

"Dis place na 'ave no casualty, man. You want di General 'Ospital." The driver pulled out and turned the taxi round. "Or di Cottage 'Ospital."

Wesley's guts clenched as he wedged himself back in the corner of his seat. He knotted and unknotted his hands, twisting his head as if he had to count every building they passed, tortured by the slowness of the cab however fast it went floating through the night, wondering, *what hospital? What fucking hospital?* and looking at the meter, thinking, *I haven't got enough money,* and thinking the ride was going on forever. But then they were pulling up outside the General Hospital and the driver was saying, "Five pounds eighty, mate," and Wesley was dragging all the change out of his tight white cords' pocket, raking his knuckles raw on the seams, his eyes wild by now, saying, "I only got three pound twenty, man, I only got three pound twenty," not thinking at all, just staring crazily into the man's eyes, daring him to fight him over it, holding onto his money tight, "that's all I got, man," holding it against his crotch, "that's all I got." And the driver, seeing something he needed not living in Wesley's eyes, was saying, "Cool it, man, cool it. Jus' give I de tree pound, man. Give I what you got." And Wesley had offered it to him and he had taken the money from Wesley's outstretched palm carefully, not touching Wesley's flesh.

The cab pulled away and as it left the madness drained out of Wesley and off into the night. He looked up at the sign above him marked CASUALTY and slowly climbed the steps to a pair of glass double-doors. He had never been in a hospital before.

The noise of the street cut out as the doors floated together behind him and was replaced by the suppressed sounds of the hospital. The air was warm and antiseptic and felt as if it had been breathed by many people. Stifled by it, Wesley unzipped his jacket and let it fall open. All around him was the faint but permanent smell all institutions have; of stale bodies never quite swabbed clean, like chrome bed-pans — shiny but always soiled.

The nurse on reception was friendly and helpful and gave him directions to a waiting area. They were simple and clear, but he forgot them because he couldn't really listen to her talking, not when she was just talking words like she had been, just words. So he had to peep into several unlit rooms before finding the sterile waiting area with its chipped Sixties easy-chairs and low occasional coffee tables. Sharon was sitting there, blankly staring at a magazine. There were several other silent, tired-looking people in the room too, all of them waiting. For the bad news. Several pairs of eyes looked up at him as he pushed the door open. Sharon smiled a strained smile and held out a hand to him. He gripped it and sat down beside her. They hugged. He had never needed to be held so much, and neither had she. Her perfume surrounded the two of them like a wreath of incense. They sat like that for several minutes, breathing in harmony, just needing each other and answering that need. Wesley thought about Floyd, tall as a mountain, dark as the night, and bright as a star, and held Sharon tighter. She answered him, their cheeks pressed together, gliding on tears, as close then as any two people could ever be, and still. After they had reached that stillness they released each other and Sharon spoke. Her voice was calm, her phrases well-rehearsed.

"He's on life-support, Wesley. It was a massive cerebral haemorrhage. They don't think he's got a chance." Her eyes were liquid. "Tony's in there now," she whispered.

"I loved him. Jesus I loved him," he said softly, looking at the ground as he spoke. Sharon touched his arm.

"Please," she whispered, "just hold onto me."

It wasn't until eight o'clock that morning that the doctors decided that Floyd James Philips was irredeemably dead. He had technically died on 18th February 1987, at 22:01, three minutes, thirty-three seconds after arriving at the hospital. The three of them, Sharon, Wesley and Tony, hard-eyed and worn out, were guiltily glad to be released from their hopeless vigil, and from the mouthing of the words which were all hopelessly loaded with saccharin. Only silence had sincerity, and then only if it meant more than just a lack of words. If this was a film, he thought, the camera would be turning in the empty hall of the theatre now. It would pan round onto a bunch of red rosebuds still glistening in their cellophane wrapping, but trampled out of shape. It made him think of the poppies on Poppy Day. He didn't care about the war, but the poppies seemed right — red drops splattered on the grey marble, but peaceful now, no longer soiling or disordering it.

They said goodbye to Tony, and then they walked across the common, going very slowly, arm-in-arm, saying nothing. There were no tears; their time had passed and not yet come again. The sky was lit by a predawn light and their tired eyes picked out colours from the grey; the purple and white of the crocusses and the yellow of the daffodils against a dull-green expanse of lawn. Wesley felt at that moment that Sharon's touch was his only hold on life, the only real thing he had. He pulled her closer to him. She glanced round at him then, but she didn't say anything.

The street-lights at the edge of the park were still buzzing orange, lighting the housefronts with a deadpan, stagey light. Soon they came to Sharon's house.

"You'd better come in," she said. They were at the door and she was fishing the keys out of her bag. He shrugged.

"Yeah." His arm was still round her waist, though loosely now. She raised a finger to her large, bow-shaped lips as she carefully opened the door, and they crept inside.

The small, narrow house felt full of sleepers' breath, dark and warm and drowsy. Sharon turned on the large white table-lamp in her parents' tasteful, toning living-room and placed her crumpled white-leather handbag on the gleaming sideboard. It sat there squatly, like a bean-bag on a highly polished floor. Sharon rubbed her neck, furrowing the brows of her broad forehead as she touched herself.

"C'mere," he said, moving round behind her. She shifted her pose, letting her jacket slide down her arms and onto the floor, allowing him to rub her hardened neck and shoulders. Under his hands he could feel the knotted tension gradually seeping out of them.

"Better?" he asked. She didn't answer and seemed to be deep in thought, looking down at the carpet, her face in deep shadow. His mind was full of red blood, as still and roaring as the deep and silent sea. In a moment she looked up and her blood answered his. He took her in his arms, thinking *life and death*, and the thought grew in rhythm with his breathing. He kissed the back of her neck and felt her exhale, shuddering. Then she twisted her head round and they kissed a desperate, longing kiss. *Is this wrong?* he wondered, but at that moment he was Floyd, and his body was Sharon's body; he was the medium ridden by the loa, Floyd sitting on his back, his strong hands on Wesley's shoulders, guiding him, passing through him. He felt Sharon's fingers at his breast and moved his hands slowly up and down the outsides of her thighs, inside her skirt, caressing her smooth skin. They sank to their knees in a tangled embrace, struggling out of their clothes like butterflies from their chrysalises, tearing the fabric even, in their desperation. She bit his lips and pushed him onto his back, her nails cutting into the skin of his shaved chest, him massaging her breasts as she slid on top of him, looking down on him, young and wise, with her wider-than-possible eyes, her cheeks silver with tears, watching his face contort as they strained like two halves of the same bow, stretching and stretching around its outward curve.

They made love silently in her parents' house, below their bedroom, keeping it all bound up inside, their bodies screaming for them as they reached a shivering fusion and flared with a wild electrical charge like tree-tops in the wind, even in the rain.

At the moment Wesley's thighs locked against hers, and his hips jerked upwards and he flowed like ectoplasm, he knew that Floyd had passed from him into her, and that the eyes that looked down at him wet with emotion and washed clean with tears were his as well as hers. He touched her face gently then, knowing it had been more between them than sharing and it had been more than need: It had been rebirth.

Afterwards, they had lain there in the dark, naked and fearful and trembling in each others' arms, reborn out of tears, oysters out of pearls.

All that feeling was gone now, five years later on, and Wesley felt only emptiness inside. He thought about suicide again; under a bus, under a train, under the Underground frying on the line, plugged into the mains or a gun in the mouth, like giving death a blow-job, if only you could get a gun, but he realised that he had gone beyond those choices for now.

His stomach rumbled. He wanted something to eat. He looked up and down the dull High Street he was standing in, looking for a Macdonalds or something else quick and easy, but all he could see was a chalked-up blackboard. Its title was arty, CAFE VERDE, but the menu read:
All lunches £2-50
Spaghetti Bolognese
Lasagne
Roast Chicken
Plaice
All served with Salad or Chips

He crossed the road and followed an arrow up a side-alley. A second arrow pointed down a wrought-iron staircase to a glass door in a cellar-wall which had been wedged open. Above it CAFE VERDE was spelt out in a semi-circle, the letters framed by a curly Art Nouveau design, yellow on green. The paint was peeling. Wesley stood in the doorway looking in, his stomach groaning as he smelt food cooking, crumpling the ten- pound note in his pocket until he was no longer sure if it was money or just a scrap of paper.

Chapter Four

MUSIC FLOATED OUT of the doorway to meet him, and each note thrilled him like crushed ice poured onto hot skin. It was Billie Holiday, singing,

> *I'm travellin' light*
> *Because my man has gone*
> *So from now on*
> *I'm travellin' light,*

and her voice took his breath away. He didn't know it was her, wouldn't have known who she was even, but the way she sounded it was like nobody else had ever opened their mouth and sung before. The words opened in his mind like white gardenias, new, and sung for him alone:

> *He said goodbye*
> *And took my heart away*
> *So from today*
> *I'm travellin' light.*

His feet were aching so he sat down at one of the round plastic tables. He had walked a long way that day. The plastic was printed to look like marble.

> *No one to see*
> *I'm free as the breeze*
> *No one but me*
> *And my memories.*

Wesley reached for the menu. Prices had been whited-out with Tipp-Ex and rewritten in biro. Soaring above him, Billie's voice was sad, but he knew she was smiling too:

Some lucky night
He may come back again
So until then
I'm travellin' light.

Somewhere a record clicked off. *No one but me*, he thought, *and my memories.*

It was small and run-down, the cafe, and not busy. A middle-aged couple sat by the servery, him not looking at her but reading a paper, perhaps because they had argued because she had dragged him to a restaurant not a pub, only to find by the time the arguing was over that other places had stopped serving, only to find themselves here, both cheated. Next to them an old woman was eating a lettuce-and-tomato salad. It made him think of how Sharon would shred half roast-chickens into mayonnaise with flaked almonds: real salads.

A group of students were posing at another table, smoking cigarettes and drinking filter-coffee. He watched one of them, a girl whose orange hair was tied back with a piece of black lace, as she laughed and waved her cigarette around. Her lips were painted into a cupid's bow with purple lipstick and she was wearing mostly black; a nice, well-off girl trying to be hard, but with not enough hard living behind her to carry it off. She was lucky, he thought, and she didn't know it. But he liked her for that luck, and because, in spite of everything she tried, she still wore her vulnerability on the outside.

"Ready to order?"

The waiter stood over him, his greasy white jacket touching Wesley's arm. Wesley shifted away from him slightly.

"Yeah. I'll have the lasagne."

"Salad or chips?"

"Chips."

He ordered a Coke to drink as well. The waiter scrawled on his pad, tore the top sheet off, folded it and put it on the table.

Wesley looked at the bill without interest. He wanted to leave, get out, go anywhere, but he forced himself to stay because he knew there was nowhere else to go to; that this was it. He felt hot from walking, or from a fever, so he slid out of his jacket and hung it over the back of his chair. After a moment's hesitation he unzipped his overalls too, and slipped his arms out of them, folding them down to his waist. Now I'm really here, he thought. But his bare arms just made him feel stripped and vulnerable, like he was showing too much on the outside. A drop of cold sweat ran down his side and he shivered, feeling ill. His eyes ached as if he had been up all night, and they were hard like lumps of marble. If he closed them he knew he would start to fall, so he stared down at his hands instead, lying on the grey marblette, God's hands moving through the clouds in mysterious ways. But not really; not even for an instant.

He turned suddenly. Had someone called his name? He looked over at the chattering students and one of them looked up and seemed to meet his gaze. He was a black youth of about twenty, Wesley guessed, and he sat slightly back from the others, wrapped in an army greatcoat. Cigarette smoke twisted up lazily in front of his face but his eyes met Wesley's steadily and, for no reason Wesley could understand, his heart began to pound. But maybe the youth was just short-sighted. Wesley flicked round the room and back and met that same pair of eyes again, looking golden in the yellow light. Little thrills ran through Wesley's chest then, and he felt he could drown in those eyes. Even now he was struggling for breath, forcing his lungs to work when they just wanted to rest and lie still. The young man's skin was very dark and smooth, like plain chocolate. His neck and face were thin, his eyes large and slanting and his nose broad. His woolly hair was short but needed a cut and was untidily brushed back from his forehead. His large, sharply-defined lips made a broad band across his face. It was a very still face, handsome if he's not beautiful, Wesley thought, or maybe beautiful if he's not ugly. Wesley felt very strange looking at the young man's face, like he saw his whole life reflected in those eyes, eyes that were for him, and at that moment only for him. The youth smiled then, at something one of his friends had said, and looked away.

No, Wesley thought. But without those eyes he was a drowning man clutching at straws. He heard the rustle of the loa like wasps on paper, coiling around him cold and white, and with the pale and anguished faces of Jesus, Mary and Saint Sebastian. And they began speaking to him, whispering in French words he couldn't understand, the whispering the wind. And through the wind a figure came walking towards him: Floyd like a scarecrow, wild and striding through the stalks of cane burnt into Hell's black whistles, and beneath a bruised electrical sky, or (his body) a church in the wilderness, fire in the sky and straw in his sleeves. Then dry as tinder he was burning, burning at the foot of a black cross, for no reason save walking in the storm; for daring to walk in the storm. Bang bang bang went the hammers driving the nails in, bang bang bang like gunshots in a Southern night. And then the rain began, hiding all that, soaking it all in a second and glittering white like diamonds or a shattered windscreen, and cold and hard as diamonds on his head and face, and he was shouting *help me* as he fell like Lucifer, but there was no-one to help him as he entered the darkness and sank.

Chapter Five

SHARON WRAPPED HER hands around the cup of coffee till it burnt her. Then she pressed them against the cool plastic of the table she was sitting at and drew a deep breath. The anger she had felt today, that was the anger of many days, weeks, months, passed out like the heat through the palms of her hands.

She sipped the coffee. It was strong and bitter. She shuddered and spooned a little brown sugar into it, tasted again, pulled a face and put in a little more. The third sip was bearable. She didn't really like black coffee, she liked cappucino with grated chocolate on top, but taking it black was a few calories less, and that made her feel self-disciplined. Not that she really worried about her weight; she liked her full hips and her full breasts that made her a woman not a girl, and a woman not a clothes horse. But still she had got into the habit of eating a bit less than she wanted, and she had never eaten sweet things.

That was because of my mother, she thought, *because of what she said when I was small, when I wanted to be the fairy princess in the book, with big blue eyes and no waist. I pointed to the picture of the princess and said, "Me, mummy," and she laughed (dressed in a navy-blue dress with white cuffs and wearing a white three-pointed hat), and said, "You're my big strong girl who helps me carry the shopping-bags home." Then she hugged me and kissed me on the forehead. And Daddy looked through fromt he bathroom where he was sleeking back his hair and straightened his black bow-tie that he learnt to tie himself (out of pride, she knew, out of wanting to be successful from the inside out, no faking it), and smiled a band of white without gold. "You'll soon be as strong as your dad," he said, looking in the mirror, not looking at me. He came into the bedroom, touching his hair. I could see his nipples dark through the whiteness of his shirt and smell his aftershave. He put on his black tuxedo and hugged me against it. It smelt of dry-cleaning. His hands gripped my shoulders tight and I knew he was nervous.*

"My big strong girl," he said.

Sharon always remembered that evening, and years later her mother saying how pretty she was as she plaited her hair into short, fat plaits, the two together in Sharon's mind because she always said pretty and never beautiful.

23rd June 1982

It was a hot summer afternoon. The laurels gleamed a dark, rich green, secretive against the bright sunlight, casting long blue shadows across the yellow pavement that turned purple on the grey asphalt of the road. The air smelt of old grass-clippings, and the shadow of the railings outside the school lay across the paving slabs like a venetian blind. A hard, dark boy was lounging there against the railings. He kissed his teeth as she passed (holding her books in front of her breasts, wishing her skirt went past her knees instead of riding up above them), but she walked on by him, snobby then and shy too, because she was the dentist's daughter, the girl who went to church every Sunday, the girl who put her hand inside her knickers and felt ashamed because she hardly felt ashamed at all.

He called out, "Hey!"

She turned to look at him, a ragamuffin boy arched against the black-iron railings, sports bag by his feet, his hips aslant and forward, black school trousers tight over his thighs and crotch. She couldn't look at his face, but she kept on standing there, wanting to be street, wanting to be solid, letting the sun dazzle her from behind his head. Then she turned away from him.

"Hey girl."

"What d'you want?"

"C'mere."

His voice was hard but there was laughter in it. He cocked his head on one side, looking young and cool but with a smile in his scowl. She wanted to go to him but she was too proud and too afraid. The dentist's daughter who had never had a proper boyfriend, who had never had sex even though she was fifteen, whose best friend Sarah was pregnant and was going to have an abortion. She started to walk away from him then, into her long blue shadow, holding her schoolbooks tight against her.

"Hey, bitch," he called after her, his voice only hard now. Stung, she whirled to face him. He had followed her a little way so they were only about eight feet apart. They breathed in time, watching each other. She looked into his black eyes that were secret like the laurels in the bright light and didn't tell him to fuck off like she had been going to. Instead she said,

"You're Floyd, aintcha. Floyd Philips, right?"

He ignored that.

"You got beautiful eyes," he said. His voice was very low and soft. "Kind of like sphinx eyes, like Egyptian, African, you know what I'm sayin'?"

Sharon looked down, blushing, thinking was he bullshitting her, knowing he wasn't or he wouldn't have followed her even one step, would have saved his pride and his cool and stayed against the railings, hanging loose. Finally she looked up at his handsome, savage head and saw that he couldn't meet her eyes. He was looking down and kicking at the ground, his hands in his pockets.

"So I'll see you around, yeah?" he said. He glanced at her with his laurel-dark eyes to see if she was still watching him and then, satisfied, he turned and jogged off without waiting for an answer.

"See you," she called after him. The sun felt hot on her head and her heart was pounding. The laurels were glittering darkly against the cobalt-blue sky and inside them birds were chirping and chattering.

Sphinx eyes.

She'd never been to Egypt, but she'd seen pictures of Egyptian art; finely drawn profiles with big cat's eyes that made their faces beautiful and mysterious. She had loved Floyd for seeing that mystery in her, and when Floyd had died she had seen something like that in Wesley's eyes, and she had loved him too.

But now it had all gone stale and she didn't know what to do.

This morning had been the worst morning yet; starting with her stumbling out of bed with the clock-radio yakking away loudly. She had pulled on her dressing-gown and gone and stood in the green light that filtered through the roll-blind in the living-room. Below her Wesley had lain contorted on the sofa. He had been drunk on sleep, his mouth slightly open, lips papery, his breath filling the room. Needing time to herself, Sharon had gone and washed her hair. When she had finished, he was still asleep. He had looked like a stranger to her then, and she hadn't wanted to wake him. But thinking that, that he was a stranger, this man she had lived with for four years, and loved, and made love with, had filled her with fear, so she had shaken him gently by the shoulder.

"Wake up, Wesley," she had said.

"Thanks," he had mumbled, his head full of sleep.

But touching him had been like touching someone else, and her mind had flooded with bad thoughts as she drew her hand away.

She had felt so trapped in the flat that morning: It had seemed even smaller and pokier than usual, and in the middle of it Wesley lying there, sleeping the sleep that she felt showed a total contempt for her.

After waking him, she had gone to the kitchen to cook him bacon and eggs, despite hating the smell of the frying, and despite knowing it was soaking into her clean hair. She had set the food down in front of him and he had eaten it without a word. And then he had flung it all back in her face (her effort, her giving what little there was still left), by lighting up a cigarette, when he knew she hated her hair to smell of cigarette smoke. She had told him to put it out, so tired of being ignored, and he had just got up and walked out of the room, like he was in the right, like she wasn't meant to speak.

Fuck you, she had thought as the door slammed, anger flaring up inside her. It had been there a long time, and now she asked herself, *how long?* The woman on the front of *Cosmo* smiled up at her blankly, her skin perfect. 'Ten Tips For Holding Onto Your Man,' in big white letters. *How long?*

Sharon was supposed to be going to lunch with Vanda, the salon's top beautician, but Vanda had had to pop to the Ladies; she had heavy flow. Sharon had gone on ahead to get them a table. She wondered if she could get through the day just on coffee, but decided against it. "I'll have a salad with Vanda," she thought.

She was sitting in a salad bar in the top of Marks & Spencers. It was crowded with dull, ordinary people, mostly women, mostly shoppers and secretaries. People she might have been. But she couldn't have stood to work in some drab little office as clerical support with secretarial skills, where life stays on one dead level and you wait for your looks and the years to bleed away among the coffee stains and dried-out felt-pens. She knew because she had tried it, and every day, every hour, every minute spent in that office had made her feel like a failure, like someone who had dreams but not the courage to cut loose and chase them.

And then one day she had cut loose.

And the others she had worked with, like the people here, without dreams and without passions, she had nothing to say to them and never would, because they had never loved, or hated even, had never felt savage joy in their sex or the colour of their skins, and were wan in the face of Ethiopia.

She looked at the women around her then and felt oppressed, not by their minds but by their bodies; by the insistent pull of their wombs and the milk dribbling from their nipples (Sarah's stained bra, she remembered, and her nipples cracked and sore from breast-feeding. "Is worth it, gal," Sarah had said, "cos pickney is life you know, and woman na woman without that bringing forth a life.") But looking at them, subservient to their bodies and almost certainly to their men, (or if not to their men's cocks or fists or money, then to the world men make), Sharon felt consoled and no longer foolish. Almost free. She slipped her shoes off under the table and rubbed her heels where the new leather had worn holes in her stockings.

She hadn't really wanted to meet Vanda for lunch, but when Vanda suggested it she couldn't think of any reason why not. Except she didn't want to see Vanda's spotty yellow face or her masses of black wavy hair (that everyone said was so attractive but Sharon privately thought was just coarse and needed a good styling). And she didn't want to hear about Vanda's wedding plans; the crepe de chine candy-pink dress; the amount of food and the cost of it; the guests like Granny Rose who was coming all the way from Antigua, who Vanda had never met before. Or how Ray was so good to her, so thoughtful and kind. She felt resentful in advance.

Maybe she'll be able to keep off it, she thought. *Maybe we'll just talk about the TV or talk shop.* But she wasn't hopeful.

It set Sharon thinking back to her own wedding-day. Why did she recall it with such feelings of anger, she wondered, and remember the ugly invitation cards before the smiling faces of friends and relatives? Was it just that the lift had been out of order this morning and she'd had to change out of her heels and into some trainers for the stairs, and the trainers had made her feel vulnerable and child-like? That trivial anger? No, she knew that wasn't it at all; it was something much deeper down. Her whole life felt like it had been falling apart for ages now. Not in the way it does in those fat, generation-spanning best-sellers, where you find out that your sugar-daddy lover is your real biological father, but in a small and almost invisible way, like paint flaking off an untreated patch of damp. She realised she had been watching it flake for a long time now, doing nothing about it, and that made her feel helpless. Everything in her life seemed to have got tangled and knotted up, and now she could hardly bear to move because each move she made just pulled the knots tighter. She wanted to step outside it all and breathe, but she didn't know how, how to untie the knots. Back then, she thought, when she had said yes, it had all seemed as clear as a mirror reflecting a clear blue sky.

Their wedding day: February the 10th, eight days before the anniversary of Floyd's death. Somehow it had had to be before; without speaking, she and Wesley had decided it. They had been cloven together then, like two halves of a single seed sunk in the hot, wet earth, joined on a night of violence and darkness. Thinking back to it now she felt she remembered a storm; cold rain needles icy against their sweaty skins, soaking them in white. And there was lightning too as they stretched out and Wesley's head banged against the floor with a thump and then another thump and another and another and another as they pounded the violence of the night into each other until the night like the sea flowed inside Sharon and flowed out again black but white-mantled, filling her to her fingertips and the tip of her tongue and then spreading out into a pool of shadow, a stillness that left her empty and free. They had lain there, she and Wesley, too exhausted for guilt even, their faces wet with tears as they held each other in that stillness.

She had been surprised by her lack of guilt, because she knew that if she'd told anyone what she'd done, that person would have been shocked and called her a slag. Even Sarah. And how could she have explained herself? It had been so inevitable, that night, so much to do with need and nothing at all to do with right or wrong. *And that's what they all say*, she thought.

Back then she had been sure that they needed each other like eyes need the light; that that need was what had decided them to get married — not for the passion that was gone, and that neither of them wanted to feel again — but for the closeness that came after it in those days as quiet as the lilies in the church.

And she had come home that day after kneeing that guy in the balls in the tight world of the office she was working in then, not hurt herself by his hand on her tit (not a breast but a tit beneath his hands and his contempt), but for a moment she had been all women everywhere so she had had to knee him. But she had missed and the air had gone out of the room, making it just another office, unbearable. Then she couldn't breathe and his face was red but still smiling stale and yellow, like her knee and her breasts were just a joke and it was all just a come-on, and in her anger she filled the room and she had never felt so hard.

And Wesley had been there when she got home and she had said "Help me," and he had taken her in his arms not needing to challenge her or dominate, but just holding her the way she wanted to be held. With him she didn't have to fight to keep her place, her hard-won place, on the iron surface of the thundering sphere that ripped her nails raw every time she slid, and with a gentle touch he reached inside the torn core of her being and gave her a little peace. And she could let go and float like a baby in his waters.

In the end perhaps she had rejected all he had to give her and chosen to be strong all the way round: no chinks in her walls and no windows in her buildings. Perhaps it was she who had chosen to step back; perhaps she was to blame for where they were now. But she knew that wasn't a true explanation of what had changed between her and Wesley: he had moved away too.

Sometimes she felt as if she had never even touched him.

There was that time that she had watched him, she standing in the kitchen doorway, he sitting in the lounge on the brown dralon settee. It had been a quiet Saturday afternoon; the TV was on, showing the sports round-up after the news. Wesley had turned the volume down low so there was just the screen green with the racing results. He sat sprawled out in a pair of faded jeans and an American football shirt, hands dangling between his legs. The muscular curve of his thighs did not excite Sharon as she watched him sitting there, not like it had once done. Once, it had been poetry.

There was an empty red mug with hearts on it sitting in front of him on the smoked-glass coffee-table. It was like looking at a painting of a man watching TV, except for the flicker of the screen, which flung out green eclipses that sickled round the curves of his face and body. But Wesley wasn't watching the TV, he was staring out of the window.

From where he was sitting there was nothing to see; no buildings, no trees, no birds even, just the square of dull grey sky through dirty glass. Sharon stood leaning against the doorway, letting the water boil behind her, and watched Wesley. The rule she made herself was that she had to watch him until he turned and looked at the TV. Then she could stop.

But he didn't look away, and the seconds and the minutes ran down over her like drops of sweat. After quarter of an hour had dripped by she thought she would go crazy and her arm prickled with pins and needles from where she had been leaning on it. Defeated, she went back into the kitchen, picked up a plate and smashed it on the floor. And waited.

He hadn't come in, but when she went into the lounge later on he had asked, "You alright, Sharon?" And she had said "yes" quite lightly because there had only been a few tears and they were washed away down the sink by then.

It wasn't being ignored that hurt her, not really, and she

wasn't one of those women who have to have a man looking at them all the time. What hurt was the fact there was nothing to see through the window, nothing for her to see anyway. And that meant that a hidden part of him had been shown to her, and only by accident. He hadn't meant to show it.

He seemed to spend a lot of time staring out of the window, staring at the sky, enough to make her ask him sometimes,

"Why're you staring out the window, Wes?"

He would look at her, shrug, and talk about something else, the shrug sometimes irritated, sometimes not. Not that she really expected an answer. She knew she was using the wrong words even if she didn't know what the right ones would be. She had imagined writing in to *Cosmo: Dear Irma, my husband is always staring out of the window and he won't talk to me about it.* She couldn't imagine the answer, however.

The week before, she had gone to see Sarah, who was still one of her closest friends. There was something about Sarah that made it easy for Sharon to confide in her, maybe because she had lived through divorce and abortion, so she wasn't ignorant about life. And since both those things were failures, she had passed up the right to judge what other people did too. So Sharon didn't find Sarah's worldliness a threat because it was nothing that she wanted, but still she very much respected the wisdom that Sarah had gained from what she had lived through. Sarah was a good listener too; you could tell from how she watched and what she said that she was really thinking about what you were saying.

So Sharon was sitting there talking and Sarah was listening, her eyes never leaving Sharon's face. To start off with, Sharon's words had been cool and detached, a mirror of how she wanted her life to appear. But the words quickly started to get away from her, shimmering and shivering with repressed emotion until she couldn't give them shape and only tears would come.

Sarah had taken Sharon's knotted hands and then hugged her, rocking her like a child, her touch Moses' staff on the rocks of the desert, keeping the torrent flowing. Sharon's face burnt with crying and shame.

"You must think I'm a total fool," she said a little later, after blowing her nose in Sarah's hanky and pulling her coat protectively round herself. Sarah shook her head, concentrating.

"I just don't know what to do," Sharon added.

"Eh-eh, no knowin' what to do na make you foolish, gal," Sarah said briskly, gripping Sharon's hands and shaking it to get her full attention.

"Wesley na know 'im own mind, you know? An' 'im can't tell you ting 'im na know 'imself. Is not you a blame."

Sharon found it hard to meet Sarah's eyes, but she made herself do it for a moment before looking away.

"I know," she said evenly, tightening her hand around Sarah's, struggling to let go of her guilt.

"I know is 'ard," Sarah said gently, "but you mus' try an' give 'im space fe work ting out in 'imself. We all 'ave ting we can't share, you know."

Sharon nodded, looking down at her hands.

She had known Sarah was right because Sarah really liked Wesley and wouldn't put him down just because it was the easiest thing to do. It was Sarah who had said that Sharon should marry him. Even now, Sharon had to admit that, at the time, she had been right.

It was stupid, she thought (mocking what actually meant quite a lot to her, only once again the words were not enough to bear the meaning), but she still felt now what she had felt then; that it was wrong to live in sin. Even if she never went to church now she was grown up, that honesty or decency was still important to her. It was really her who'd proposed to Wesley, by talking about the advantages of marriage and how it made sense and so on until he had finally asked her. Her parents had met him a couple of times before, and they seemed to approve, because even if he had been a friend of Floyd's, and even if they didn't approve of that, Floyd was dead and thus exonerated, and some of his bleak halo of light shone on Wesley's face. But Sharon didn't care very much whether they approved of who she married or not; it was none of their business. It had stopped being their business from the time they had said she couldn't see Floyd and had banned him from the house. And always their voices so apologetic as if their prejudice and snobbery were some divine authority that they were ordered to obey. She remembered screaming at her mother, and her mother acting all hurt, saying,

"But a *boxer*, Sharon, how could you go out with a boxer?" pretending it was the violence she hated, the brutality of the fight, the career and not the individual. But the truth was she hated Floyd because although his eyes shone with intelligence and his mind and tongue were sharp, he didn't speak nicely, didn't admire her status or aspire to her values. And she had been afraid too, because he was so near to the line where life and death are closest and each is at its most vibrant, and she had spent her life creeping away from that edge, that violence.

Even her father — not ashamed but proud of the black men who fought in the ring or even outside it, who wanted to be part of that fight, less honest in that desire than her mother, perhaps — hadn't wanted to bring the danger so close to home. And it was him who'd told her she couldn't see Floyd again, struggling to be a man in the face of another man.

They didn't know she had slept with Floyd and they were sensible enough not to ask. Their virginal daughter defiled by a blackheart boy. But it hadn't been like that of course: he had been shy, she had had to encourage him. There had been a little pain but then it had become something more, and more than the movements they were making, the light inside the touch; something secret. All stretched out on the back seat of a car that was borrowed.

After a boxer, anyone in any sort of reputable and regular employment sounded good to her parents (even if he wasn't a doctor, even if he wasn't a church-goer; just, please Lord, not some ragamuffin yout, and not drugs). Wesley's good manners and good looks more than made up in their eyes for his non-professional status on the wedding-day.

Recently Sharon had found herself wondering what if Floyd was still alive? What would they be doing with their lives? What would they be doing right now? And she would blush even if she hadn't imagined anything sexual, the heat of the blush an echo of the heat of the ecstacy that he had given her with his hands, his dick and his heart. It was those blushes that made her realise how much of a compromise what she had with Wesley was. As the passion between them had slowly faded away, all that remained was the time and the feelings they had shared. If that was love, it ended up being like the love of brother and sister, not husband and wife. Not lover and lover.

It would never have been like that with Floyd. it had always been raw between them, stripped naked and with their wounds open, loving and hating their nakedness with a passion but never withdrawing from it, she always reaching that part in Floyd that in Wesley would never be open to her.

Sure, it would never have been perfect, she thought, remembering the bruises and the broken windows, and shouting until she thought her throat would burst; and maybe they would just have ended up turning the knife in each other and watching the wounds bleed. But it seemed to Sharon that would be better than what she was doing now, falling slowly into silence and nothingness. Thinking about Wesley now, she found it impossible to remember the times when they had talked into the small hours, him holding one of her small, slim hands between his large, heavy ones and looking deep into her eyes.

It made her think of all the things everyone tells you about marriage: kiss romance goodbye and stand by for drudgery. But that wasn't true for her and Wesley; she had more of a career than he did, and he accepted that. Sure, she cooked and cleaned, but she got home earlier than he did, and besides she regularly sent him off to the laundrette. And he didn't complain about watching her knickers go round and round in the tumble-drier, or about washing his socks and vests and underpants separately so all her things were fresh.

She couldn't help but smile even now when she remembered the morning after their wedding, when he had jumped up in bed, shaken her awake, looked into her eyes and, with a grin on his face, asked,

"D'you feel any different?"

It had been six o'clock in the morning, and she had smiled back at him before drifting back into sleep, her hand entwined with his.

She had wanted a church wedding. Like a little girl she had wanted a twenty-foot train, everyone in grey morning-suits and top-hats, and a white rolls-royce to ride in. She did get the church wedding: her parents' church all whitewashed white inside, light and airy, with motes of dust that bore no bad memories for her anymore, but hung in the sunlight like specks of gold. For a moment it had all felt like a homecoming, and she had been like a little girl, full of wonder and belief. But then the sun had gone behind the clouds and she had become her woman-self again, whose body was vaster than the church and whose experience would not fit inside it. Who was her own mystery. And so she had walked down the aisle with her body the temple, knowingly.

She couldn't recapture now the excitement and the fear she had felt in the days before the wedding. Originally she had thought that once Wesley proposed to her, that would be it; that the wedding ceremony itself would just be the signature to the letter, deft and done without thought or effort. But as the day got nearer she had become more and more nervous as she realised how important it was for her, and while her mother was telling her the plans she had made, Sharon began to be afraid. Part of her fear was the knowledge that she was no longer in control; that she'd said she would marry Wesley and everyone had taken her at her word and booked the church and arranged the food and invited everyone else. Part of it was something else.

Sharon wore the hat her mother had worn at her own wedding, a little pill-box with a white feather and a net veil. Her wedding-dress was very simple, like a Twenties dress, with a drop waist she was just slim enough to wear. Sarah had made it for her, out of a length of satin that Sharon had bought herself. It was white satin, and she was dressed all in white on the big day, not for the virgin she would never have wanted to be (because of denying Floyd, which she would never do), but because it meant a fresh start. It meant something new.

All the little memories of that day, many good and a few bad. Like the invitation cards her dad had got printed, vulgar with silver and gold, and lettering in red that was really ugly, but she knew it had been expensive for him to have them done, so she had pretended to like them and just had to live with the fact that everyone who came to the wedding would have seen them. Or like the wedding-cake, enormously rectangular and white, with silver letters on the top and pillars on its sides, and no little figures of the bride and groom. Or Tony's pretty daughter Floella throwing up on somebody's coat, she couldn't remember whose. And of course Wesley's friend Mikey's band playing lovers' rock at the reception, keeping the political content to a minimum, and Mikey singing a ballad he had written for them, accompanying himself on a guitar — she didn't remember any of the words but they had sounded sweet then, and Mikey's voice had been sweet too. And Wesley large and handsome and smiling, looking well wikked in a double-breasted navy suit which had a cut like a razor-blade, a yellow rose in his button-hole, and black shoes that shone like glass. She remembered just after the moment of slight fumbling as they exchanged rings: It was an odd feeling, as if she had never worn a ring before.

She ran her finger around the plain band of gold as she sat in the coffee-bar, thinking about the things it might have meant to her; the purity of marriage maybe, or a link in the chain of women's slavery. But what was topmost in her mind was that the gold that she touched was really Wesley's. At the back of some drawer there would be a receipt that was his, for however much it might be, she didn't know. It wasn't the cost that mattered anyway; what mattered was that it was him who had paid for it: it was his. And it was on her finger always, and for always, and bound to be on her spirit-finger too, her church finger. She touched the gold again, realising then what she hadn't realised before — the power of rings. Bob Marley had been given a ring by the Emperor of Ethiopia that he never took off, she had read somewhere, even though it burned him sometimes. She could believe that now: the power of a ring. She could feel sweat tingling under the gold for the first time in years, as if the ring was a scab coming loose; as if now that the wound beneath it had healed, it was time for the ring to drop off.

She pulled at it slightly. *It would only take some soap*, she thought to herself, *or some vaseline. I just have to slip it off (the ring the only physical bond between us now, the rest, the chairs and glasses just money to be split), just slip it off and it'll all be over between us.* But did she want to finish it? It was nothing to do with freedom, it was nothing to do with hope. Or despair. Or hate. She drained her cup to the bittersweet dregs. Where was Vanda? she wondered, feeling distracted and irritated.

The ring was more than debt and obligation though, to Wesley, her parents and the church. It was betrayal too. And she had known that the moment she had signed her name, her new name, in the book, Sharon Brooks, in an uncertain hand, both halves new and unfamiliar. She had betrayed then, and been betrayed. Her name had been taken from her, and she had given it away, that taking raping her, and that giving the betrayal of Floyd, Floyd James Philips' name. And by being taken without giving, but giving in too, she had betrayed him twice. And in her dreams she did not face him but turned away, denying his name as if she had never heard it spoken.

Sharon Brooks. Sharon Brooks. Sharon Brooks.

But then there had been nights before the marriage when she had stared into the dark and watched the crosses floating on the ceiling blossom and fade until daylight sent them away, and other nights when she had cried herself to sleep, hating Floyd because she loved him, hating him for being dead. That time she hadn't been able to stop sobbing and had started to choke, running to the toilet to vomit, her throat and eyes and nose stripped raw and burning, almost fainting over the bowl, then pulling the handle and stumbling back to bed.

She had slept for a whole day after that, not waking up until six in the evening, and her mind had felt clear and empty on waking, as if she had somehow vomited away the razor-blades that had been stuck inside her head.

Looking back, she saw with a fresh clarity what a mess she had been in.

Marrying Wesley had been a way out of herself, a sort of healing. He had been gentle and undemanding, had given her space. Now she wondered if what she took for care had only ever been indifference. But after a while you can look into someone's eyes and be sure of what you see in them, so she knew that wasn't true because she had looked into his eyes and seen the care. For a time it had been like that between her and Wesley for everything, but now their eyes rarely met, and his had become impenetrable. She wondered what secrets he was keeping. She had told Sarah about that feeling, that there were secrets, and Sarah had replied, "The best-kept secrets is the ones you don't know you're keepin'."

Sharon had known that was true, and it made her think that was why words had failed between them; because there were no words for Wesley, because there was nothing for him to describe. But not only words had failed. They rarely touched now, just a kiss in the morning and maybe at night. When you share a bed with someone it seems impossible that you don't really touch, Sharon thought, but all it is is my backside against his or my arm against his. Like people on the Tube: not touching really.

Last night he hadn't got in until late. She had woken up at the rattle of the key in the lock and lain awake in the dark, waiting. She heard the sound of piss splashing into the toilet water. There was no flush, which might have been thoughtfulness on his part, or drunkenness. This was followed several long minutes later by the sound of the light-switch clicking off. Then there was silence. She waited, fully awake now, and then slipped out of bed, pulling on her dressing-gown before opening the bedroom door. Wesley was lying curled-up on the settee, drunkenly asleep and despite it all she wanted to do something for him, so she went and got a blanket to put over him, pulling it up to his chin. Then she went back to bed and lay awake, thinking.

Despite it all. Despite the unforgiveable things.

It happened yesterday, on Sunday, the only time Sharon and Wesley spent more than the fag-end of the day together; when they were actually in each other's company for longer than a two-hour stretch.

In the morning Sharon had thought about going to church. It was just habit really, to think about it anyway. She hadn't actually been for years, not just to an ordinary service that wasn't a wedding or a funeral. Besides which, she realised that when she did think of going, it was church which she thought of going to. Church. Not even God. So she put it out of her mind and stayed in bed reading a magazine instead.

When she was a little girl one of her teachers had told the class that she was an atheist. Sharon remembered wondering how someone as intelligent as a teacher could not believe in God. She had felt then that it had something to do with the teacher's being white. Now she just thought the teacher had been stupid to bother saying it, even though Sharon didn't believe anymore herself. Trying to remember what it felt like to believe was like trying to remember what it felt like to be a virgin: almost impossible to feel again the ignorance and the need the ignorance created. But if she sank back far enough into herself she could remember that sense of burning wildly from the inside out, burning white and not pure in her faith and untouchedness, needing to feel the pillar of fire, the pillar of the church, deep inside her, that created even as it cleansed her sense of dirtiness. (Then soaked by sweat and wetness, blood and come, the tarnishing fire put out forever by experience. And she had come out steaming like smelted iron from the water, with a new faith that shone within her doused fire like polished steel, and so she had put away her cross and her childish things.)

Her parents had been disappointed when she stopped going to Church when she was sixteen, but they had never tried to force her to go except with the hurt in their eyes. That hurt had deepened all the time she was going out with Floyd, and began to heal only when she got married to Wesley. She used to wish sometimes that they had been more angry over her backsliding and shouted at her and argued and not let it go like they had, because that would have given her something hard to kick against when she needed it: a springboard out of herself.

"Your folks're like jelly," Floyd said to her once. "Stick your anger in 'em and you think you made a hole. When your anger goes, the hole goes. Like sticking your fingers in a jelly. When you take 'em out, the holes close up."

So they always thought of jelly and anger as being close to each other. Like the time she had chucked in a secretarial job because the bloke was a racist and to her face too, and she had been blazing mad with anger and had gone round to Floyd's flat and thrashed around swearing blind. And he had slipped out after making her a cup of tea and brought back a jelly from the corner shop. He produced it unexpectedly on a plate, green and shiny and quivering, and looked at her dead serious. She had looked him straight in the eyes and his po-face hadn't wavered. And then she couldn't help but laugh, and he laughed, and they laughed her anger away.

Afterwards they ate the jelly off each others' fingers, feeling unexpectedly shy and self-conscious. And then they made love.

Like on all the Sundays Sharon spent with Wesley these days, she found his just being there irritating. Perhaps she still worried about him too, perhaps that was the root of her irritation. Or perhaps she had stopped caring by then. She couldn't be sure. All she did know was, she found him irritating.

Sarah and her new boyfriend Rafe were meant to be coming round that afternoon, and even though they didn't actually turn up until the early evening, because they had said the afternoon that meant Sharon and Wesley were tied to the flat, and to each other. Sharon made it bearable for herself by pretending not so much that everything was alright, but that she hadn't noticed that everything wasn't alright, and that Wesley hadn't noticed it either. But the harder she pretended, the more impossible words became between them.

Until that afternoon words had still just been possible.

Sharon had deliberately spent a long time in the bathroom getting herself ready. If any room in the flat was hers, it was the bathroom, a territory delineated by soaps and scents and bath-crystals, shampoos, conditioners, cleansers, make-up, hair-dye, even nail-varnish and remover. She had put a little pink rug around the base of the toilet, and in the cupboard above the sink, Wesley's deodorant, razor and toothbrush were crowded out by her tampons and the boxes of multi-coloured tissues she got given as presents. The bath-mat, black and white with elephants on it, was a present she'd been given by a boyfriend she'd had when she was fourteen, Sam. Sam. He'd been so nice, so serious, with his earnest brown eyes and his razored parting that she'd felt like a slag for not wanting to go out with him. After a while she'd had to say, "I want to have fun, Sam, not sit in every night watching the TV." And he hadn't understood because she couldn't put it into words, that it wasn't that she wanted to sleep around, and she couldn't bring herself to say, "I'm not ready for a regular boyfriend," either, because that wasn't exactly true. It was that his passivity and lack of ambition threatened her deep down inside, like being a housewife cleaning up after your man, like having babies and washing nappies and filling pouting mouths, or like lying there while he does it, bored and complaining. Like not existing as herself at all.

But she couldn't have said that then, couldn't have put it into words. All she could say was that he was 'too nice,' and ask him not to call round anymore. He had never called her a slag but she had felt like one. At the time it had been awful, but now the bath-mat had become a symbol of her strength and self-worth. And its presence made the bathroom more definitely hers.

Wesley's personal space was inside his head.

When she finished drying herself, Sharon wound one fluffy white towel round under her armpits so it just covered her up and another smaller one around her head. Then she walked out of the bathroom towards the open bedroom door. The bathroom door opened noiselessly. As she stepped into the hall she glanced round towards the living-room and saw Wesley standing there, facing the window, a silhouette against the white glare outside, the sort of light it would hurt your eyes to look at too long. He was twitching his head, shaking it like he wanted to shake something out. Like he wasn't quite sane. Sharon stifled the urge to cough or make some other noise, and watched.

After a few seconds he stopped twitching and seemed to just be staring out of the window, still and silent as a statue, hugging his shoulders with his hands. *Did he see me? Did he see me?* Her heart was racing. She didn't dare to move because the next move had to be silent, completely silent, so she just stood there with her brain not working, paralyzed. Then she realised that he could turn round at any second and find her spying on him. Any second, and it would be much more embarrassing to be caught standing shivering in the hall than to be a flash of white fluff at the back of his mind.

Holding her breath she took two quick steps into the bedroom, her heart thudding against her chest. Once inside, she stood listening for several seconds, hearing nothing but the pressure in her ears. Gradually outside sounds, of cars and children's shouts filtered in, but the flat itself was filled with silence. She unwrapped her towel and sat down on a corner of the king-size duvet that covered their bed. It moulded coolly to the shape of her buttocks. She patted tentatively at her hair with the other towel. Then, angry at being afraid to do what she wanted, to go where she wanted, even in her own house, she snapped the radio on, asserting her presence. The coarse rasp of static, the incoherent jangle that always comes out of a radio until you get used to it, tore through the silence:

> Hot love
> Crazy love
> You're the one I'm thinking of...

As Sharon applied her make-up, putting it on lightly and with professional cool and detachment, all her thoughts floated away from her, so when she walked into the living-room, her mind was a curious blank.

Wesley was sitting on the sofa watching the TV, an old black-and-white Western.

"'If we cut the wagon loose, we can make it to the ford.'"

"'You do that son, I'll make sure Lavinia and her paw got rifles.'"

He didn't look up when she walked into the room which made her bristle with anger immediately, not out of vanity or wounded pride, but because he was acting as if she didn't exist. As if he had the right to decide that. It seemed so arrogant and condescending of him. So she walked into the middle of the room and switched the set off. Silence. His eyes swivelled up to meet hers, pretty eyes, unreadable eyes. They didn't pull memories out of her anymore, his sphinx eyes, they just made her feel tired. She looked past them and said,

"Come on, Wes, I've got to get the front room tidy for Sarah and Rafe."

He exhaled in a way which was not quite a sigh, not quite anger, and pushed himself up onto his feet. Then, without a word he started to walk out of the room. Sharon blazed in anger.

"Hey," she said, "are you going to mend the medicine cabinet or what?" (her voice saying with the edge of a whine *help me*, but not going far enough to say *I don't want you to be a man*, still not threatening that, still within the boundaries; offering the hinge and not the duster, the screwdriver and not the hoover, but whining now by holding back), "You said you were going to do it months ago. Like always."

He turned round and slapped her hard across the face, hard enough to knock her to the floor in her surprise. She sat where she fell, her mouth open, face stinging, eyes pricking with hot tears. The only thought in her head was, *now he'll rape me, now he'll rape me*. He towered above her, thick-set and powerful, his broad chest swelling like the moon's horizon, his face somehow in shadow as he looked down on her. She couldn't think, couldn't act. Brain dead, she could only sit there and wait for it to happen, her legs spread, skirt rumpled high up her thighs, indecent, provocative. The room behind him seemed compressed and tight, the V of the ceiling a devil's crown of horns for his head, haloed by a white star; the light-bulb glaring raw from under its paper shade, a present that Sarah had given her. A Habitat shade. It was brown. She liked it. But the brown, the brown of the armchairs never looked quite right in electric light, but you know how it is you can never be bothered to change it once you've bought it oh God. She could hardly breathe. She couldn't breathe. Everything stood still. Her chest was going to burst it had gone all hard, like wood.

Then he gestured in a helpless sort of way and stumbled out into the hall. She heard him pull his leather jacket, the one she sometimes wore, off the peg and sling it over his shoulder.

"I'm off out to get some cigarettes," he said, but he wasn't speaking to her.

The door shut and he was gone.

Sharon sat there, still not moving, just breathing shallow breaths. The seconds ticked past and her panic gradually receded. Suddenly she felt foolish, sitting there on the floor. She struggled to her feet and straightened her dress and hooked her shoes back on. She looked around but no, the flat had not been smashed up and no one had kicked the door down. Everything looked just the same.

She went to the bathroom and methodically removed her make-up and bathed her face in cold water. Then she put ice on the bruised side. It wouldn't look too bad, she decided. If she was careful she could hide it with make-up. She didn't want Sarah to see it. The towel felt hot and rough against her chilled, bruised skin.

Wesley came back as she was putting her eyeshadow back on. A touch of gold. She had once put it on his eyelids and they had looked at each other, grinning stupidly, his eyes sphinx eyes like hers.

"Here," he said, lightly tossing a packet of Benson & Hedges onto the table beside her. And then it was too late for words.

And that was what had finished it between them, even though with Floyd there had always been fights: he had hit her and she had hit him back and sometimes she had even hit him first. But that fighting like wild animals, that extremity, had been so much a part of their relationship that she had accepted it, that knowledge of the cage; the shining violence that had been another reason why her parents had hated Floyd. She had never told them about the cracked rib. They hadn't said too much anyway, because even to them it was obvious that she wasn't a doormat. Everyone knew that she had blacked Floyd's eye once. But what they didn't know was that it hadn't even been in anger. It had all been a game, a game of holding back. And Wesley had never so much as laid a finger on her, could never lay a finger on her, because of Floyd.

But he had, and so everything was changed between them. She felt no hate for Wesley, even after that. Only a little love and a little sadness. And that was all she felt right now: no fire, only embers.

Without her setting out to do it, she realised she had come to a decision: It was over.

She wouldn't be leaving Wesley; they had left each other a long time ago. And it was like all this time she had been waiting at a bus-stop, and now the bus had arrived all she had to do was to get on it. It was a happy thought, and for a moment she was wreathed in perfection, caught up in a vision of herself that made her feel free.

A heavy camelcoat was flung down on the back of the chair opposite her.

"Sorry I'm late," said Vanda. "Fancy another coffee?"

Chapter Six

WESLEY WOKE SUDDENLY and in blindness, not knowing if the dark was just another dream. As he stared, his eyes open like opened crabs pale and ruined in their shells, crosses started floating upwards past him, black and invisible in the opaque blackness. His eyes ached, bruised like the crabs' flesh by the salt water of his tears so he closed them, but the crosses kept on moving upwards like he knew they would. Even if he was blind, he would always see crosses. He kept his eyes closed and listened to the silence rushing past his ears like the sea. The gutted crabs rolled and turned over in the surf and he slowly faded into sleep.

When he woke up again he felt tired but no longer drained; just the tiredness you get from sleeping too long. He yawned and stretched his aching back, wriggling around on the lumpy mattress to try and get comfy again, pulling the quilt up over his shoulder. But he didn't feel sleepy anymore. He rubbed his hard, crisp eyes. His breath tasted stale and he was bursting for a piss. An eddy of cold air stole over his sticky back as he sat up on his elbows and looked around. *Where am I, anyway?* he wondered.

Someone had lit the room while he was asleep. A jointed desk lamp with a missing spring that was sitting on the threadbare carpet by the bed pushed shadows up the walls and onto the ceiling, where they clustered like the sails of boats around the wire of the empty light-socket. The lamp's flex trailed across the colourless carpet to an adaptor wedged into a cracked plug. Wesley could hear soft sizzling noises coming from the plug.

The room was long and narrow like at some time it had been partitioned off from a larger one, and there were light rectangular patches on the walls where posters or pictures and a wardrobe had once been. All the furniture looked old and battered; junk-shop furniture.

The mattress he was lying on sat under a window at the end of the room where part of the roof sloped down. Thin, dirty-yellow satin curtains with straggly dark-green leaves embroidered on them hung over the window on a piece of flex stretched between two nails. The nails had split the white gloss on the woodwork and he could see caramel-coloured wood inside. The curtains didn't keep the light out from the street, just changed the colour of it.

Despite the friendly orange glow of a little one-bar electric fire that faced the bed, the air was still icy and Wesley pulled the sheets up around him and the green paisley eiderdown up to his chin. He watched his breath mist the air and wondered where he was for the second time, the cold increasing his urge to piss.

Across the room from where the mattress was lifted off the ground by bundles of yellowing newspapers was a chest of drawers with a purple paisley shirt hanging out of one of the drawers, one sleeve touching the floor. On top of it sat a packet of Bic razors, some Gillette shaving foam, shampoos and conditioners, cocoa butter, and a shiny wooden bowl with gold chains hanging over the edge of it. Next to that was a photograph of a middle-aged white couple in a pewter deco frame. They should've been smiling but they looked more like they were being dazzled by the sun: their eyes were in shadow.

In the far corner of the room a faded plum-coloured velvet curtain on a rail made a makeshift wardrobe. Next to the curtain was a spindly little round-bottom chair with a perforated hardboard seat which had a dirty green army greatcoat draped over it in stiff and awkward folds. Wesley looked at the coat and wondered who it belonged too. The metal buttons were tarnished and the seams were splitting.

On the floor beside the bed was a red mug with white hearts on it and a little cold coffee in the bottom, and lying next to the mug was an open pad of paper, A3 size, with a drawing on it. Wesley leant over to get a proper look at the drawing.

It was a picture of him, lying in bed; just his head on the pillow and one shoulder sticking out from under the quilt, done with coloured pastels or crayons. *It must've taken hours*, Wesley thought as he looked at it. That made him think that someone had been watching him for hours, and he felt uneasy.

He knew it was him in the drawing, but he didn't know if the likeness was good. All the face except for the lips was a blur of smudged pastels and his closed eyes were just curling blue lines. But the lips were sharply and carefully drawn, made bigger perhaps than they really were, and shaped as though they were kissing sleep. Whoever had drawn him could really draw, he reckoned. All the colours were soft, and the picture should have been tranquil, but here and there were flashes of harder lines behind, and in the wall behind his head were restless patterns like knotted climbing plants. On the quilt-cover too the paisleys blinked and fluttered like uneasy butterflies. Even Wesley's closed eyes in the picture had a tenseness to them, like someone closing their eyes tight against a nightmare. But it wasn't Wesley's nightmare.

He reached out and turned the page over to see if there was anything else in the pad, but it was empty. On the back of the page someone had written in green pastel and in a rapid, scrawling hand, *like sleeping beauty he sleeps imprisoned by a wall of thorns that prick him like bad dreams.* He flipped the pad shut and put it down. It was like he had read someone's private diary and he felt embarrassed. Or maybe like a burglar who finds himself right in the heart of somebody's house without knowing the people who live there.

He rubbed a hand over the back of his head then the front, making his hair feel cleaner and more springy. Just as he was lying back on the bed, the bedroom door opened and a young black man walked in, the young guy who'd been sitting with the students in the cafe. He saw Wesley propped up on one shoulder.

"Hello man, how're you doing?" he asked. "I didn't wake you up, did I?"

Wesley shook his head.

"No, man, I was already awake."

"Al*right*." A piss-take American accent.

The young man grinned and his grin was like a new moon rising, touching the room and Wesley's face with silver. The mask-like quality his face had had back there in the cafe, where it had meant so much to Wesley, disappeared as his nose crinkled above his smile, and laughter lines touched the corners of his oriental eyes.

Wesley looked up at him thrusting his hands deep into the pockets of the outsize frayed tweed jacket he was wearing. It had leather patches on the elbows, but the stitching that held them on was fraying and coming apart. Underneath that he had on a baggy cream jumper with sleeves sticking out past the sleeves of the jacket and hanging over his hands. His skinny skin-tight legs ended in light brown disco boots that were heavily seamed above the toes. He looked vulnerable in the large jacket, like a cute kid dressed up in grown-up hand-me-downs, but touched by punk, touched by the hardness of the street.

Wesley saw that he was nervous at being looked at. His eyes flicked round the room and he swallowed before he spoke.

"I just came to get my sketch-pad anyway," he said, pointing to where it lay on the floor. Wesley picked it up and handed it to him.

"It's good, man," he said, his eyes on the young man's eyes, trying to see something and trying to give something too. But there was a wall.

"D'you like it?" the young man replied, as if he too was trying to climb the wall. Wesley nodded. "I did it while you were asleep," he added. Then: "Well, when you were keeping still. Man, you had *some* nightmares. I wouldn't've done it but I just thought someone better keep a eye out for you." He was embarrassed now and couldn't look at Wesley.

"That's alright, man. Thanks." Wesley was talking as casually as possible, trying to put the young man at his ease. "Suppose this makes you me guardian angel, yeah?"

Another quicksilver smile. Wesley caught onto it and smiled back. "I'm bustin' for a piss, man," he said. "You got a bathroom round here?" He swung his legs over the side of the bed and sat up slowly. Pain knifed through his head and he winced.

"Are you alright, mate?" He was squatting facing Wesley looking concerned, his voice soft and slightly uneven, nervous still.

"Yeah." Wesley's voice was a whisper and he closed his eyes against lights that were suddenly too bright. He sat on the edge of the bed, willing the pain to go. Slowly it faded and he opened his eyes. The young man offered him his hand. Wesley took it and was pulled to his feet.

"Christ, it's cold," he said, slapping his bare arms.

The young man went and rummaged in the chest of drawers and pulled out a grey tracksuit top, worn white in patches with so much washing. He threw it across the room to Wesley who caught it and, stretching up his aching arms, pulled it on. It was small on him but it stretched. He felt warmer and immediately he felt warmer he felt stronger too.

The young man was looking and smiling again as Wesley lowered his arms to his sides, and there was an openness and wonder in his eyes where they had been closed and smokey before. He glanced down at the floor then up at Wesley. Wesley met his intent gaze for a second, then ran his eyes round the room.

"How did I get here, man?" he asked, wrinkling his brow. "I don't remember —", but he wasn't sure how much he didn't remember. For a second he had a flashback to somewhere white and dazzling. He was Floyd, dying on the operating table, his mother letting him . . . no she wouldn't've let him die, no way, man, but later — later, yes, he did die. Floyd was dead, Wesley was dead — No. . . . He covered his eyes against the brightness of the light. *No.* He opened them. Everything was as it had been a second before.

"The doctor said you'd just fainted, you should just lie down for a bit. He said to take you home and I didn't know where you lived so I brought you back here."

"Yeah?" Wesley said. The young man's comically worried expression made him smile softly. When he smiled, the young man smiled too.

"You want a cup of coffee or something?" he asked. There was almost laughter in his voice. And maybe a touch of craziness.

Wesley nodded. "Sweet, man," he replied. "You got a name?"

The young man nodded. "I'm Paul," he said.

As he moved his head slightly, Wesley noticed a row of five steel studs running the length of Paul's left earlobe. They caught the light and looked like tiny stars in the night of his ear.

Chapter Seven

YOU NEVER GET free, Paul is thinking, *you never get free but then sometimes (or maybe just once, maybe one chance is all you ever get) you get a chance for freedom, and although everything in your life (in my life) tells you not to decide, not to take it, and always be passing by on the other side of the road, you know This Is It.*

And you do something because you know this might be the only chance there is and if you don't it'll prove them right and if they were right you would've cut your wrists a long time ago, so you do something. And then for the first time in a long time you start to feel alive and life is suddenly very frightening but the fear feels good compared with the nothing you were feeling before (I was feeling nothing before). It feels like ecstacy.

But the day had begun so differently to that; another like so many recently, grey and featureless.

The painting he had been working on was a failure, had come out stillborn. Despite the sinewy textures and garish colours it had no real life; it was just paint on canvas (even though all paintings were that, all Van Goghs, all Soutines too). But this one didn't live, not even in the paint. He wondered if he was up to giving up on it and scraping all the paint off so he could start something else that afternoon on the same canvas. But the canvas would never be pure again. The stains would always show through.

Today he felt that painting could never express what he needed it to express, that his extremity needed knives and razors to reveal itself, cutting not just through canvas but into his own flesh. And maybe nothing he had done had ever been honest either. Maybe all the spattered paint had just been masturbation. Looking at the canvas he had given up on, it became a soiled sheet, pinned up like an old man's nappy, to shame him for soiling it by being desperate and naive enough to believe that art could mean something, that art could be the balance.

Back then, when everything had been flat and black and lifeless, painting had been something good. It had been something he could do, however valueless he felt, that seemed honest, or as near to honest as he could have got. And as he had put the colours on the hardboard he had known he was an artist, that he would be an artist. And although he knew that there was nothing inside him except that slight, cold hollowness he had always felt since his life had fallen apart, his hand moved anyway. So he became a painter despite that knowledge.

Six years ago art had saved his life, and for six years it had gone on saving him. But now he felt there had been no real growth inside, and that all he had learnt was nothing more than sleight of hand. And when nothing came, and all he had was that, the paint turned to mud on the palette and he felt things slip away like sand between his stick-like fingers. His heart would race then and he would find it hard to catch his breath.

Paul heard loud voices coming up the corridor. He stood where he was and waited. There was a casual knock on the door. It opened before he had time to say "Come in." Joanne, Mary and her boyfriend Steve crowded into the small room.

"Hey, that's really nice, Paul. It's coming along really well," Joanne said brightly. Paul smiled, almost laughed; it was so Joanneish. Mary and Steve smiled too.

"We're all going for a coffee, Paul. You want to come?"

"Where were you thinking of going?"

"The Cafe Verde does really good filter coffee," Mary enthused.

"And you can just sit and talk for as long as you like," Joanne added. "Go on, Paul."

She put her arm in his, all mock-serious, her beautiful green eyes opened wide, orange bow-lips slightly parted, and her look made him realise that he did want to get out of the studio and get some air into his lungs. He laughed.

"Okay, okay, I'll get my coat."

He wound a long white muffler round his thin neck and pulled on a pair of grey woollen gloves as they clattered down the stairs, then out through the swing-doors into the cold, clean air. It felt colder than it was because the building was so badly overheated. Even in January Paul had his window open a couple of inches.

"And then of course they can't afford a life model," Mary was saying. It had all been said before, of course, but none of them could stop gnawing the old bones. There was always a little marrow left. Only Joanne stuck up for the college, and she couldn't paint or draw properly. He'd heard she only got a place through sleeping with the interviewer. He thought it was Mary who had told him that. But he knew it wasn't true: Jo wasn't a slag, only young and pretty. And if you're young and pretty then aging men with little hair think that if you sit on a chair in front of them you're offering them your thighs, your crotch and every curve of your body just because they can take you with their eyes. Who could not be a flirt or a dyke or a prude to eyes like those?

The tutor who had interviewed Jo pinched first-year girls' bottoms in their studios, and the first assignment he had set Paul's class, and every first-year class he taught, was to paint a nude self-portrait, life-size or bigger. He used the paintings to humiliate everyone, and prove he still had if not a cock then something that would do just as well. Authority. He had asked one boy if he had a cock because his painting had him with his ankle crossed to his knee and shielding his crotch, and one girl about her tits because she had painted herself with her arm reaching out in front of them to paint the canvas. The tutor liked words like *cock* and *tits*. He kept all the paintings too. Paul only found his reddened, twinkling eyes bearable because he saved most of his twinkle for the female students, but Joanne seemed to actually like him. She saw his hand-on-back-or-shoulder helpfulness as helpful, and his eyeing girls up as only natural and forgivable, almost lovable. It made Paul's flesh creep.

Jo was one of those people who can almost be good friends if you take them as they are. If he had expected anymore of her than a limited but voluble enthusiasm and machine-gun clatter of gossip, he would almost certainly have ended up loathing her. A friend of his who had shared a studio with her for a year now disliked Jo so much that she had to leave the room if Jo was there. She tries too hard, he thought. Like when she had tried to get off with him at a drunken party, too drunk to stand up, pouting and mumbling in a little-girl voice, one hand slopping Cinzano over someone else's carpet, the other fiddling with the zip of his jeans.

"You want me don't you? You *want* me."

And he had held her so he wouldn't have to answer, just as drunk as she was, and they had fallen asleep wrapped round each other, and when Jo awoke the next morning she had the feeling that they had made love and she felt happy. And he couldn't bring himself to tell her that if her touch meant anything to him, it was only because he could close his eyes and dream of someone else, so in the morning he had kissed her cheek before leaving, and smiled for her. But no "thank yous". No lying.

Perhaps he only liked her now because she felt that he was special to her, and in some way she always let it show.

When she was drunk she would cry and tell people about her sad life, forgetting the pain even as the words slurred out of her immaculately made-up mouth. So he knew there was something there. But it never came out as anything creative;

just cigarette smoke and tears.

Every couple of days she would come into his studio and talk while he painted, chewing gum that was meant to take nicotine stains off your teeth and pushing a mass of bleached-blonde (now orange) hair up out of her eyes. He wondered how she could paint with hair in her eyes. She also wore Indian bangles which clanked like rolling Coke cans if she moved her arms at all. Everything about her said *I am not an artist* to him. But she was his best friend at college. And sometimes she really was his best friend.

He only knew Mary and Steve to say hello to. She was a short, attractive girl with cropped black-dyed hair, a loose black jumper, baggy black trousers and patent leather DMs. She was always trying to be tough, tough as men and being like men, never quite getting beyond it to just being herself, as if she needed a shell. Part of it, Paul knew, was that her best work was in delicate watercolour, the traditional preserve of the most wan and anaemic ladies of leisure, which made her own creativeness a knife to turn against her if she wasn't hard enough. Her feminism didn't seem to go beyond an attitude, he thought. But maybe he was writing it off too easily because he only saw it in relation to what she painted. And he more than most people knew that paintings could be dumber than the dead.

Steve was a plain-looking youth with acne and badly-cut mousey hair who wore cords. He was a graphic designer and didn't talk much. When he did talk, when he got drunk at some student party, he talked about money and cars and prestige jobs. He was like all the people Paul knew at college; mostly nice and well-meaning, but foolish and ignorant too, and vibrant with the superficiality of youth. But Paul had never felt young the way they did; walking and talking as if the whole world was in their hands, flying on a carpet of credit cards and untarnished dreams. He was only twenty-one, only a year older than any of them, but if felt more like a lifetime.

They cut through run-down backstreets, perfect illustrations of sharply-etched urban decay, and the setting for a thousand gritty thrillers; angles arching towards the sky and grey concrete, stained by washes of acid rain, meshed over by the black tangles of fire escapes. In the cold the scene had a purity, not of subject-matter, but in the starkness of its lines. There was no smell, no wind and nothing human here. The cold created a glass shell around Paul, through which crumpled newspapers and cardboard boxes were visible only as abstract designs. It made him eager to scrawl with black and grey ink across smooth white paper which like glass would absorb nothing.

"Paul," Jo nudged him, "you were miles away! I said, do you want to go rollerskating next week? Go on. Mary's friend Trevor's got a car and he'll take us. He's the one who got Steve that terrific blow last week, you know?"

"Jo," Mary complained mildly, "Trevor doesn't like people knowing he deals. And he doesn't really, just a bit on the side, and like only if he knows you."

"He sold some grass to a mate of mine," said Steve, "and it was all fucking rosemary. Ten quid that was. Lee's such a dick-brain he wouldn't've noticed if I hadn't said anything."

"So are you coming rollerskating?" Jo remembered to ask.

"Yeah," said Paul. "Why not?"

He wondered why the others were on the course. They hadn't seen what he had seen, had been too busy talking about drink and drugs and parties to actually look at what was around them. Maybe they had only chosen art because they weren't any good at anything else. But he couldn't believe that that was all of it; that they could paint or sculpt without feeling what they were doing, or without any kind of need for it at all.

Their attitude burnt Paul more intensely today because the need that he felt was failing to be answered by scrubbing paint into cloth. The idea that it ever could have done seemed like a joke: clever at first, but stupid if you thought too much about it. He felt his isolation from the others increasing, and he worried that it was the beginning of another breakdown, another six months under the shadow, staring at a wall blurred with tears.

There wasn't anyone he could talk to about that, only people like Jo, who would smile brightly and say, "I know exactly how you feel, Paul. What you have to do is just snap out of it. Have some *fun*," and invite him to another party. Or other people who sounded more sincere but meant the same thing in the end. Besides, talking couldn't help when he felt like that, not really; pouring out the words didn't change anything. It was just a pressure valve, and the weight of the valve itself was too great to allow any of the pressure to escape.

The Cafe Verde was popular with the art students because of its art nouveau sign and its cheap filter coffee. They sneered at the dull, pubby sub-Italian food it served, but swilled coffee back by the cafetière. The place was never full, so there was no pressure to be on your way until the dim lighting and dull decor became oppressive. One time he and some friends had made plans, elaborate ones, to buy it and do it up, just a daydream of course, but they had all talked as if it was something that was really going to happen. The cafe would be filled with green things, right down to green liqueurs and spinach pasta. And a waitress in red, just to add a Fauvist touch. But then Mary had pointed out that the customers would never be green or even red, and that had made them all feel slightly depressed. They had all wanted to hang onto the idea somehow, even if it meant the restaurant having no customers. A restaurant without customers. Paul had felt sad then that art always seemed to end up meaning so little. The plans for the cafe were just masturbation; a sterile release that gave birth to nothing.

They chose a corner table at the back of the cafe and sat down. Paul got the corner seat and since no one wanted to sit facing into the corner, he had an uninterrupted view of the whole room.

The cafe was almost empty, but that was standard for a Monday. An old, senile-looking woman was eating lasagne, and a pissed-off middle-aged couple were waiting for their order to come. The husband was pretending to read his paper while the wife fingered the stainless-steel cruet set and tried to make him feel guilty for ignoring her. There was a clatter as a pock-marked young waiter banged through the steel doors from the kitchen, carrying portions of meat-&-rwo-veg for the couple. He set the dishes down on the table in front of them with a clunk and disappeared back into the kitchen.

Several long minutes later he emerged to take the students' orders.

"Filter coffee for four and a grapefruit juice, please." Jo's voice was precise and a little sloaney, her manner condescending but polite. It would never have occurred to her that the waiter might despise her for it, despise her for having the world in the palm of her hand, and letting it roll away and smash. She had the lack of humility of one who had never been humiliated. And today she was wearing her Labour Club and Workers Against Racism badges.

Paul sighed and offered his cigarettes around, lit them with his old Zippo petrol lighter. The weight of it made it pleasant to hold, and he liked flipping the lid open and flicking the wheel. It was as calming to him as a rosary was to a nun. He put it back in his coat pocket carefully. He had only two possessions he valued, and the lighter was one of them. Normally he didn't let himself get attached to things. He was afraid of being hurt if they got lost or destroyed, afraid to give any thing, any object, the power to do that to him. But the lighter, he had become fond of that anyway.

The only other thing it would have bothered him to lose was the photograph of his foster-parents that he kept on the chest of drawers, the only remnant of his life with them he still had. As long as he knew he could throw it away, he had control over the man and woman in the picture.

The coffee arrived. Mary poured it out, dark and steaming, into the thick china cups. Paul helped himself to milk from the sort of small chrome jug you always find in cheap cafes, and spooned some fly-specked brown sugar out of the matching bowl and into his cup. The coffee was boiling hot, even with the milk, and strong, but soon he was able to gulp it down and only burn his throat a little. Feeling warmer and more relaxed, he unwound his scarf and sat back in his chair.

The arrival of the coffee and the lighting of cigarettes produced a lull in the conversation that Paul welcomed. He gazed idly at the cafetière. Its shape appealed to him: squatly glassy and cylindrical, on spindly little legs, and with a chrome lid and plunger. He pushed the plunger down a little, watching the grounds being sunk back into the darkening liquid. But he wasn't a child anymore and he couldn't live in the sinking grounds. They weren't enough.

He looked up when he heard the cafe door opening again and saw a black guy standing in the doorway, framed by sunlight, a good-looking man of maybe twenty-five, in a boiler-suit and a leather jacket, and with a shaved box-haircut. His skin was a gun-metal grey where the scalp had been shaved, and the sight of it made Paul's skin prickle on the back of his neck. He imagined touching it, just with the very tips of his fingers, just reaching out and touching it.

The man looked edgy and nervous. He stood shifting from one foot to the other, staring into space like a soldier on parade. Then he blinked and looked around him, chose a table against the wall and sat down at it. Paul looked at his round face, large, well-defined lips, his smooth dark skin and beautiful black eyes. It was an opaque face, but for a moment Paul saw a flash of something violent and collapsing and chaotic there, something dangerous. But he couldn't stop staring, however rude it was, however dangerous, and the chaos and the violence drifted across the room and into the windows of his eyes, filling his mind.

The man unzipped his black leather jacket, took it off. He pulled his open white boilersuit down to his waist. He was wearing a light blue tee-shirt which stretched tightly over his bulging, body-built chest. Cloven shoulder-muscles dived elegantly down between the curving triceps and blocky biceps of his upper arms. His forearms were corded with muscle and sinew. A gold watch glittered on one wrist. From where he sat, Paul could see the man's arching thighs and big round ass. He had never seen a bodybuilder before, not that he could really look at, only pictures he had jerked off over.

The man was more beautiful than any work of art, more electrifying than any line, more resonant than any colour. And for the first time, Paul really believed that. It wasn't just a clever idea, it was a divine revelation. He wanted to paint angels with wings that touched the corners of the world.

He didn't want to paint.

He wanted to go over to the man and talk to him, to be all brotherly, touch him on the shoulder and say, "Hi, man, how're you doing?" Casual not loaded. Or spill some coffee and say, "Sorry, man, I'll get you another," and sit down and take it from there and smile and show the starlight in his teeth. Or walk over dressed in silver, take him by the hand and say, "My white horse is waiting, man. Let's go." And they would ride, the man's hands around his waist, bathed in the moonlight. All Paul had to do was speak to him. One black guy greeting another, that easy. Only the man kept catching his eye and glancing away, and Paul felt that tightness in his chest he felt when he knew he wasn't going to do it, the sickness in his gut and crotch.

But he kept on looking, willing the light not to fade.

"Paul?" It was Jo's voice. "Are you going senile?"

He looked round at her quizzical face and couldn't help smiling.

"Well, pay attention then, this is really important you know. Did you know that Jackie Barrett's pregnant and no one knows who the father is? Someone said it was yours."

He didn't know if she was just ribbing him.

"We'll know when the baby comes, yeah?" he said, touching his face and smiling again. "If there's a likeness."

"I think she's having an abortion," Mary said.

Paul stared into the bottom of his cup brooding over that,

allowing himself to drift along in their conversation for a bit, but then he started watching the man again.

His look had changed since Paul took his eyes away. His eyes seemed glazed now, and he twitched his head every few seconds as if he was disorientated. Perhaps he's on drugs, Paul thought, though it didn't make sense that someone who took that much care of his body would abuse it like that. Paul watched him grip the table-edges with his hands and stare forwards, eyes bugging out of his head, all movements slow and silent, like in a silent film. Then with one hand he swept everything off the table and as the things went flying and scattering across the floor everyone's heads snapped round to stare. His eyes were closed now and he was mumbling incoherently under his breath, his whole body twitching as he mumbled. Clumsily he tried to stand, banging the chair against the wall and toppling the little round marble-topped table forward. It hit the floor and the marble top cracked in two on the hard orange tiles, and that seemed somehow strange, like something in a dream.

The man slumped forward onto his knees like he was going to pray. Then very slowly he curled forward until he lay on the ground in a foetal position, tears squeezing out of his screwed-up face.

It had all been so sudden, so shocking and embarrassing, that no one had moved. The waiter came through the double-doors and stood there gawping.

"Christ," Mary whispered. "What d'you think he's on?"

And that made Paul angry enough, gave him the strength to get to his feet. He pushed awkwardly past Jo and hurried across the room, slipping between tables, his coat catching on chairs and yanking them over, until finally he had covered the distance that stretched between them and he was kneeling down beside where the man was lying. Without thinking about it, he put his hand on the man's heavy shoulder.

"Hey man, are you okay?" he asked, his voice unsteady. There was no response. Paul's soul was aching. Slowly, so very slowly, he put his arms around the hunched back, pulling the man's heavy body partly upright, hugging him to him as he did it. He tried to speak but a lump rose in his throat, cutting the words off.

All the eyes in the room were on the two of them and Paul burned with self-consciousness and embarrassment. And also with anger: If they were all watching, then they weren't helping, and they weren't helping because they only perceived the man as one of the others, not one of themselves, because they only saw the blackness of his skin, the wiriness of his hair, or even only his boilersuit. And now they were watching one nigger helping another. He hated and despised them all.

"Come on, then," he shouted to the others, bitterness harshening his voice, "or are you just going to sit there?"

At least they looked ashamed as they edged across the room towards him.

"D'you think you can stand up?" he asked the man. No answer. "Please try," he begged as he struggled to pull him to his feet. Then finally Steve was there supporting him on the other side.

"Let's get you up, mate," he said. The girls trailed behind them, silent and embarrassed, as they shuffled over to the door.

"Friend of yours is he?" the waiter asked Paul as they passed him, and his voice made Paul's face burn. Paul ignored him and as he reached the door he heard the waiter say, "Black cunts."

"Fuck you," he shouted, but it wasn't obscene enough, he wasn't obscene enough. Then the cook stuck his head round the kitchen door.

"You going to pay for this, are you?" he shouted at them. They made placatory gestures. "Yea, well that ain't gonna pay the fuckin' bills, is it?"

He glared at them and they kept on moving.

"Yeah. Fuck off. And don't show yer fuckin' faces round here again, right?"

The door closed behind them with a firm click.

"It's not as if the tables are ever full anyway," Jo said the moment they were outside. She sounded upset, about to cry. But Paul had no time for Jo's little griefs.

"We better call an ambulance, yeah?" Paul said. "I can go with him, say I'm family or something. I mean," he caught Steve's inquisitive eye. "I can't just not go, can I?"

"Yeah, well, rather you than me," Steve replied, presumably thinking, *I guess it's a black thing*. Mary ran off to the phone box at the corner of the street while Steve and Paul swung the man's heavy body so that he was sitting fairly upright on a low brick wall.

"Shit." Paul hurried back down the steps to the cafe as quietly as he could, ran in, grabbed the man's jacket from the chair it was draped over and ran out again. When he got back to Steve and Jo, Mary was out there too.

"Not out of order yeah?" Paul pulled a disbelieving face.

"999 calls only," Mary replied. It should be here in a couple of minutes."

The few minutes dragged out into quarter of an hour, then twenty minutes. *Why am I doing this?* Paul wondered. He wished the others would go away instead of standing there wanting to go but too spineless or too guilty to admit it. At least the man was quiet, not quite unconscious, staring down at his own feet, his mouth moving occasionally but no words coming out of it. Now that he was no longer perfect, Paul felt protective towards him. They draped the jacket around his shoulders to keep him a little warmer while they waited.

Finally the ambulance pulled up. Two paramedics in green uniforms climbed out of the cab. The white one opened the ambulance's double doors and climbed inside. The black one, a plump young man with a shaved head, came up to speak to Paul.

"He just fainted, seemed to just — he curled up on the ground like a baby," Paul said. "I don't know why," he added, redundantly. The paramedic nodded, looking at the man. He touched him on the shoulder.

"Can you hear me, mate?" he asked. The man didn't respond. "Archie?" he called, looking away to the ambulance. His colleague stuck his head out through the double doors. "We better take him in."

"I'm riding with him, yeah," Paul said.

They sat in Casualty for half-an-hour before a doctor saw them, a brisk, patronising but competent man in his thirties, who shone a light into the man's dark and secret eyes and said,

"You'll be alright." And to Paul, "Just get him home and tucked up in bed."

"That's all?" Paul asked, feeling almost cheated. "What's the diagnosis?"

"A fainting spell brought on by exhaustion in an airless environment," the doctor replied cursorily. "Or by being worried, or rundown, or most likely a combination of all three. It's perfectly commonplace. The *prognosis*," he continued blandly, "is complete recovery with a little rest and sleep. Okay?"

And he was gone. Paul helped the man to his feet, in an odd way enjoying taking the weight of his body as they slowly left the hospital. At the door they stumbled and almost collapsed. Then Steve was there, pulling them upright.

"I thought you might need a hand, so I came on down," he said. "What's up?"

"We need to get him back to my place," Paul said.

"Yeah?"

"He needs rest. I don't know where he lives."

Steve looked at Paul obliquely. "Let's get him over to the taxi rank, then," he said. Then, "don't worry, mate. I can cover the fare." Paul looked away, embarrassed.

"Thanks," he said.

They manoeuvred the man awkwardly into a waiting black cab. "He ain't gonna throw up or nothing," Steve said to the uneasy-looking cabbie.

The cabbie pursed his lips and pulled out. "Where to?" he

asked grudgingly. Paul gave his address.

It only took them ten minutes to get there. The driver had been quick, bouncing them about on the fawn leather seats.

"That'll be four-eighty," he said as they were struggling out of the cab. Steve pushed a fiver through the window.

"Keep it," he said.

"Thanks, mate." The cab pulled out abruptly the moment Paul slammed the door behind him. If it wasn't for being so broke he wouldn't have let Steve pay for any of it let alone the whole lot, but once again he had to just feel grateful.

They stumbled awkwardly up the broad, open stairwell, and were gasping for breath by the time they had lumbered up to the first floor with their burden. Almost overbalancing, they staggered up to the second floor, where they had to sit on the landing to get their breath back. While they were sitting there, Steve looked around him.

"This place could be really something. Used to be a hotel, did it?"

Paul nodded. It looked like it had been some hotel in the Forties that had got closed down or gone bust, and then the council had bought it up but never had the money or the will to do anything with it. Now it was a squat.

They struggled slowly up the remaining flights of stairs and down a long, unlit corridor, finally reaching a battered white door with a heavy padlock on it. Paul unlocked it, putting the padlock in his jacket pocket. They edged through the door sideways.

"My bedroom's at the back." Paul pointed with his head. "We can put him in there."

He grunted with exertion as they slowly lowered the man onto the bed. He lay there quite still as if he was asleep. Paul unlaced his boots and took them off, pulled the blankets and eiderdown over him, up over his shoulders to his chin. His leather jacket had fallen to the floor. Paul took it and put it on a hanger behind the curtain that passed itself off as a wardrobe. The leather was soft to the touch, and well worn. He and Steve went back into the living-room, shutting the door behind them. They stood in silence for a moment.

"Why?" Steve asked, puckering his brows. Paul looked away.

"Because," he said. "Because he needed me, man. No one, no one's ever needed me. My whole life I've been a spare part. Surplus to requirements." There was bitterness corroding his voice.

Steve looked down. "You shouldn't run yourself down, mate." He glanced at his watch. "I'd better go."

"Yeah. Thanks for the help, man. Really."

"No big deal," Steve replied. "It's you that's gotta look after him." Paul nodded. "Anyway, I'll catch you later."

"Later."

Steve hurried off to try and catch his two o'clock lecture. Paul looked at his watch. Five to two. No chance. As he listened to Steve's footsteps disappearing down the corridor he shook his head slowly, and sat down on the punctured grey settee that he had bought for a fiver from the junk shop across the road. He had sewn a suede patch over the spring where it had torn through the seat and now it was quite comfortable to sit on.

Now he was on his own, fake, clichéd thoughts swam through his head, about how stupid he was for taking the responsibility of someone who might be mad or drugged or ill, and how people might say that he was very brave too, not thinking that they were talking shit. Because he had only done what he had to, and all that meant was he was still a human being.

He went into the little galley kitchen and rattled around in the pile of oily tin takeaway trays until he found a mug, rinsed it out and made himself a cup of coffee. The kitchen was beginning to smell.

Back in the front room he unrolled a sheet of white paper on the floor, smoothing it out from the centre with his palms. He emptied the contents of a carrier bag out beside it: Charcoal, grey pastels, Indian ink and a dip pen, other stuff. What he wanted was everything that was black and grey and white. And maybe in the end glass for the sky, he thought. He wanted to recreate the street as he had felt it that morning.

But it was all too dead and grey, and however delicate the lines he drew might be, they were clumsy and coarse compared with the lines that made him turn his head towards the bedroom door. He gave up on the drawing and screwed it up, went to wash his hands above the dirty plates. And then he thought, *I'll draw him*, and he realised that the other drawing had just been running away, and that was what had made it a failure. He found a smaller pad, picked up his box of pastels and walked over to the door. Stifling an urge to knock, he opened it and crept in quietly. He put the pad, pastels and coffee down on the floor and plugged in the fire before settling down on a large velvet cushion. Then he opened the pad and started to draw, making careful lines on the white paper, pulling a likeness out of smears of colour imitating light and shadow. He began on the man's fine and sculpted lips, kissing them with the pastels, and worked outwards, meshing traces of colours and shadows into the pattern of the eiderdown, covering the wall as well with a detailed design.

The tutors said Paul's work was too decorative, as if he could have left the patterns out. But the ornate weaving of the pattern was the ritual magic that made it what it was: order painstakingly woven over the heaving void. He carried on working the lines until it was finally done. Then he put the pad down and wiped his hands on his trousers.

He was pleased with the likeness as he didn't do portraits much. Not even self-portraits. Particularly not self-portraits. He looked at the patterns he had made and they seemed to him to be in a state of flux, changing as he watched them, chaotic. But he knew that they worked themselves out somewhere beyond the edges of the paper. He closed his eyes, worn out now and bored, and stretched.

It had taken Paul over six hours to do the drawing, and his hands were dirty with streaks of different-coloured pastels.

The man had slept all that time, sometimes as still as the dead, or more shallowly, moaning and stirring and putting an arm up over his face. Or frantic, thrashing his head around and muttering under his breath, and finally drifting restlessly back into deeper sleep. One time he had begun to sob, and Paul had gently shaken him by the shoulder, half to wake him, half to rock him in his sleep. He had left slight marks of purple and yellow on the light blue tee-shirt.

Looking at the drawing again, that was meant to be a picture of sleep, he realised it wasn't peaceful at all; the patterning was sharp and harsh, hemming the face in swathes of barbed wire. He flipped the page over and wrote on the back of it, *like sleeping beauty he sleeps imprisoned by a wall of thorns that prick him like bad dreams.* The chalk broke on the last word, falling in splinters on the floor.

He turned the drawing face-up again, dropped the pad, and rubbed his aching eyes. *I'm out of milk,* he thought. The 7-11 was open twenty-four hours now but he could do with shaking the pins and needles out of his cramped legs, so he decided to go right away. He didn't like the idea of leaving the man though, however deeply he seemed to be asleep; he was afraid that he would get back and the man would be gone and he, Paul, would have failed to see it through. But that would be true whenever he went, so he struggled to his feet, feeling stabs of pain in the backs of his knees, and rubbed his hardened thighs. He needed a piss too so he went to the loo at the end of the hall.

Leave a note, he thought as he came back into the living-room to get his coat. He tore the corner off an old figure-drawing, scribbled on it, *Gone to get some milk, back soon, Paul,* and put it on a small round table in the middle of the room, pinned down by a glazed yellow vase with dried and dusty sunflowers in it. He hesitated for a moment by the door, weighing the padlock in his hand. But he didn't have the right to lock the man in even to lock the vandals out, so he just left it pulled shut. There was nothing worth stealing in there anyway.

He hurried down the stairs and out into the night. He felt like running, because if the man wasn't there when he got back and he could've been quicker and could've caught him on the stairs at least but hadn't, he would want to die. He didn't know how honest the feeling was, but he felt that he was falling in love with the man asleep in his bed, in love with his beauty and the pain that danced above him. He wanted to go crazy with that feeling and spin down the street like a new coin, fresh and shining, but he knew that he had to stifle it instead, and hide behind the wall where he was free from pain and free from feeling too. But something shone out anyway, and still the air was sweeter than it had ever been, and he wanted to run and run until he became the wind in the cold air.

And the grey streets seemed like gardens to Paul, asphalt lawns and turned earth, rubbish strewn like flowers across the grass; and torn paper was wood-doves and nightingales, and the sounds of the city were their singing beneath a neon sunrise. All those things that had died to him as they were he could find here and live with: the hedges and birds and colours and summer memories in the cold, full of white clouds and blue skies and sunshine.

And families like traps.

He hadn't wanted to be able to remember any of them: His mother, not his real mother, his adopted one, and his not-father, and their two children, his not-brothers Mark and Michael. The same initial. He used to think *how stupid*, but now he knew it was worse and cleverer than that, it was one of her power-gaining devices. Like the food she cooked every day in the homely-looking red-brick designer kitchen and had placed in front of Mark and Michael since they were blotchy purple pallid babies purposely to make them fat, so they would say to their respective wives, *it's not like Mother used to make*, and come home every Sunday for a sizzling roast. And because they had got fat and he had always been thin she had forced him over and over again to eat more than he wanted, almost more than he could keep down, so that now he never ate more than once a day and would have preferred to look like a starving Ethiopian than be able to pinch the slightest amount of fat on his flat belly, and float like an angel on cigarettes and coffee rather than be pulled down to earth by a good, solid meal.

It was a long hot summer day and the sky was a cobalt blue. The leaves of the plants were a dazzling green, and the hot earth rose in a hazy dust when Paul kicked it. He must have been nine then, or maybe just gone ten. He was playing at the bottom of the long, thin garden, the bit where they grew vegetables and had a few fruit bushes that never produced anything that wasn't either green and bitter, or rotten. Paul liked that part of the garden best because it was cut off from the lawn and the house by a tall, manicured privet hedge; it was private. His father clipped the hedge every weekend, and he mowed the lawn every weekend too so that it had stripes on it. The hedge was so thick you couldn't see through it except for a brown bit where part of the plant had died. On the other side of it Mark and Michael (never Mike) were playing on the lawn, kicking a ball around. Mark was a year older than Paul, Michael a year younger, but they were both bigger than him: not just taller but broader and fatter too. Sometimes he wondered why. Mum and Dad were short and not really fat, just overweight. Even Grandpa Joe, who liked to let people know that he thought blacks were genetically inferior to whites but by God they were good at running and throwing the javelin, even Grandpa Joe who was six-foot-four, was as skinny as a rake and narrow-shouldered too. So that couldn't explain the boys looking like they did. The real explanation was they were pigs, which was given away not just by their round bellies and sagging behinds, but by their rosy pinkness and their snub noses. They even squealed when they played or fought. Paul used to hope for the moment when his parents would realise that they were pigs and take them to the butchers and turn them into sausages, but that was only until he realised that his parents had no love for him, only despite, and getting rid of Mark and Michael would do him no good at all.

It was then that he started to hate himself.

He poured a fistful of warm grey earth onto the knees of his dark-blue dungarees and it made him think of funerals. He picked up another handful of dust and let it trickle over his crotch. Then he quickly dusted himself off, abruptly self-conscious and aware that he could no longer hear the other boys playing. He looked around quickly, scanning the paved path that followed the fence all the way round the garden, squinting at the large hydrangea with its spheres of pink blossoms. He knew they couldn't be hiding behind the compost heap or the stick beans; only he was slight enough to be concealed by either, and so they couldn't be spying on him from that end of the garden. But the game was spoiled, and he sat there, disconsolate, feeling inexplicably close to tears.

Suddenly Mark and Michael ran out from behind either end of the hedge, whooping. He sat there, his shoulders hunched, ignoring them as much as he could, until they shoved him face-down onto the dusty earth and fell on him, pummelling and kicking him, but aiming more to humiliate than to hurt. And when he was pinned down Michael said in a sneering, childish voice,

"If you eat this dirt maybe you won't be such a *nigger*," (because the dust was grey).

"Yeah," Mark added, jabbing him painfully in the small of the back. "Maybe you wouldn't be so thin."

He struggled but couldn't free himself from the heavy, sweating bulks on his back.

"Gerroff, you're hurting," he shouted in a loud voice that was neither command nor supplication, just pained, and loud enough to carry a risk of parental attention.

At that moment their mother called out from the patio, "Lunch is ready, kids."

Mark and Michael jumped up, leaving Paul to pick himself up. Before they ran off to the house, Mark waved a plump finger at him.

"You better not say anything," he threatened. "Or else." As if he would have bothered anyway, Paul thought as he dusted himself down. He would never sneak on them; it would just make things worse. Like the fact he had a bedroom of his own made things worse, even if it was small, because Mark and Michael had to share one. He used to be glad when it was bedtime because then he could be sure of being on his own, but even then the other two might burst in while he was undressing to embarrass him and to take what he had away from him. And nothing was his own: He remembered when they had discovered the word *nigger* and kept on saying it with a spiteful relish and Mark had written it in blue pentel on Paul's Michael Jackson poster and then, frightened Paul would let his mother see it, he had made Paul rip the poster up and put it straight into the outside bin. Paul's parents had bought it for his birthday, which made it worse telling his mother that he had swapped it for football cards because he was sure she would have seen it in the bin because he had forgotten to drop anything on top of it afterwards to cover it up. He left the space bare where the poster had been.

Like on many nights, that night he had cried himself to sleep, desperately trying to stifle the noise of his sobs. And because he had just been a child, he had never wondered why they were like that, had just accepted that life was hell, that the torturers were no more free than the tortured were, and that they had not chosen to be cruel. But later he saw more clearly their selfishness and malice and he could never forgive them for it.

The last news he had heard about them, in a letter he had never answered, was that one was going to join the army after doing his A-levels and the other was doing something in a building society. That was four years ago. And he knew they would be now just like they used to be: smug and self-satisfied and reading the *Daily Mail*, with enough money by now to be back in suburbia, where it all happens behind locked doors.

"Come on, Paul," his mother shouted. "It'll get cold."

He wasn't hungry at all. In fact, as he stumbled up the path he felt a little sick. He prayed that she wouldn't comment on his dusty clothes and hair because he couldn't bear it if she did. He walked past the ornamental pond with the newt in it and onto the patio they'd had done last spring.

"Oh, Paul," she sighed, her voice and eyes heavy with reproach. "What have you been doing?"

He hung his head, his cheeks hot with embarrassment. Surely she couldn't be so stupid as not to guess what had happened?

"I must've fell over," he mumbled.

"Well, it's on the table," she said. "Go and wash your hands, there's a good boy."

Why did she say that? A good boy? All it made him think was that he wasn't real to her. Not a person. Not a human being. A good boy who was always bad whatever he did.

He went into the breakfast room, where they always ate lunch. The dining-room was for special occasions only, and was plush and dark green with fat velvet curtains that blocked out half the light. They didn't even eat in there on Christmas Day.

The breakfast room was light and airy, with yellow lino squares and a red formica table, all loud kitchen colours and wipe-easy surfaces. Paul's place at the table was in between Mark and his mother. Mark and Michael sat either side of Father, like the righteous, excluding Paul, denying him the privilege. But it wasn't just their doing. Even when Michael had been ill in bed and so a place was free, their father had not deigned to move his hand and call Paul over and say, "Come sit by me, Paul, for tonight at least." He had just asked how Michael was, nodded and carried on eating. And Paul had carried on sitting where he was, chilling slightly inside.

The food had already been dished up and the two brothers were eating heartily by the time Paul sat down. His plate was smothered by three pork chops and six boiled potatoes, covered by a mound of garden peas. His mother was watching him as she chewed so he hid his revulsion and started to eat. He thought of the grey dust turning to black mud in the washband basin and leaving black lines in the cracks on the soap and that made him feel really nauseous.

"Do eat up, dear." His mother again. He had blocked out the smacking of lips and the slurping of water and eaten, but still much more slowly than the rest of them. Their plates were licked clean, and he still had a chop and four potatoes to eat.

"Come on Paul," his father this time. "Don't keep the rest of us waiting."

He forced the food down, mouthful by mouthful, his eyes downcast in shame, not wanting to see Mark and Michael's contempt for him. But this was one time they never gloated over because by now they wanted their puddings. In fact he had probably inadvertently prevented their premature deaths by heart attack by giving them a breathing space every Saturday and Sunday. During this interval, which had become an expected, but never accepted part of the family ritual, his mother would make lists and his father would fold his arms and stare into space while Mark and Michael fidgetted.

Finally Paul would be able to clink his knife and fork together and push his plate forward. And then their mother would bring in the pudding. Today it was peach melba, made with lots of ice cream, and in addition she helped everyone to double cream. He got given the biggest portion. Had she noticed? Was it deliberate? Did she hate him that much? The others were already tucking in, and there was no way of avoiding it, so he too began to eat, amazed that no-one noticed that his face was contorted with disgust and anguish.

"May we get down, please?" asked Mark. They were tired of waiting for Paul to finish, and since their parents were tired of their fidgetting, their father said, "You may," and they ran off, heedless of indigestion, to play in the garden.

That left Paul alone with his parents, who refused to move until he had finished, either out of a desire to impress etiquette upon him, or a sadistic urge to humiliate him. To his own surprise, because it seemed like a never-ending torment, he finally crammed down the last of his peach melba and said,

"May I get down, please?"

His father nodded and he walked slowly from the room.

As he stood on the patio in the hot sun, Paul realised that he was about to throw up. His stomach hurt with every juddering step he took, but he managed to duck round behind the hedge before vomiting wetly onto the grey earth, turning it black beneath a tide of yellow. His throat burned and he could taste the vomit in his mouth, but he felt relieved.

Then he realised that Mark and Michael had watched the whole thing. Michael stood there staring while Mark trailed off towards the house. Paul felt tears of rage and frustration running down his face. He wanted the cracked earth to swallow him up. But since it couldn't, he just stayed where he was, waiting. He wished he could throw up again, but there was nothing left inside him.

Mark ambled back a minute later.

"Mum and Dad want to see you," he said, as if he hadn't told. Paul looked up into their mindless faces, trying to remember Mark crying when his gerbil had died. But then he remembered that on the same evening Mark had thrown a Dinky toy in his face and cut his forehead open. He had needed two stitches.

He stood up and started walking towards the house, his feet dragging on every step, trying to make the journey last until the sun winked out and everyone was dead. But nothing had changed and not a second seemed to have passed by the time he stepped through the french windows into the long living-room where his parents were sitting in their Parker Knoll recliners. They must have seen him the moment he entered, but they deliberately ignored him, forcing him to make the first move. He hung his head, unable to speak. After several long, painful seconds as he managed to say,

"Did you want to see me?"

Already he had made himself a liar. Even *why did you want to see me?* would have come close to being a lie, because he knew why. He wanted to run away and he was afraid that he was going to cry, but he just stood there not crying.

It was his father who finally spoke, having put down his paper and taken off his glasses and put them away in one of those glasses-cases that snap shut when you touch them.

"The lads tell me you were sick after lunch, Paul," he began, his voice serious, his words half-truths and deceptions. "You should tell your mother, or me if she's busy, if you're feeling ill." He paused. "Have you been feeling ill, Paul?"

It would have been easy to lie, such a relief, but he couldn't because he knew that they would know it was a lie, even if they chose to believe differently.

"No, Dad." He felt ashamed because whatever happened now would be his fault; he could have avoided it with a word, pushed the festering mass down below the water-line again and gone and laid down in his room. His father sighed.

"I just don't know what to do about this," he gestured vaguely, "behaviour of yours. Your mother thinks it's just naughtiness" — her eyes were fixed on him — "but I disagree. Is there anything you'd like to tell me?" Jesus Christ, what did he want to hear? What did he expect to hear? Paul shook his head. His father seemed disappointed.

"Is it because your mother's here?" He spoke as if their gender gave them a special closeness.

"No," Paul said quietly, his voice low and embarrassed. There was another pause, during which he became aware of the ticking of the pendulum-clock that hung next to the brick fireplace, and his every breath seemed offensively loud and slimy with saliva. He fidgetted uneasily.

"The thing is, Paul," — his father's words came out like a prepared speech — " it hurts your mother's feelings. She makes a lot of effort to cook nice food and make everything nice, and, well," — a pause, out of embarrassment or for dramatic effect? — "sometimes we feel that you just throw it back in our faces. We just want what's best for you."

So there it was: Guilt. As soft as fur and sharp as knives. He would rather have been called names, beaten, or sent to his room, anything rather than this. He wanted to fall on his knees and say *I'm sorry I'm sorry*, not because he wanted their forgiveness but because he was sorry that he had ever been born. It was not the plea of the adolescent, crying because no one understands him. He cried because they didn't understand themselves or what they were doing to him. And that made him hate them too, because you don't have a right to ignorance. He hated them where his heart was reddest, even knowing what hate could do; how hate could burn him worse than any fire his parents might devise. But it was in him anyway, beyond his control and permeating out from his heart and poisoning his flesh, contaminating him and staining him forever.

Perhaps it was that contamination he was trying to paint out now, whenever he picked up a brush. But art could never be enough for that. All he could do when he painted was illustrate the pollution he felt in ornate patterns, over and over again. His painting offered no possibility of transcending his pain; it was only a delicate and beautiful straitjacket that stopped him from tearing at his own flesh. And because he could see that now, he needed something more, a genuine purification and a genuine healing. A beginning in an end.

Before he had left home, he'd used to wonder why they had adopted him. That was before he'd read Stokely Carmichael, Malcolm X and Eldridge Cleaver, and learnt about liberal white guilt, and he had felt a terrible shame with every page he read because he had been implicated in their crimes. He had become the object of their absolution. Or worse, he had merely been the stage upon which they had sought to exorcise their guilt. It became obvious why they had hated him. And the less he became what they wanted and needed him to be, some sort of Sidney Poitieresque star of the establishment, the more they had had to hate him. He had felt dirty for years and he realised that it was their dirt.

Sometimes he would wonder what it felt like not to always have all those bad thoughts at the back of his mind. And in his waking dreams he had dreamed about the Black Panthers and their crazy, beautiful racism, for he too needed salvation.

He had thought after leaving his parents and with the arrogance of adolescent necessity, of writing a letter to them, explaining what was wrong with them, but all the churchy words he would have had to have used would just have sent them off uncomprehending to their weekly worship, to say words made meaningless by their familiarity and make prayers no-one was meant to hear. He even wrote the letter once, reread it later and tore it up, because the words were never big enough.

One thing he had asked in the letter he already knew the answer to: *Where was I born?* and the answer was twice; once between a pair of black but nameless thighs, and for a second time before a pallid psychoanalyst in a pale-green office, a man wearing a kindly, bearded mask, who had said when Paul had looked wildly round the room,

"No, there's no couch."

And Paul had looked at his lying face and hated him for the couch in his head.

And Paul had gone week after week to listen to the man's lies and avoid talking about himself. And yet for all his lies the man had dragged a truth out of Paul that he had denied in himself, and reduced him to silence because of his own words. But that moment of hope was quickly choked by other lies that sprang up like weeds on any clear soil, that left him jerking off over girlie mags every time he needed a wank, and almost hating women and certainly hating himself as he held his dick over the page so he was looking at that not the body beneath, and waiting for his come to spatter the shiny paper.

He had stopped going to the centre when they had wanted to put him on more than the routine antidepressants that had been flattening out his soul for two years and six months. Even the antidepressants were lies in the end. He had seen people at the day centre who kept on like that, their eyes flickering, their steps unbalanced, the gyroscopes in their heads thrown out by pills, people who seemed to have said goodbye to the normal world forever. Sometimes, unwillingly, he heard their stories: eleven years in and out of institutions; five abortions; crippled livers from ODs; twenty years inside. And the bad poems he wrote about all that, he left them behind him in the day centre when he left.

He had walked out one day across the bright green lawn beneath the summer sun and never looked back. The summers seemed brighter back then, but the brightest summers of his youth would always be cold and grey to Paul.

It was after supper and the sun shone more in their eyes now than it had when it was higher, flashing white behind a speckle of leaves. It was still hot and they scuffed up dust with their trainers into the close evening air as they walked across the heath, leaving it trailing behind them in a widening cone like the smoke from a wrecked aeroplane. The heath they were crossing wasn't wide; it only ran for several hundred yards between two small, well-heeled housing estates, but it had mounds and dips and gorse-thickets and groves of silver birches in it. Sometimes he hated going there because he was afraid of finding a dead body white flesh peeping through the leaf-mould a black glove sticking out like on TV, but when he forgot all that he loved the heath and wanted to stay and play there all day.

In the middle of the heath was a large old oak tree they all used to climb. He could always climb higher than Mark or Michael, but he was careful never to get too much higher and risk making them jealous. He used to want to disappear up out of sight among the leaves, but he knew that someone would quickly call him back, and when he climbed back down again that things would be a little worse than they had been before, subtly but undoubtedly more bitter and estranged. He wanted to climb the tree now, sit astride the smooth bole, the wood polished to a glossy sheen by a procession of eager hands and feet, but he felt too old, and he knew Mark and Michael would laugh at him if he did.

Despite the heat Michael had insisted on wearing his new black plastic bomber jacket, and his face was red and shining from being too hot. Wearing the jacket with the shorts they all had on just made Michael look stupid, but Paul didn't dare to rip the piss out of him. He was hot just wearing a tee-shirt, and Mark's straw-coloured hair was turned dark by sweat and glued to his perspiring forehead.

They said nothing as they ambled along, which seemed like harmony compared with how it was between them usually, but even so Paul's heart would pound every so often, in anticipation of some new tedious practical joke. Sometimes even just suddenly running ahead and refusing to walk with him seemed to really entertain them.

It was about a half-mile walk from their house to the youth club if you cut across the heath, or a mile if you went around it. Their mother didn't like any of them to walk across the heath on their own, especially after it got dark; forbade it. Paul had only done it once. It had been raining heavily, and he could hardly find the familiar paths. With every step he took he had become more and more convinced that somebody was following him. He had walked all the way, though, too frightened to run because to start to run might be the trigger for whoever was there to make his move. And then he would no longer wonder whether it was just his imagination that was following behind him because it wouldn't be. He had reached the other side of the heath gasping for breath and wet with sweat, hot inside but chilled by rainwater, feeling like he was drowning in the water-logged air.

That was just one more thing the other two had done to him; deliberately sneaking off early out of the youth club so he would have to walk the extra half a mile home, implicitly daring him to cross the forbidden ground.

Most of the summer holidays were still to go, but Paul was

already looking forward to the new term starting. He didn't like school much, but anything was better than days and days of Mark and Michael twisting the knife. At school they were all in different classes. He didn't do sport with them either, which was a relief because although he was a good footballer and good at basketball too, he was skinny and they could've got him back for all those things on the rugby pitch. Michael once said he wanted to tread studs into Paul's face and kick his balls in.

Paul didn't want to be better than them, or worse. Either would make his life a misery. It was bad enough that he was good at drawing *(only girls do drawing)*, when they had no talent. He hid his drawings in the bottom drawer of the chest of drawers, underneath the navy blue trousers he never wore. He didn't wear many of the clothes in that drawer, so his mother hardly ever opened it. It was the only secret place he had, apart from under the wardrobe, which was so narrow that you raked your knuckles pushing them into the gap between the bottom of it and the floor.

The club was a rectangular corrugated-iron building with a flat concrete roof. It was next door to Saint George's, the over-sized red brick church they attended as a family every Sunday, where you had to sit still for forty minutes and you couldn't talk or draw or go to the toilet or anything except crease the pages of your hymnbook, and you looked at Christ on the cross and it really didn't mean anything even though you believed in God because everyone believes in God especially if they're afraid of the dark and for Paul life was dark and getting darker.

Sometimes swarms of midges would flicker in a sunbeam, and he once wondered if angels were like that, floating around on the edge of visibility: present, but you could never really see what they looked like. That was before he had come to hope for angels that came in a more tangible form, in the night. But he had never really believed in angels anyway; it was just his mind wandering in the sterility of the dry church air. He would get hard-ons in church too, thinking of nothing, signifying nothing. And yet, despite all that meaninglessness, there was something there, even if it was really nothing more than his own spirit turning inside out and using its ribbing as the struts of the church. Maybe all churches were nothing more than that, he thought. He would look over at Mark and Michael then, but they remained untouched by it all, and unsuckered too.

The unlocked padlock hung from its hasp. Mark gave the door a firm shove so it wouldn't jam halfway open and they went inside, Paul entering last. Not many people were there yet. Steve, the young curate, was taking bottles of squash out of a Boots carrier bag and lining them up on the "bar". He had his everyone's friend uniform on, worn blue jeans and a brown leather jacket with unfashionably wide lapels, and his wavy black hair was untidily pushed back from his tanned, friendly face. He smiled as they came in and carried on with what he was doing.

Two kids of around Paul's age who he knew only by sight and not really to speak to, were playing table tennis. He noticed that Steve had made a sort of splint for the leg of the table that had got broken when one of the older boys had jumped up onto it, at a disco where drink had got in. Since then it had been held together by a wart-like lump of Sellotape, and it would collapse at least twice every evening. The splint looked pretty solid.

This evening Steve had also brought a dartboard as he had promised and he went out to his large, second-hand hatchback to get it. He only had three darts though, which slowed things up badly. The older boys hogged it anyway. Steve started off trying to arrange it so that everyone had a turn, but it ended up being so long between turns that most of the kids lost interest and went off to do something else. Paul didn't even bother trying, not when Mark and Michael were so keen.

None of Paul's friends had turned up yet except Michelle, and she wasn't paying any attention to him; she was giggling with her boyfriend Gary while they waited their turn at the dartboard. They were both sixteen, four years older than Paul, so he had no right to be jealous of Gary for going out with Michelle, but he was anyway. He hated the way they looked at each other with big cow-eyes, and he was sure that Michelle never used to giggle so stupidly before she met Gary.

Until she had started going out with him, Michelle had been Paul's best friend at the club. She would get close and talk to him about what she thought and what she felt, always with a smile, laughing when he was too serious, telling him not to frown. She was the only one who had made an effort to be friendly when he first started going, not like the others. Apart from him she was the only black person there too, well her father was Jamaican and her mother was Irish. He was a bus-driver, she was a primary-school teacher.

Paul had only met Michelle's mother once. She was pretty and very sharp and smoked all the time, waving a cigarette around in one hand, talking quickly and with an Irish lilt, always saying, "You must."

"You must study, Paul, if you want to know what you're doing, and why." Or,

"You must travel, Paul, get to know what people are like. Be broad, Paul, be a citizen of the world."

He'd never met her father or even seen a picture of him, but sometimes he would imagine her father's hands, large and chocolate-brown with calloused pink palms, and square gold rings on his fingers, resting on his lap, on blue serge maybe, or denim. Just his hands, though. Paul never looked up at his face.

Michelle was very pretty. She had her mother's eyes, her father's skin, and long black wavy hair from both of them, and she was popular with all the other girls because she never bitched. Sometimes before she met Gary she had used to act as if she was going out with Paul and call him her loverboy, which embarrassed him, but he liked it anyway. She would hug him too, in front of everyone. He never told her, but he loved her very much.

Now she was going out with Gary, everything had changed. She had still broken into a wide grin when she saw him that evening, asked him how he was doing, but that was it really; she hadn't listened to the answer. So he knew they would never steal the red De Lorean from the showroom down the road, the one with the gullwing doors, and drive out of town to somewhere new where nobody knew them and live in a tall house with six cats and a parrot like they had been going to.

He went off to talk to some kids who were in his class at school. They were the sort of kids you could spend time with and have a laugh with, but you couldn't ever talk about yourself to them. It wasn't that you had to be hard; you just couldn't be soft. They could never be special friends like Michelle used to be, and she wasn't special anymore.

Mark ambled across to Paul.

"We're going to play cricket with Harry and Rick," he said. The *and you're not invited* went without saying.

"See you later."

He would have to walk home on his own now. That made him want to hang around the club for as long as possible, to put it off. An hour or so later the friends he had been talking to decided to leave, leaving him standing there alone. Soon there was only him, Steve, and Gary and Michelle, who were playing darts. Soul music was playing on the radio, giving the room a late-night feel. Then Gary and Michelle said their goodbyes and left, holding hands coyly. Paul looked at the darts, which had been left stuck in the board. He felt indecisive.

"Can I help tidy up?" he asked Steve. It would give him a few more minutes before he had to go.

"That's good of you, Paul," Steve replied. "Could you collect up all the plastic cups, please?"

He started collecting the cups, one at a time, trailing backwards and forwards across the room, occasionally trailing over to the paint-spattered sink to empty out the half-full ones. It didn't take long though, however slow he was about it. He looked around for Steve, to see if there was anything else that needed doing.

Steve was standing in the doorway, leaning against the frame, watching him. Immediately Paul caught Steve's eye he felt uncomfortable.

"Want a game of darts?" Steve asked. He sounded casual, but the question seemed unusual somehow. He walked easily across the room and pulled the darts out of the dartboard. Paul watched his hands. They shook a little as he jerked the darts out.

The darts were steel with union jack fins, the lino floor was grey speckled with black and white which you thought at first might just be flecks of paint but turned out to be a printed pattern, and Steve's brown leather jacket catching the yellow light along its folds and creases was a shadow against the lime-green walls flecked with yellow where the paint had chipped away. It was all very clear and sharp and for a moment Steve's hand had trembled against it.

He started lobbing the darts at the board, oblivious to Paul's presence for a moment it seemed, holding him there by ignoring him, trapping him with the game. Each dart hit the board with a dull thunk, sawdust sprinkling the floor beneath. It was only subconsciously Paul noticed that Steve was pulling the darts out without counting the score before offering them out to him, point first. Paul took them gingerly, took up a position in front of the board, and started throwing. The first dart scored a one. The second hit the ribbing and bounced off onto the floor, clattering noisily in the silence, The radio had been packed away for the night.

Steve watched him bend over to pick it up. He threw the third dart. It stuck in. Steve stepped forward and pulled them out before Paul had a chance to tot up his score.

"Go on, have another go," he said, smiling oddly. Paul accepted the darts again.

"Look along the line you're going to throw." Steve mimed the gesture. Paul nodded and held up a dart. Steve gave his shoulder a friendly squeeze and left his arm hanging there. Paul threw. The dart bounced off the ribbing and impaled itself, point-first, in the lino.

"It doesn't matter." Steve turned to face Paul, putting his other hand on Paul's other shoulder. Paul wanted to run away, but there wasn't any real reason, so he stayed where he was. He looked into Steve's face, which was full of incomprehensible emotions. He could see flecks of dandruff in Steve's thick black hair. His heart was in his mouth.

"I am your friend aren't I, Paul?" His eyes stared into Paul's, and Paul could only nod dumbly and wonder why he was so afraid.

"Your special friend?" Paul didn't react at all, and Steve's expression was subtly altered.

"Come on, Paul, you do want me to be a special friend, don't you?" Paul nodded. He could feel himself trembling. Steve's hands slid down to Paul's waist. Then Steve kissed him, his coarse chin and wet lips against Paul's mouth, his tongue pushing in and violating the pink inside. Paul gagged. Steve's large tongue tasted acrid and sour and went in far too far. He wanted to throw up because his mouth was full of the tongue. He could hardly breathe. Steve's large, pale hand began feeling around the front of Paul's shorts.

Suddenly Paul was struggling with all his strength to get away. With a wriggle and a twist he was out of Steve's grip and free. He bolted to the door, ripping at the handle not getting a grip grabbing snatching not seeing ripping the door open banging his face on the edge spinning and stumbling away from the building from the yellow-lit doorway. And behind him Steve a silhouette shouting,

"If you tell anyone, I'll kill you," then shutting up very suddenly in the silent stillness of the night because his voice had carried and might yet reach the nearby houses past their curtains and into the respectable ears of the mother and father inside, but reverberating around inside Paul's head for not minutes or hours or days but months and years.

He pelted down the street, his arms and legs flying, the balls of his feet bruised by the tarmac, blinded by the cold air, his head yanked back, tumbling like a runaway ferris wheel, then falling on all fours at the edge of the heath and heaving his insides up onto the roots and leaf-mould, acid burning his throat and leaving his mouth sour.

He lay there in the suspirating dark then, listening to his heart beat like thunder while white light like lightning flashed before his eyes, and within that his ears were straining for the whisper of a sound and his eyes twitched for a shadow moving in the shadows.

Gradually his breathing slowed, and he wiped the snot from his nose and mouth. His hands and knees were dusty. He wiped his hands on his shorts as he stood up and dusted his knees with them. He walked home through the streets around the edge of the heath that night, under the brightest lights. But the nearer he got to home, the smaller he felt. A new fear rose in him: They would be sure to ask him why he was late and what was wrong, and he couldn't tell them or Steve would kill him, and he didn't want to anyway because he felt so dirty. He thought of running away, but where to? He thought of drowning himself in the water-butt next to the garage, but a dead bird was rotting at the bottom of it. Each of these thoughts was just a pretend escape that only brought him closer to the street he lived in.

He pressed the doorbell, his feet shifting on the crunchy gravel path. He heard the melodic tone sound softly in the hall. If it had been a buzzer, he didn't think he would have had the courage to press it. His father answered the door in his cardigan. Paul couldn't bear to look up at his father.

"I'm sorry I'm late," he mumbled, and before he got any further he was crying again. His father shrank back a little, and by doing that he diminished himself forever in Paul's eyes and became like a little beetle with nothing but pus inside.

"What's the matter, Paul?" His voice was concerned. Paul wanted to hug him but he couldn't. He just stood there, arms at his sides, snivelling. His mother came to the door and she did hug him, saying,

"There, there, it's alright," and the moment passed and his tears stopped. He could hear the television in the sitting-room, and he was glad that Mark and Michael were more interested in the film than in him.

"Go on up to bed," his mother said gently. Later he realised that she told his brothers that he had got flu. It was almost the only time he had ever felt close to her, but she ruined it all by asking what happened. He might even have loved her if she had let it alone instead of sitting on the end of his bed and looking betrayed when he didn't want to talk about it. Eventually the guilt she stirred up in him forced him to say, in the quiet of his room and lulled by the tick of the Mickey Mouse alarm clock left over from when he was younger,

"It was Father Matthieson." A pause, but there was no escape. "He touched me."

He would never have said it, would have told any lie rather than the truth, if he had known that they were going to drag him over to Steve Matthieson's house and force him to repeat the accusation to Steve's face. And until that afternoon he would never have believed how evil Steve was.

His mum and dad got him in the car without telling him where they were going. He couldn't refuse to get in, though maybe if they had told him, if he had known for sure, he would have tried to run away right then. Right then, not later.

He had been to Steve's house before with some mates, one Christmas Eve after carol-singing, but he didn't even realise they were in that neighbourhood until the car was pulling up in front of it. It was a small, cosy terrace, slightly shabby and over-furnished, with a bookshelf in the front room full of intellectual books with titles that were just words to Paul, and a garden that needed weeding.

His father knocked on the door. Three even raps — business not socialising. Steve opened the door and, to Paul's dismay, rather than looking shocked, he smiled and invited them in.

His parents stepped over the threshold and he looked at their backs and felt that he was caught in the web of a malicious conspiracy. He followed them inside. As Steve closed the door behind him, he winked at Paul. Paul's heart lurched. That wink confused and terrified him. He felt like he was going to piss his pants, the water sliding down inside, just a drop maybe spilling out and soaking into the fabric of his pants as he was tangled in a web sticky with honey and saliva and left hanging there naked and blistered from piss-rotted under-pants tangled around his ankles that had been torn down for everyone to have a look.

He had been made to stand up and repeat what he had said to his mother to Steve. And when he had finally whispered it, he had been foolish enough to think his ordeal would be over; he expected Steve to deny it. But Steve said, in a voice full of concern,

"I hoped it wouldn't come to this." His father seemed about to say something, but Steve nipped it in the bud by raising his hand sharply. "I hope you won't mind me betraying a confidence, Paul," — *He was talking to him!* Paul's eyes goggled. He stood there with his mouth open, staring — "You see, the thing is," he addressed Paul's parents again. "Paul's had something of a crush on me — perfectly natural in a boy of his age — and he admitted it to me last night, after waiting for all the others to leave. I don't know what he expected." His voice trailed off speculatively.

"Anyway, I said to him that I felt I ought to tell his parents and I'm afraid he got very upset and ran off and I'm afraid what he told you is some sort of revenge on me. I don't know what he did tell you, but kids aren't so naive nowadays."

Behind the earnest concern he was laughing like a devil. Paul felt sick, he actually felt his gorge rising. He was going to puke everywhere, all over his nicely-pressed school uniform and all over Steve Matthieson. He willed it down, hearing but not listening to his father apologising, his mother apologising, even Steve grotesquely apologising for what he had had to do, all of them shrivelling back into their shells like bloodless snail-horns, shrivelling away from each other, shrivelling away from him. The conspiracy was complete.

The three of them sat in the car in silence as they drove back home. No one said a single word. But Paul's ears were filled with the roar of insanity.

He felt as if his life had ended. His parents had betrayed him, and as well as hating him because of their guilt, because he was black and had not transcended the dirt that made him black despite their all-embracing whiteness, they hated him now because he was sick in the head; had sunk, got dirtier, and was a wicked little liar who tried to destroy the lives of decent ordinary men, stain them with his filth. His world became bleak and dark, and his capacity for feeling died. He lived in a small empty space, touched only by coldness and despair. His schoolwork fell apart and his friends dropped him. Even Mark and Michael left him alone. He would play truant and go down to the railway line and watch the trains pass by, full of people going somewhere, but empty too because the carriages never did more than rattle backwards and forwards, iron on iron, going nowhere, waiting to be scrapped.

They sent him to the psychiatrist's and he was put on a course of antidepressants. He flushed the second course down the toilet and felt better for regaining a bit of control over his life. Then there was the psychoanalysis, once a week for fourteen months, until he was fifteen and a half and stopped going. He had hated the therapist, and yet it was him who had found out the truth, which was that as Paul ran to the edge of the heath he realised that his prick was stiff and that amongst all the disgust there was something that he wanted there. He had lied about that one for months until the lies became so stale and meaningless that he told the truth, almost as a variant on the lies, just another lie really as he was saying it, but the moment it was out he realised that it was the actual truth.

But the truth didn't help. It wasn't an answer. It just started more lying and more deceit, because then not even the analyst would believe that it had been Steve doing it and not him, and that the dirt was inside Steve, and not Paul.

So he stopped going to that. But at the same time he was going to an art therapy class as well, which he carried on with. He would draw grids on the fresh white paper with thick black paint, sharp clean lines with no overlap between black and white, and black lines and squares in shiny black enamel. And when that was over he had started to try to draw real things -- furniture, plants, hands, never faces, trees and buildings. It was hard but it really meant something. And when he threw the black paintings away, he felt a little lighter than he had before.

That gave him the strength to run away from home when he was sixteen. He did shitwork, lived in hostels and then squats and painted in the evening. He got four O-levels, and when he was seventeen he started a foundation course in fine art, working at McDonalds six nights a week to get money to live on. Things got easier when he got onto a degree course, because by then he had been living on his own long enough to get a full grant. So he handed in his Happy Hat and his badge with three gold stars on it and his name, Paul, along with the slogan, *I'm here to help you.*

When he felt really lonely he would go and buy a burger in one, not because he recognised the faces — staff turned over every couple of weeks — but because he knew the system, how it worked, and because, since McDonalds is the same the world over, he might just as well have worked in the place he was sitting in at that moment: the people, their attitudes, would all be just the same. It was the nearest he felt to belonging to a place, to a group of any sort. Nearer than he felt to the students on his foundation course, anyway. They were girls who wanted to go to parties and maybe get laid before settling down with babies and a mortgage and had chosen art rather than a secretarial course as a good stop-gap, and boys eager to get drunk and desperate to lose their virginities before they were eight-

143

een. And they had done a Fine Art course maybe because they got a grade two CSE in Technical Drawing. And while he had to do what he was doing, while he was compelled, they could stop anytime they wanted. So he had nothing to say to them.

Only the tutors interested him at all. Even though most of them were failures as artists they still had something to teach him, even if it was only how not to succeed. What Paul found most striking about almost all of them was how naive and soft they seemed for their years, that their shouting and drinking and factory paintings were just shells for molluscs who had never had bones or a spine, that their radical views were no more than manure to feed their working-class roots with, and keep them strong. But they were no longer the tree the roots would've grown into left to themselves. Looking at his tutors' lives and their work made him believe that all great art must come from suffering and nothing comes out of an easy life except complacency.

One of the tutors on the foundation course had been black. Paul hadn't liked him at all to start with; had hated his arrogance and swearing and the lack of manners that seemed like a pose adopted to attack him with. The unbelievably named Levere Street, who cultivated the words *fuck* and *shit* until you couldn't imagine a sentence meaning anything without them. In retrospect perhaps Paul had simply been afraid of him and his short natty dreads, his Black Power attitude and American-style violent posturing, afraid because of the challenge that his presence was to Paul's sense of self: "Do it bigger, man, more garish, more *Afrikan*," "Them flowers are cissy, man. Grab it by the balls and make it *scream!*" "You gotta speak, man; moan; *wail*."

All Levere's words had a poetry that was crude but vital and immediate, a poetry made to wring something out of you. He always believed, and that was what drew Paul to him, despite everything else. He believed that anyone could do it and frequently did. And he believed that Paul could be a revolutionary. He introduced Paul to the writings of Stokely Carmichael,

H Rap Brown, Malcolm X, Franz Fanon and Huey P Newton. And Levere's faith in them and in his own race was simple and ennobling enough to give Paul a cause not to believe in (which would never have been enough), but to live by.

So he grew his hair into baby dreads and painted large paintings of revolutionaries with insufficient technical skill. And he worked for a while in a screen-printing collective that produced posters for political meetings. But one by one the colours ran out and they weren't replaced. Eventually it folded up with a lot of bad feeling, and Paul wasn't sorry not to have to go there every Wednesday at nine in the evening any more and listen to the injustices of the world pouring out in a wash of technical jargon. Sure, he agreed with it; he saw things how they were. But it didn't make him feel more at one with himself as a Black man, because Levere denied what Paul most needed from him; to believe that what he painted represented his race as much as any expanse of Afrikan red and green and gold. But Levere was a Black man who painted, and Paul was a painter who was Black, so to Levere Paul's art stood for nothing: "This piss out your dick ain't Black just cos your dick is," was what Paul's work meant to him.

There was only one time that Paul had got to see some of Levere's paintings. He often forgot that Levere was a painter, not a social engineer-cum-political philosopher, but when he did remember he would get quite curious about what Levere did with a paintbrush.

One Wednesday after coffee Levere took Paul into his office to pick up some leaflets which he had left in the adjoining storeroom. As he opened the office door the phone started to ring. He answered it, at the same time handing Paul a bunch of keys and gesturing for him to open the storeroom up. Paul unlocked the door and went inside. Levere was laughing on the phone in the other room and Paul felt embarrassed at the idea of hanging around in there while Levere was talking, so after taking a pile of leaflets off the top of a filing cabinet and stuffing them into a plastic bag he waited where he was.

There were some small canvasses leaning facing the wall. After a moment's hesitation he went and gingerly flicked through them. They were small and lumpy and abstract and grey, with letters stencilled on them in black. On one the uneven black letters spelt out a girl's name, *Maria*. On the others they were just words that only meant something to Levere. He looked at the skin of dust stuck to the lumps of encaustic which stood out from their flat surfaces. They were sad paintings; just looking at them turned him inside-out. He leant them gently back against the wall, feeling upset without quite knowing why. It was only as he was running down the street with Levere to catch a bus that Paul realised: Levere's paintings had shown him he could never be a revolutionary.

Soon after gaining that knowledge he'd had to move on to other things. But by then he had found out that anything he did could be a weapon, and that his new tough skin could be armour. Once again he had been reborn. And he had learnt the history of Doctor Yakob: that he was the centre of his own universe.

But it was not the politics, the slogans and the bandwagons that so totally transformed his way of thinking; it was the fervour that produced it, the aesthetic, personal and political, of Black muscularity and Black power. He dreamed of the brotherhood, the beautiful brotherhood of the Black Panthers. How many nights had he lain there, his prick stiff and aching, imagining that one of those men so hard and black and beautiful and vulnerable might tap on the window, wanting to be let in, to hold him and need to be held by him, burning with desire to fuck him, to do everything to him, saying, *you are my beautiful brother and that's why I want you*, and also, *through wanting you I can fuck this badness out of you*, and proving it by the thrust of his hips? Sometimes Paul would be content with the physical gratification in itself, but on many nights he would lie there unmoving afterwards, tears sliding out of the sides of his eyes in silver lines across his cheeks, a pool of thick, semi-opaque white fluid cold on his belly.

In all that time he had never sought anyone out, never even tried. Partly it was because he didn't believe that he had a right to his own happiness, all that psychoanalytical bullshit, but also he could never rid himself of the fear that all he would find in the corners of gay bars and clubs would be men like Steve, who wanted to take, and would take even while they were pushing it in, and that if he went there he would find himself trapped in a dark corner stinking of piss and semen being groped and squeezed by greedy, unwelcome hands. And then he could never be just a man who wanted another man again. So he turned away from the fear of being labelled and sat dreaming in his squat, all on his own, watching the TV, his reality limited to people who lived on the curved grey screen, the fantasy figures on the pop shows who tease you for a few minutes and then disappear with a twist of the videographics. But perhaps the most fundamental reason he feared the clubs and the gay scene was that they threatened him with the one rejection that would really destroy him: To stare into shining black eyes and dream, only to find them glassy and cold the morning after; only to find he had been used one final time.

Sometimes it made his life seem like a dream, because what would make him feel most real would never happen. And then that man had stumbled into the dream, black and muscular, beautiful and vulnerable, and for an idle moment Paul had poured all his hopes into that man, bringing him into the dream, removing him so far from the familiar world around him that Paul was able to catch his eye and let it go again, as if his eye was a perch and the other man's bird-eye would keep returning to it; like in a dream.

But after a while he had realised it was just a dream, just a game and that he didn't have the guts to actually do anything. And then the man had freaked out and collapsed and needed somebody's help, and Paul had been somebody there to give it.

But what was he going to do now?

Perhaps it didn't matter. Perhaps the man would have left already. He fumbled in his pocket for the keys. They were caught in a rip in the lining and he had to wriggle them out. He cradled the carton of milk awkwardly in the crook of his arm as he turned the handle, pushed the door open, went into the hall. After being outside, the air in the hall felt warm on his face and hands, though his breath still misted it as white as cotton wool.

He ran lightly up the stairs, his heart beginning to pound as he reached his floor his corridor the door of his flat. The door looked just like he had left it. Or was there some subtle difference, some slight change in the air, some broken hair to show that someone tidy had passed through that way a few minutes before, closing it behind him and vanishing into the night?

He reached out and touched the doorknob, and he could feel the pounding of his heart pulsing against his fingertips. And still he couldn't tell, even as the door swung silently open and moved the still air.

The room was just as he had left it, down to the last twist of dust and pressed-down fibre in the carpet. But had the light from the naked bulb briefly broken on another man as he was leaving? The note was where he'd left it, unfingered under the yellow vase. He crumpled it up and threw it in a corner, setting the milk down on the table where the note had been. And then he looked at the closed bedroom door.

He slipped off his coat and went to the door and opened it.

The man was still there.

He was awake and propped up on his elbows when Paul came into the room. His dark eyes were slightly bleary, their corners glinting with the crystals of sleep. It was strange for Paul to see someone else in his bed, and it made him think of the times he'd jerked off looking in the mirror, a self-affirming act that said, *I can be my own lover. And if I can be my own lover, I can be someone else's lover too.*

But all he could hope for would be to make the man his friend. And that would be fine, and that would be safe, and it wouldn't go any further than that.

"Hello man, how're you doing?" he asked. "I didn't wake you up, did I?"

"No, man. I was already awake." Casual, friendly.

"Al*right*," Paul said, in an American growl. He couldn't help but smile looking at the man; his gentle face and shy eyes; his eyebrows shooting up, opening his face; the curve of his arms, his soft lips. But the eyes still made him nervous.

He couldn't think of anything to say.

"I just came to get my sketch-pad, anyway." Boring. Safe. The man handed it up to him.

"It's good, man," he said. He's talking to me, Paul thought, he wants to talk to me. *Say something!*

"D'you like it?" Keep talking. "I did it while you were asleep. Well, when you were keeping still. Man, you had *some* nightmares. I wouldn't've done it but I just thought someone better keep an eye out for you." *Shut up*, he thought, *stop babbling*. He flushed hotly.

"That's alright man, thanks. Suppose this makes you me guardian angel, yeah?" His voice was soft and low and friendly, and his eyes pulled another smile out of Paul. *He wants to talk to me!*

And he wanted the bathroom and Paul helped him stand up, offering him his hand and grasping it firmly. And he was cold and Paul found him an old tracksuit top that he didn't wear anymore, that he wouldn't have to ask to have back, and he threw it to the man. When he stretched up to put it on he was so beautiful; the outline of his body, his thighs, the curls of hair over the ridge of muscle in his armpits so perfect, that Paul glowed with happiness just looking at him, just being there. He wanted to dance or laugh or run or all three of them together. And the man asked how he got there, and Paul told him about the hospital, and about taking him home. Telling that part of it made Paul nervous, but the guy just smiled and so Paul smiled too.

"You want a cup of coffee or something?" he asked. *Yes yes yes* his mind was saying, and the light from his eyes shone in the man's eyes and made them glow hazel.

"Sweet," he said. Then: "You got a name?"

Paul nodded. "I'm Paul," he said.

Chapter Eight

"I'M WESLEY," Wesley replied, shaking Paul's hand firmly, not wanting to let it go, finally releasing it a moment before Paul might get embarrassed, not realising how much Paul wanted to hold on too.

As Paul turned to leave the room, Wesley glanced curiously at the photograph in the pewter frame again. The white couple were standing in a large garden with a stripy lawn, their eyes squinting against the bright sunlight. They were both in their late forties or early fifties and both a little overweight. His hair was light grey, balding over the crown. Hers was permed into a mass of short orange curls. Just ordinary people. He wondered who they were: A girlfriend's folks, maybe? In the photograph the sun would always be shining too brightly.

He didn't want to know really, not about the girlfriend, so he didn't ask Paul, who was in the other room by now. Wesley followed him through and closed the door softly behind him. He had to rattle the knob to get the snib to move.

"Don't bother," Paul said. "Someone painted it up."

He disappeared into a small kitchen and left Wesley standing in the middle of the room, looking around.

The walls were covered with sketches and drawings that had been up there. There were a lot of naked women, not like out of girlie magazines, not so glamorous; only a few of them were even a bit good-looking. Mostly they were old and fat and sagging a bit. He wondered why Paul had done them, these drawings of unsexy women in the nude. The rest of the drawings were views out of windows, streets, furniture, things like that.

There were also three large paintings, all about the same size. four feet wide and six feet high, nailed up on the bare chipped walls. Like the sketch before, he couldn't say if they were any good, but there was something about them that sent little thrills through his chest. The first painting was the most colourful of the three. It was a mass of tangled greenery, rich and vibrant, hung with brightly-coloured flowers, like it was meant to be the richness of life. But through the tangle Wesley could see skulls' eyes staring out, and on the skulls little crosses were painted. It could have been Floyd's painting: Paul could've painted it for Floyd. Wesley looked at it, full of wonder. He didn't need to ask to know that it was Paul who'd done it, who'd done them all. The painting was bright like stained glass in a church, maybe the first real church he'd ever been in.

He looked at the next picture. It was a piece of canvas, covered with black butterflies, none larger than the size of his hand. There must have been hundreds of them. Some were made out of feathers or fabric, most were painted or stencilled. There were one or two real butterflies as well, dyed black. He looked at it blankly. If it had a meaning, he didn't even know how to begin to look for it. He turned away from the picture towards the kitchen. Paul was standing there, watching him, steam swimming lazily out of the spout of the kettle he was holding. There was a stillness about him as he stood there, and when he spoke it was like he was reading out a speech.

"They're mutants," he said. "Because of industry and technology. They were made to fit in, but they're freaks; like they're natural and unnatural at the same time. But they're beautiful anyway. Sometimes — " He stopped mid-sentence, afraid to give himself away as weak or foolish, or perhaps just afraid to give himself away at all. Wesley stared, thinking that he must have been going to say, *sometimes, I feel like that*.

Looking at Paul he thought of Floyd and his own private pain, and of how he had never been quite able to share it. He took a deep breath.

"Yeah. I know what you mean, man," he said. He looked back at the butterflies again, then glanced back at Paul, who was looking at the floor. "Yeah," he added. "Look, man, I know what you're saying. I really do get it." He was almost angry. "Believe me." Paul lifted his head and there was a surprised look on his face. Like Floyd he had a beauty about him, a delicacy undercut as it had been for Floyd by its source in violence, like a razor-blade. And in both of them there was a poetry that other people didn't seem to have, that gave them smiles like trains rushing out of the night.

Wesley reached out tentatively with the trembling tips of his fingers and stroked one of the feather butterflies. It felt like an eyelash. The real butterflies looked too delicate to be touched. He exhaled through his nose, and the movement of air stirred the feathers.

He stood back and looked at the third painting, which wasn't the sort of stuff he would normally bother with: Red, yellow and white lines were scraped and dragged over an uneven black background, cutting across it vertically like they had been done with a ruler. Wesley only looked at it now because he knew from the drawings on the wall that Paul was a good artist. He tried to find shapes in the black like faces in the peeling bedroom door from when he was a kid. There was nothing else he could do with it. The black was scarred and knotted unpleasantly and the little twists of paint caught the light and glistened like they were still wet or the black was sweating. The twists radiated outwards, giving the black form a halo of pain. And it was seeing that that made him realise that if the painting was turned on its side it would look like a boxing ring, with white blobs smears of faces in the background and a dark form tortured in black and lying behind the ropes.

The more he looked, the more sure he was that that was what it was meant to be. Again he felt sure that Paul was painting the colours of his life, and again he felt like he was in a church. Like he had found the church that he had always believed in, one without crosses.

"You don't like it," Paul said, watching Wesley's blank expression. "I think abstracts are fakes. Most of them. But just a few got something you couldn't show any other way apart from like that. That's how they've got to be." He stopped. He could've said more, but he didn't want to put Wesley off by being too impenetrably arty, too pointlessly intellectual.

Wesley's reply took him by surprise. He flicked a glance at Paul.

"It should go sideways, man," he said evenly. Then he looked down at the ground. It was his turn to say less than he meant to. When he looked round he saw that Paul had gone back into the kitchen. He could hear the small sounds Paul was making in the little room -- the squeak of his trainers as he moved around on the lino, the clink of mugs and spoons, rustling around for teabags and then the soft sound of the hot water being poured. It all seemed frozen in time and made as solid as a bee caught in amber. He felt as if he was floating a long way from everything. He shook his head like he was trying to shake water out of his ears and swallowed. His throat felt very dry and ached as if he had been shouting.

"Where's the toilet, man?" he called.

"Turn right out the door and it's right in front of you. The lock's busted."

"Thanks."

Wesley walked unsteadily down the corridor. He closed the toilet door behind him. There was a stale smell of piss. The socket was bare, the bulb long ago taken or busted, but enough light to see by filtered in through the small frosted window from the yellow street-lights below. He unzipped and began to relieve himself, looking down vacantly at the steam rising off the stream of urine. His bladder felt hard, and as it emptied he felt stabbing pains in his gut. His neck ached and his head throbbed in the cold, the bone shrinking, pressing against his brain. For a moment, a blink, it all went black, but he hadn't fallen to the ground or even buckled at the knees, so it could have only been for a fraction of a second. He had heard somewhere that if you faint, however long you're out for it will only feel like a couple of seconds.

He rinsed his hands in the small enamel sink and regretted it instantly because there was no towel and the water was so cold it felt like being scalded. He shook the drips and wiped his hands vigorously on his overalls. The biting cold made him jog back to the living-room.

Two mugs, a brown one and a red one with hearts on it, sat steaming on a tin tray, a teabag in each. There was a blue-and-white bag of granulated and an unopened carton of milk on the tray too. The tray was sitting on the floor in front of the punctured grey settee. Paul had set up the little one-bar fire next to it.

Christ, Wesley thought, *is that all the heat this place has got?* Not like the flat, with a radiator in every room. That made him think of Sharon walking from the bathroom to the bedroom with just a towel wrapped round her, and she seemed to him then to be someone he had left behind a long time ago, and who had herself gone on in another direction.

"You got a towel?" he called back. Paul emerged from the bedroom with a large red towel and handed it to him.

"Sit on the sofa," he said. "I'd put on a record but it needs a new stylus." He directed his gaze at a battered music centre whose smoked-glass look lid was dusty and white with scratches. The oversize speakers sat on either side of the sofa. Wesley shrugged and sat down. Paul handed him the red and white mug after fishing the teabag out with a spoon.

"We've got some like these at home," Wesley said. Sharon had bought them.

"You live with your family, yeah?" Paul asked. *Don't press too hard*, he was thinking.

"No man, I'm married," he replied. "For three years now."

"What's she like then, your wife?"

"Oh, she's great, man, you know, she's pretty but she's

154

clever too. She's got ambition." He wondered why he was saying this, defending her. He felt like he was really defending himself. The words didn't sound like they were describing anyone he knew, and especially not someone he had been married to for three years.

"Do you reckon you're still in love with her?" Paul asked, gazing at Wesley's face which was made more beautiful for having had that experience that Paul would never have, and more mysterious too. Wesley shrugged.

"I suppose," he replied. He felt annoyed because Paul was trying to put him in a box.

"Look, " he said, "I left her today, right? And I don't know if I want to go back."

He knotted his fingers together, making a church, stared down at them. His heart was pounding and at the back of his head between his eyes a little white light was beginning to burn. *I could run*, he thought, *run and run*. But his body felt heavy and he didn't want to move: He wanted to stay.

"Sorry," he whispered.

Paul cleared his throat. "That's okay, Wes," he said, reaching out to give Wesley's shoulder a reassuring squeeze, and Wesley saw that Paul's eyes were shining as he was sure his own must be; that he had touched something in Paul too. Then he felt suddenly guilty and afraid. What right did he have to be here, away from what was left of his life, even if it looked like nothing, to dump all his personal shit on someone else who had already put himself out a long way for a guy he didn't even know.

"Look, man, I better go," he said apologetically. Paul's hand fell from his shoulder, and Wesley felt lonely without its presence. He stood up.

"Your jacket's in the bedroom." Paul's face was a mask again, like it had been in the cafe, and a million unasked questions ran through Wesley's mind. He went and got his jacket and pulled it on, walked to the door, looking all the time at Paul's mouth because he couldn't look in his eyes but he couldn't be so rude as not to look at him at all.

"See you," he said.

Paul held his hand up and opened it. His mind was empty. Perhaps his soul was dead.

Wesley hurried down the stairs. He felt confused and guilty. He had betrayed Sharon and now he had betrayed his new friend, and all he was doing was running away from both of them. But he couldn't run away from the betrayal; he couldn't run away from himself. And for a second he was floating there above the stairs and pulling a revolver from his pocket, pushing it into his mouth and blowing off the back of his head then falling slowly to the floor blood spurting twisting round him like a winding-cloth. And then stillness and no feeling. But he didn't have a revolver in his pocket, and anyway he didn't want to die; he just wanted to do something to deaden the guilt.

He realised that an off-license would still be open somewhere, and he had enough money feeling it crumpled in his pocket yes it was still there, to buy a bottle of whisky and keep himself warm, and numb that part of his mind that wouldn't stop burning. And when he had bought it and left the empty bottle in the gutter like a fallen star he would walk home through the cold night, singing like Billie Holiday or maybe just shouting obscenities that meant to say the same things and show the same pain, hoping and willing that the pigs wouldn't stop him smiling out of their blue lights and fluorescent stripes and say *Where are you going at this hour sir (nigger spade coon black bastard) burgling mugging raping and get in the car because Did you tell my fellow officer to fuck off Oh dear that's not very helpful is it You're going down the station,* not tonight because he couldn't stand it, not any night, but tonight he really couldn't stand it and he might kill somebody or break some face at least. But he wouldn't be stopped and he would get back to the flat alright and pitch drunkenly into bed beside Sharon and then it would all be over.

But was that how he wanted it to be? He was going down

the stairs more slowly now. The last flight before ground level. *Was that how he wanted it to be?* He let his mind run back over what had happened that morning. He didn't have a job anymore. Right now he didn't care, but tomorrow he would. But he couldn't imagine tomorrow, what it would be like, what would happen, or even where he would be.

Something had to change.

He took a last unsure step and he was in the shabby entrance hall, facing the hardboarded door.

He had to make things change.

But knowing that didn't help him know what to do, so he stood where he was for a moment, ignoring his mind (talking so quickly the sound ceased to be words and became the humming of bees), and listened to his body, let his body make the decision. And as he stood there he realised that what he felt was cold and tired and hungry and foolish and alone, so he turned and slowly began to climb the stairs again. He went quietly up the passage to Paul's door, paused a second listening, and hearing nothing, knocked. The first knock was too quiet, the second too loud in the empty corridor.

He remembered once picking up one of Sharon's fat romances and flicking through it, reading the ends of the chapters to see how graphic they got. One bit he remembered from somewhere near the end went something like — *their eyes met across the finely-polished oak dinner-table and with a thrill that went deep inside her, Agnes realised that Philip did truly love her.* And they lived happily ever after, most probably.

But real eyes are never as revealing as that, and when Paul opened the door to him, all Wesley could see in his eyes was a secret blackness he had no right to look into, and all he could read in them was what his own doubt and guilt had put there. *Maybe he'll just slam the door in me face,* Wesley thought. *I wouldn't blame him.*

And Paul, who had been electrified by the first timid knock, stood frozen now in the doorway, wondering, *Did he just come back because the door is mortice-locked? Did he just come back for the key?'* wanting that not to be true, wanting Wesley to have come back to see him, but not daring to hope it. So he stood there, waiting for Wesley to thrust out his hand and ask for the key like he expected, and Wesley stood there not asking for it, waiting too, waiting for Paul, looking shy like a little kid who wants to give a present but gets too embarrassed to hand the present over. Paul couldn't help but trust that look, and he could feel Wesley's loneliness and vulnerability flow out towards him along it. He wanted to hold Wesley very much.

"Come in," he said, stepping back a little.

"Thanks."

As he brushed past him Wesley gripped Paul's upper arm and look straight into his eyes.

"Hey man, look, I'm sorry," he said. "I didn't mean to be rude or nothin'. It's just been a fucked-up day, you know? I got the sack this morning. For punching out the foreman." And that wasn't half of it, but it was all Wesley wanted to say for the moment, and for the moment it was enough. He realised that he was gripping Paul's arm a bit too tight so he loosened his grip, but when he did Paul didn't try to pull away, just stayed there, staying close. Wesley didn't let go of him.

"Look, maybe you'd better stay here tonight." Paul was speaking quickly, still looking straight into Wesley's eyes. "You were pretty out of it in the cafe, you know."

"Sure I'll stay, man." It sounded as if he had decided before Paul opened his mouth. Paul smiled. It was his turn to be shy.

Wesley looked towards the kitchen. "You got anything to eat round here?" he asked. "Man, I'm starving."

"I was going to get a takeaway," Paul replied. "There's a Chinese round the corner." He dug into the pockets of his jeans. "I've got about three quid." He looked at Wesley, who pulled out the crumpled tenner.

"Great," said Paul. "Let's go. You like Chinese, yeah?"

Wesley nodded. "Safe, man. Yeah." His mouth watered as he thought of shredded beef, soy sauce, fried rice, chasubal dumplings and squid, and his stomach sang as Paul went to the bedroom and returned pulling on the army greatcoat Wesley had first seen him wear. He tugged the padlock out of his pocket and gestured to Wesley to go on ahead of him.

They hurried along the cold street and cut through a deserted new housing estate, feeling like gunslingers staking out a ghost-town as they stumbled over the frozen ruts of mud. Then they went down a side-alley and onto a long and deserted shopping street. Paul pointed to a neon sign at the far end of the street.

"That's it," he said.

Wesley looked at him with a grin. "Race you," he said.

Before Paul had a chance to answer Wesley had sprinted off, so he had to run too. Wesley ran like an athlete, everything pointed forward, making lines like a silver fish. Paul pelted after him gracelessly with his arms and legs flailing, the greatcoat flapping like a broken wing behind him, his eyes on Wesley's big ass drawing him on. And Wesley slowed and Paul caught up with him, and they were in front of the takeaway heaving and gasping for breath, almost choking on the cold air. Wesley spat into the gutter.

"D'you feel good, man?" he asked, still grinning broadly.

Paul thought about it. "Yeah," he coughed. "I feel good."

"Safe, man. Safe." Wesley gave him five and grabbed him round the shoulders and they went into the takeaway like that, laughing loudly. It was already crowded inside though it hadn't gone nine o'clock, and even with the door propped open it was steamy and warm there compared with the night outside. They ran their hands along the surrounds of the polished steel hotplates, warming the tips of their fingers.

It was hard to decide what they wanted; there was always too much choice on Chinese menus. Eventually they settled on sweet and sour pork, beef and ginger, fried rice and beansprouts. Wesley paid the fat, pretty cashier and they went and leant against the wall in line with all the other people waiting for orders. Every so often they turned to look at each other and grinned inanely. After ten minutes of hungry waiting their order was called. Paul pushed past the people who had filled the place up while it was being cooked and grabbed the bulging paper bag from off the counter. It felt good and hot. He and Wesley jogged all the way back to the flat with it in the hope that it wouldn't have gone stone-cold before they got there.

Some of the sweet-and-sour sauce had leaked out and was soaking through the brown paper, but they were home long before the bag ripped. Wesley sat down on the sofa. He cleared the tray on the floor with one hand so he could put the bag down somewhere where it wouldn't stain anything. Paul went to the kitchen to get some plates to eat off. They didn't match. Nor did the cutlery.

They unpacked the bag and picked the lids off the still steaming foil trays, their stomachs rumbling and their mouths watering as they tipped the food out onto their plates. Paul poured out some sauce from the split sweet-and-sour carton and then licked his fingers.

"Would you like some more tea?" he asked. Wesley nodded, already eating.

"Only if you're making it, man," he replied after swallowing. He watched Paul going off to the kitchen, noticing the shape of his legs and how small and neat his buttocks were. He felt much better with food inside him, warmer and more confident. When Paul came back, he said,

"So you're a painter, yeah?" Paul nodded. "You want to do it for a job?"

Paul's brow furrowed. "I suppose," he replied. "I used to be sure, but now I don't know." He deliberately avoided Wesley's gaze. Even a few months ago he had been sure. Paul carried on talking and as he talked Wesley looked at his face and he could see the whole world reflected in that face:

"I started painting because I had a nervous breakdown, like, as therapy. I was good at it, people said I was good, so I carried on and got into a college. It's a dump. Well, it's alright really, but they don't really teach you anything."

Now it would be easy to talk; he could shit on about the

college for hours. But he didn't want to. Instead he fumbled for a question to ask Wesley.

"What was your job, Wes?"

There was a pause. Wesley looked away from him.

"Just factory work, man. Shitwork. I used to stack tins of paint, you know, drive one of them forklift trucks. It was okay, but I don't want to be doing shit like that forever."

"What would you like to do, then?" Paul asked.

Wesley shrugged. "I dunno, man. Something that pays I suppose. I wouldn't mind running me own business, you know, 'be your own boss.' I nearly did once. We were going to buy houses, do 'em up, and sell 'em for a profit. A mate of mine had it all worked out, what sort of houses to buy and everything. It never got going though. Geezer got in a car smash and broke both his legs and by the time he got out of hospital he'd gone off the whole thing." He paused. "I'd like to do something where you're free, you know? Not answering to no-one."

"I'd like to travel," said Paul. "I've never had enough money to do it with. The only place abroad I've ever been is Amsterdam, and that was with a college trip. But Paris or Italy. I'd like to go somewhere like that, where it doesn't rain and it's not so fucking cold, yeah?"

"Would you like to go to the West Indies?" Wesley felt aware of the class distinction when he asked that. Some people wanted to be white and English. After a moment Paul said, "Yeah," but he sounded hesitant.

"Have you got family there?" Wesley pushed. *Don't be a snob, man,* he thought, *don't be a wannabe. Be proud man, be proud to be Black-West-Indian-African.*

Paul hesitated again. Then he said, "I don't know. I was in a home since I was two. I don't know who my parents were. It made me bitter for a long time. I'd like to know I guess, but I don't think it matters very much." He felt tired talking about the old stuff; it was too much like the psychoanalysis. And the new stuff was still hurting. "You saw the photograph in my room? They adopted me when I was seven. I don't see them any more." Wesley shook his head in sympathy. "I don't know why they did it. Made me feel so bad. Like I was a changeling, you know? Something nasty left on the doorstep." His eyes darted and met Wesley's, holding them there. He looked away and laughed and said,

"I think I'm going to cry." Tears slid out of his eyes even though he was still smiling. "Sorry," he said. "I'll be alright in a minute." Because he was looking away he couldn't see the tears in Wesley's eyes, but he could hear the hoarseness in Wesley's voice when he said,

"I know what you mean, man. Really."

Paul turned to face him. He reached out, slowly and gracefully, and put his hands on Wesley's waist. It felt firm and warm and didn't shrink away from his touch. Wesley was watching Paul's eyes. Paul moved his face closer to Wesley's, not breaking eye-contact, and then finally he kissed Wesley on the lips, very softly, feeling the little electrical thrill you feel on coming into contact with another human being. Wesley's lips were warm and soft against his, and Paul could feel that Wesley was kissing him too.

It was over in a moment.

Wesley pulled his head back, making a slight double chin. He met Paul's eyes, a quizzical expression on his face.

"You queer, man?" he asked, but there was no anger in his voice; it was more like almost amusement.

"No," Paul replied, speaking very softly and without emphasis. He had promised himself a long time ago that he would never be anyone else's pervert and never say yes to anyone's insult. Then he added --

"Queer as you are."

Suddenly he was very afraid. He had never done anything like this before though he had wanted to a hundred thousand times. Sure, he had kissed girls, but it wasn't the same. There had never been the right chemistry. Not like now. Now the kiss really mattered, mattered more than anything he had ever done before. He waited, hiding in a heartbeat.

Wesley was still looking into his eyes. "Come here," he said, smiling. He put his hands lightly on Paul's hips and kissed him gently and then more firmly. He could feel the warmth of Paul's forehead as it touched his own. He didn't think about what he was doing; he didn't need to. All he knew and all that he needed to know was that the loneliness that had been with him since Floyd had died was finally gone. And he realised without articulating it that this was what he had always wanted from Floyd but had been afraid to try and take. Then, remembering it was another man he was kissing, he pulled back, thinking that Paul would somehow be shocked. But he was still smiling, and there was a look of wonder on his face. And Wesley felt elated because at last there was someone who would really understand.

Even so, it was difficult to start talking; it seemed so long since he'd really talked to anyone. He stroked Paul's cheek with his thumb to get his attention.

"There was this mate of mine," he began. "He was a boxer. He died of like a cerebral haemorrhage in a boxing match five years ago. We were really good mates. I guess it wasn't until just now I realised how much I was in love with him." He looked down. "I always knew, maybe. But I'm not like that, you know what I'm saying?"

He looked at Paul for reassurance. If Paul laughed at him for not knowing himself, he would die.

"I know," Paul said. "You're not like anything. Hey, did anyone ever tell you you're a beautiful guy?" Wesley turned away, embarrassed. Paul reached out and put his hand on Wesley's cheek, turning his head to face him. "I mean it," he said, marvelling at being able to touch Wesley's face, feel the warmth of what he could only look at before. He wondered how painting could have ever been enough. If it had it would have been for precisely that reason — that it was distant and you could only look at it. It couldn't touch you or hurt you.

Wesley couldn't speak. He wanted to say *you're beautiful too*, but it was all too new to him. Paul understood that without the words and didn't demand them of him.

"I'll put the fire in the bedroom," he said. "Or we'll freeze to death."

He stood up slowly, sliding his fingers out of Wesley's grip, and bent over to unplug the fire, squatting down to pick it up, feeling his skin-tight jeans stretching over his ass and thighs, hoping Wesley would want to do more than just kiss. He didn't know where this gorgeous and vulnerable man would want to go tonight, but what he did know was that neither of them wanted to go there on his own. His breath misted in the bedroom as he plugged the fire in. He went over to the bed and straightened the covers. There was a spare torn grey blanket behind the curtain. He shook it out and spread it over the bed. At least it was clean.

Wesley lay back on the sofa. He felt genuinely happy. Happier than he had for years. Part of it was a feeling of freedom, being liberated from other people's expectations. Except Paul's, but the fact that Paul could kiss him after he said he'd been married three years was liberating in itself. At that moment he felt free from all the pressure that had been building up in him since Floyd's death. He didn't know if it could last, but right now that didn't matter: He was free.

He got up off the sofa and went into the bedroom. Paul had just thrown a blanket on the bed. Wesley stood behind him, put his arms around his chest and gave him a bearhug.

"Man, you're beautiful," he said in his deepest bedroom voice, and kissed Paul lightly on the ear, nipping the lobe between his teeth.

Paul shivered. "That tickles, man," he said, half laughing.

Wesley slowly released him. Then he said, "I've got to use your bathroom again, man," and he was gone. Paul finished sraightening the bed and went back into the living-room, closing the bedroom door carefully behind him to keep in the heat.

He had imagined this moment differently; among empty bottles of champagne on a bed raised up like on a stage all the sheets black silk and the head of the bed would be ebony and black pearls from a broken string of pearls would be rolling on the floor and his lover would take him on the bed where everyone could see, could see him feel a rapture so extreme that when the sun rose he would be a different person altogether.

But now a new fear crept over him, the fear of being repulsive, of Wesley knowing that he liked all that stuff that might make Wesley sick, might make him think Paul was sick.

He looked up more sharply than he had meant to when Wesley came back into the living-room. Wesley's brow puckered.

"You okay, man?" he asked. Paul nodded, swallowing slightly, pushing his fears to the back of his mind. Wesley strolled over and sat down on the sofa. He was smiling and seemed full of confidence. He put his arm round Paul's shoulders, the fingers of his large hand spreading down Paul's upper arm. He turned to kiss Paul and saw momentary alarm in Paul's eyes.

"I'm not Sharon," Paul said. "You do know that, don't you?"

Wesley nodded slightly and they kissed, like lovers this time, long and hard, as if to part would be to die.

"Come on," said Paul. He stood up, and taking Wesley by the hand, he led him to the bedroom.

The air was quite warm there as the fire had been on for several hours while Wesley had been asleep before. They embraced standing up, hugging each other tightly, a little frightened because there was no way back, but happy too because they didn't want to go back. Wesley peeled off Paul's jumper.

"Put your arms up, bwai," he said in mock exasperation, a Jamaican mother. Paul could feel Wesley's silent laughter shaking along the length of his arms and into the fabric of the jumper, bouncing a soft sheet of wool against his face. He was only wearing a tee-shirt under it, and his arms felt cold in the chilly air. He ran his cool fingers up inside Wesley's tracksuit top, feeling Wesley's stomach muscles clench and shrink away from his light touch. He massaged Wesley's abdomen, marvelling at being able to feel each different muscle. Wesley exhaled.

"Let's go to bed, man," he said quietly. He peeled off his top, letting Paul admire his smooth, muscular arms. When he was sure Paul's gaze was on them, he flexed them bodybuilder style, grinning broadly, enjoying impressing someone with the body he had worked so hard on to make it beautiful. He lowered his arms. Then he reached out with his hands and Paul's fingers interlocked with his. They both stared at the dark, intertwining fingers, the veins standing out on skin the colour of plain chocolate. The hands could all belong to one person. It could have been a power play, but since each could break the other with a word it wasn't. They just flexed their wrists, one yielding to the other, then the other way round. It was a serious game, played in silence. Then Wesley met Paul's eyes and said,

"I'm gettin' cold, man. Let's get under them covers."

They sat facing each other on the bed, each fumblingly removing the other's shoes and socks.

Paul said, "I'd better lock the door," and padded off. He was back in about half a minute, in which time Wesley had taken off his boilersuit and climbed into bed, still shyly wearing his underpants. He had never wanted to make love to anyone as much as he wanted to make love to Paul now. He knew Sharon had always thought he was a bit of a square in bed, a bit too nice, a bit dull. He wondered what she would think if she could see him here, and for a moment he believed that she would understand. But he knew she wouldn't see the beauty. The ugly church that stood in the way of her seeing was too vast. It filled her horizon.

Paul stood at the side of the bed and Wesley looked up at him, looking up at an angel. He seemed more sure of himself now. He knelt down on the side of the bed, and Wesley's eyes ran down to the crotch of his tight jeans. From its bulge he knew that Paul's hard-on must be aching as much as his own. He reached out and unzipped Paul's fly. Paul looked down at Wesley's hands, mesmerised. Wesley pulled the pieces of fabric open, like peeling a banana, and started to pull Paul's trousers down. He looked up at Paul, whose lips were slightly parted. He watched his chest moving up and down. In one rapid, fluid movement Paul stripped off his teeshirt and dropped it onto the pile of clothes beside the bed. His trousers were now at his knees, his dark smooth skin bisected by his bright yellow briefs. He turned and sat on the bed, pulled off his trousers. Then he slid under the covers and into Wesley's arms.

They were still for a moment there, and then they began to explore each other. Paul felt Wesley's hands slide inside his underpants and squeeze his buttocks and he slid a hand down the front of Wesley's briefs, enormously gratified to elicit a groan and feel Wesley's almost painful stiffness. He stifled the groan with a kiss that was deep and wet and greedy, and slid on top of Wesley. Wesley opened his legs and Paul held his hips back, gently rubbing his crotch against Wesley's, his chest already tight with excitement. Wesley reached up and fondled Paul's erection through the stretched cotton fabric. It was Paul's turn to gasp. He was also pleased because, although he didn't seem to realise it, Wesley was making all the rules. Wesley pulled Paul's underpants down. He felt the cool air on his hard-on and became aware of its weight. Wesley fondled his balls and felt that he might come at any moment, so he pressed his body tight against him. Slowly they rolled over, kissing again. Paul felt incredibly warm and safe with Wesley's hot, heavy, muscular body on top of him. He reached down and slid down Wesley's underpants. Their crotches seemed fused together wet and hot and sticky and shivering.

With his heart in his mouth Paul asked, "What would you like to do, man?" afraid still even now of Wesley being disgusted.

Wesley put his hand between Paul's thighs, gripped his ass, one finger touching his sphincter. He looked serious.

"You ever had a blow-job, man?" he asked. Paul shook his head, hardly daring to move. "It's a shame, man. You ain't even know how good I'm going to be."

And Paul cried out as he felt Wesley's lips go over the tip of his hard-on and hotly and firmly start to move up and down and up and down.

Later, after they had made love until they were slippery with sweat and panting with exhaustion, and their eyes were hard with lack of sleep, they succumbed and slept in each others' arms, warm with a warmth that neither of them had ever felt before, fitting together as perfectly as if it was the one thing that they had been made to do, each wondering how he had got to be so lucky, for that night at least.

And Wesley lay there thinking, feeling strange still, and elated too, like he had never felt when he had slept with a woman; like he wasn't made to love women, not like that anyway. And all the grind and heaviness he found when he slept with a woman was absent here, lifted from him by a rapture that verged on hysteria. And if women were the earth then men were the air and Wesley was high on lean muscularity and oxygen, a high that women could never give him, and in men loving men Wesley had found a new and crazy freedom. For it was freedom Wesley had felt as he pumped his mouth up and down on Paul's hot erection like it was the most natural thing in the world, feeling its fullness with his tongue and lips and its weight as he cradled Paul's buttocks in his hands and listened to his moans and the sound of his head thrashing on the pillow, like Paul's hard-on was God's chalice but more as he swallowed Paul that there was no taking and there was no serving, just a hurtling towards a gasping black male oneness. And it *was* to do with maleness and it *was* to do with blackness. And it was perfection.

And for the first time ever Wesley felt totally free. He had chosen to do this thing that no one could expect of him, even Paul he knew had not expected it of him. And when he kissed Paul, and when he put his mouth over Paul's hard-on, all those people who for twenty-five years had told him not only what he should be but what he was were all defeated. Because they didn't know shit. And now he was finally himself. Only himself. And free.

Paul stirred, brushing Wesley's bruised nipples. Wesley's dick twitched. He reached down and felt that Paul was hard already.

"Oh man, you really need it, don't you?"

He gasped as Paul dripped baby oil onto his chest and began to rub it in.

"Oh, man, not me tits." *Oh, man, I really need it.*

Oh, man, I really need you.

Two o'clock that afternoon

They lay there in the half-light that filtered through the yellow curtains, wrapped around each other still. Wesley turned and looked at Paul's head lying next to his on the pillow. Paul's eyes were open, and he was staring up at the ceiling. Wesley reached over and stroked his cheek. Looking at his eyelashes made Wesley think of the painting of the black butterflies. He ran the tips of his fingers over Paul's nose and lips, feeling the warmth of Paul's breath on them. Paul was still looking at the ceiling. Then he looked sideways at Wesley and said,

"You will stay, won't you?"

Wesley felt hurt by that doubt. He hugged Paul, whose body felt burning hot against his. They kept close like that for several minutes and then, because he sensed that Paul would ask the question again, needing to be reassured by words as well as actions, he said,

"I'll stay, man. I'll stay."

Paul hugged him as tightly as he could. Wesley wondered how Paul could think he might want to be anywhere else. Paul rested his head on Wesley's chest, feeling the pulse of his blood and feeling the words reverberate around his rib-cage when Wesley asked,

"Have you got anything to eat, man?"

"Bread, jam, cereal, milk and tea," Paul replied, his eyes closed, pretending he would never have to get up. Then he sat up and said,

"You stay here, I'll go and fix it."

Wesley nodded, bleary-eyed. He watched Paul lazily as he got up; the curve of the outsides of his thighs and shoulders, the lines of his neck, the shape of his hips, the grace of the whole of his slim, smooth body, aubergine-dark in the half-lit room. Looking at Paul's butt too made Wesley think of the one thing they hadn't tried last night. He thought maybe they could try it tonight. Paul turned round to pull on his yellow underpants and Wesley looked between his legs and thought that he would like to try it the other way too. Seeing Wesley watching him, Paul gave his bulge a quick squeeze and then went and picked up his clothes. Every movement he made, Wesley saw gold dust glittering off him. Paul wriggled into his jeans and sat on the bed to tug on his shoes and socks. Wesley rubbed his smooth, hard, bare back as he sat there, and massaged his neck. After he had got his shoes on, Paul turned and kissed Wesley on the lips, a long, gentle kiss. Then he stood up and pulled on his jumper.

"I'll only be a couple of minutes," he said. He closed the door carefully behind him.

Wesley lay back on the bed and stretched out, crossing his arms behind his head. He felt like he had been reborn; like he was a new person starting out on a new life, a butterfly out of a chrysalis. And everything he had done before was past and finished with; the ghosts of his life were laid. Floyd was dead after all, and Wesley had loved him, and his death had broken Wesley's heart, but he understood that now and that meant the pain was over. And now he had Paul. If Paul would have him, anyway. He stretched again, his stretching spreading his new and colourful wings to catch the sunlight.

He had missed a work-out at the gym through being there with Paul, and for the first time in months he really wanted to go; he wasn't just doing it for himself now. Now there was someone who wanted to see him pumped and trace every sculpted line and vein on his body, someone who really saw the beauty of what he did. For the first time in months he felt full of energy too.

The door swung open and Paul came back in, carrying a tray that was heavy with teapot, mugs, milk, bowls and a pile of buttered toast. He had a big box of cornflakes pinned under one arm too. The smell of the toast had reached Wesley a bit before, and his mouth was already watering. Paul bumped the door shut with his backside and set the tray down beside the bed. He bent over Wesley and kissed him gently. His big lips were warm, and his breath smelt fresh and minty and Wesley held his breath because he knew his wouldn't be. Paul didn't seem to mind.

Paul handed Wesley a mug of tea, and while he was sipping it he took Wesley's free hand in his. Wesley felt happy that someone wanted to touch him so much. He returned Paul's grip and moved his arm so that their hands rested on the dip in the eiderdown over his crotch. Paul started feeding him toast as he lay there but it was a bit slow and the toast was getting cold, so he sat up and wrapped himself around Paul and ate properly.

After they had eaten, Wesley slid out from behind Paul and stood up in front of him. He smiled from ear to ear.

"Let me show you something," he said. "You shown me your art, yeah. Now let me show you mine. My poetry, you know what I'm sayin'?"

And it was a poetry without words, that only he could show, a vision only he could reveal. So he began — pumping up and getting ripped, spreading his back and flexing his calves, his pectorals, moving like oil on glass and then freezing not like a statue but like a taut bow, still and perfect and dangerous.

"Lookin' good, man?"

Paul nodded as he watched Wesley move sinuously from pose to pose, black and supple, his skin perfect over his perfect interlocking muscles; his fluid, washboard abdominals; the little ridges that joined the spread of his back to his chest, that looked like the gills of sharks; the ridge of muscle in his armpits; his bulging chest, the nipples turned down under the curve of each muscle so they were hard to get your mouth around. And Wesley's big ass and the curve of his thighs, the twist of his waist and the size of his arms were magic to Paul, like Wesley was a houngan and these poses were a dance and his body, his African warrior body, his Black magical body, was the spell, and in its curves and secret places he could find the answer to all the questions he could ever ask and all that could ever be asked of him. And it was Paul's turn to feel that what he had seen was miraculous, and that Wesley's body was the temple of the spirit.

And then the poem was over and Wesley came to a standstill. A single drop of sweat ran down his chest in a slow silver line. Paul bent his head and kissed Wesley where the drop had run. He could taste its saltiness on his lips. They sat on the bed again and Paul put his arms round Wesley's waist, unable to speak.

"What's wrong, man?" Wesley asked.

"Nothing man, nothing," he whispered. "I just don't have the words."

"Hey, hey, don't worry, man. Just stay quiet." Wesley cradled Paul's head and rocked him. "Let's get this jumper off, man. Just be close."

They stayed like that for a while, silent. Then Paul asked, "Did you ever go in for any competitions, lover?"

Wesley laughed softly. *Lover.* He squeezed Paul's waist.

"Yeah, man. One time," he replied. "But I didn't like it, you know? I felt, I dunno, embarrassed, up there in front of a big crowd of people, trying to do my shit. It ain't me, man, posing and doing routines and stuff. The other guys doing it, they were really into it, you know? They really wanted to win and they weren't afraid to put another guy down cos they figured it might fuck up his chances. And washing the oil off — Man! I thought, never again, man, even if I won."

"You hated oiling up?" Paul asked.

Wesley laughed. "I liked oiling *up*, yeah." He remembered

172

going in for the competition, how he had felt more embarrassed the nearer it got, and how he had been relieved that Floyd and Sharon couldn't make it, even though he had come third.

Paul looked at Wesley's face and he loved what he saw; his black, shining eyes, the smooth darkness of his skin, his neat, flat nose and little ears, the gunmetal grey of his scalp where it had been shaved up the sides, his large, sharply-etched lips, his small chin, the slope of his face. A black man's face (like Paul's face, a black man's face too), and that was important to Paul; everything that made him black (more than the way his hair sprung, more than the way he moved) was important to Paul, because it meant that everything he did was self-affirming and self-purifying. Up there in that room the white world disappeared.

And being a man seemed easy for Wesley, even here, where for Paul (who never minced and never said *darling*) it was troubled and shadowed. Until now. Two black guys. And in their embrace the universe. Finally, Paul's scars were healing.

"I've switched the immersion on," he said. "If you want a bath later on."

Wesley nodded.

"Okay," he said.

Paul wanted to say *I think I'm in love with you* but he didn't, partly because he thought it might scare the handsome, smiling man sitting by him, partly because he thought he might sound stupid, mistaking a night of passion for something more lasting. But that afternoon he felt fresh and blank as if he could become anything for anyone, or for Wesley the lover he would need and always want. He had lain his own ghost to rest too, because he knew, finally, what it meant to be wanted. Now he had to be responsible for himself and make his own choices. He had moved from adolescence to manhood.

"D'you think you ought to phone Sharon?" he asked Wesley, speaking carefully. He didn't want to make himself Sharon's opposite in Wesley's mind. Wesley didn't answer his question.

173

"I mean, she'll worry about you," Paul continued. Wesley put a finger on Paul's lips.

"Ssh, man. Later, yeah?" Then after a pause: "I'll say I'm staying with you for a couple of days." His dark eyes asked, *if that's okay with you, man?* Paul nodded. "With me star," Wesley added, smiling, reaching out and grasping Paul's hand.

"What d'you fancy doing, then, star?" Paul asked, the subject of Sharon closed.

Wesley shrugged. "I don't mind, man," he said. He would be happy doing anything if Paul was there. Then he laughed and said, "I want to drink champagne on a yacht, man. And eat fish eggs." He laughed and laughed until he cried, pulling laughter out of Paul too. It seemed funny like it did when he was stoned. He sniffed and wiped his eyes with his hands.

"No," he said. "No, man, I'll have a bath, it's okay. Then we could go out someplace. Nowhere too smart, yeah?" He started laughing again. "I ain't got nothin' to wear."

He stopped abruptly. He took Paul's hand and laid it on his chest, looking straight into Paul's eyes, and said,

"That's me heart, man,"

And couldn't say anything else.

They stayed like that, listening to each other breathing in and out in the stillness of the room. Finally Paul turned and kissed Wesley.

"I never knew anyone could be like you," he said softly. Wesley stared to cry then, quietly, tears sliding out from between his clenched eyelids while Paul held him close, feeling his own eyes burning too.

Chapter Nine

WESLEY HIT THE street jangling tens and twenties in his pocket, fingering Paul's key. His hands and face glowed warmly in the cold air from soaking in the hot water. He felt clean and could smell the slight fragrance of Paul's shampoo and deodorant floating around him. The cleanliness seemed to spread out into his clothes, killing their staleness. Paul had offered him a change of everything, but there was no way Wesley could squeeze his curving thighs into trousers that were skin-tight on Paul's stick-insect legs *(the sexiest legs he'd ever seen, on the sexiest boy)*. He did borrow a pair of Paul's briefs though, and was embarrassed by the slight frisson he felt as he pulled them on.

The phone box stank of piss and the directories were all shredded to confetti. Wesley felt nervous as he stacked his little pile of tens on top of the phone. He knew he ought to have something ready to say to Sharon, some explanation for why he wasn't there and why he couldn't come back right now, might never come back, but he didn't. All he could do was just dial the number and let it happen. He lifted the receiver.

There was no tone. The phone was dead. He slammed the receiver down on the prongs a couple of times, but the phone stayed dead; the only bit of it that was working was the panel flashing *Insert Money Now. Minimum Charge 10p.* Another time he would have been angry, like when he had been in a real hurry and needed to make a call and the first box he got was 999 calls only, the second two were both dead, and the fourth

175

one swallowed his money and then went dead. He had yelled in anger, got hold of the metal flex and ripped it out of its socket. Then he had felt very foolish and had carefully replaced it on its hook before walking off.

This time he didn't feel angry, he just felt tired. He didn't want to make the call anyway.

Paul had told him there was a phone in the 7-11 so he went back there. It was next to the counter. He hadn't wanted to use it before because of that, because it was going to be a personal conversation, but now it would make a good excuse for not talking much.

On the way to the 7-11 he passed a late-night chemist's and a vague sense of guilt came over him. *Rubbers,* he thought. *If two guys are doing it, they're supposed to use rubbers.* He wasn't afraid of there being any disease in what they were doing, nothing like that; it was a respect thing, a way of showing you respected the other person. He took a deep breath and went inside. He felt as nervous as an inexperienced teenager as he looked awkwardly at the large range of condoms on the counter. Finally he chose a brand and picked up a large tube of KY jelly as well, remembering the times he'd had sex with girls, though not really remembering because those memories felt more like stories other men had told him, and the rubber had torn. Choosing the things made him feel turned-on, and then prickly and self-conscious when he went to pay for them. But the girl at the till was nice and impersonal as he handed over the money, and he didn't really care what she thought anyway. He even said 'Goodnight' to her as he reached the door.

A thin girl, maybe sixteen but not older, was on the phone in the 7-11. She had spikey blonde hair and black and purple eye make-up. There were spots round her mouth and she was smoking a cigarette. She pumped money into the slot with long, chipped red nails. Somewhere else she might have been attractive, but here the neon lights opened every pore and shadowed the bags under her eyes with bruises. Maybe she was only fourteen. He wandered round the shelves, unwilling to eavesdrop on her call. Two students further up an aisle were buying baked beans and Mother's Pride. They went over to the beer section of the drink shelf. Wesley got bored watching them pricing up different cans of lager and started looking at the shelves again. Tampons, sanitary towels, nappies, baby buds, baby oil. Grinning softly to himself, he took a bottle of baby oil off the shelf.

When he went back to the phone the blonde girl had gone, but in her place stood a frumpy, middle-aged woman. He paid for the oil at the till and then hung around the phone as if only the young could have secrets. The woman fondled the column of 10p's she had stacked up on top of the box like she was trying to wind him up, but she didn't have the nerve to shit on for ages while he was there, and she rang off sharply. She glanced up at him as she hurried out of the shop, and there was a little fear and anger in her face. *Mugger. Rapist.* Or less than that: *black, trouble, threat.* Anger flushed through him. Stupid bitch. He fumbled for his change.

He only had 40p in tens, but he didn't bother getting any more from the counter because he knew he had nothing to say.

It had just gone six and he knew Sharon should have got home about quarter of an hour ago. He stacked three of the tens on the grey metal moneybox, sitting the fourth one in the slot, and began to dial. He felt strange dialling his own number; it was something he hardly ever did. The tone sounded very loud and he moved the receiver away from his ear. The sound of his breathing was magnified in the mouthpiece until all he was aware of was that sound and the phone chirruping on the other end. There was no reply and so, unwillingly, he rang off, listening as he slowly lowered the receiver for that sudden tinny voice answering at the last moment. It didn't. He stood there wondering what to do. There was no-one else waiting to use the phone, so he waited for a minute and dialled again.

This time it was answered with a painful suddenness that

sent his heart-rate up.

"Hello?" It was Sharon, sounding breathless. She must have heard the phone ringing and run down the hall. He would have rung off just as she was fumbling in her handbag for the keys.

"Hi, it's Wesley."

"Are you alright?"

"I'm fine," he said and then stopped. He could hear the fuzzy silence at the other end of the line.

"Look," he continued, "I need some time. I've got to think, yeah. There's things I need to work out, you know what I'm sayin'? Yeah. Ah, I'm gonna stay with a mate of mine for a bit. His name's Paul. You don't know him."

There was a pause, then Sharon replied, "Okay Wes. I've got some thinking to do too. See you in a couple of days, then?"

"Yeah. Take care."

"And you. Bye."

"Bye."

He put the receiver down, and all the things he could have said flooded into his mind. But the time wasn't the right time to say them, and the 7-11 wasn't the right place. He put the remaining tens back in his pocket. The call had taken under three minutes. Somehow he felt it should have taken longer. At least he had made it, anyway. He wanted to get back to the warmth of the flat now, to Paul's warmth, to his new home. And it felt like home because everything Paul said and everything he did told Wesley that that was where he belonged.

As he went down the corridor Wesley heard Paul running a second bath and singing. He had a deep, soft voice that only sometimes wavered out of key, and he was singing 'Don't Explain.' Wesley smiled and leaned against the door to the flat and listened for a while:

Hush now, don't explain
Just say you'll remain
I'm glad you're back
Don't explain.
Quiet, don't explain
What is there to gain?
Skip that lipstick — Paul walked out of the bathroom and stopped abruptly. "Hi," he said. "Made it to a phonebox alright?" Wesley nodded. Paul seemed very edgy. Wesley wanted to kiss him but he moved away.

"Hey, baby," he said, reaching to touch Paul's face. Paul flinched away.

"What's wrong?"

Paul was silent for a moment. Then he burst out, "It's just that you've got your wife who you love and your weights so you've got a great body and I don't know why you bother with me because I haven't got anything." His eyes challenged Wesley's.

"That's shit, man," Wesley replied. "Go and get washed."

He pushed past Paul into the living-room, burning at Paul's lack of faith, and sprawled across the sofa, twitching irritably. He shifted around, unable to get comfy on the flabby springs, then tried to zip up his boilersuit. The toggle stuck and he swore. He yanked at it impatiently and it snapped off in his hand. He swore again and threw it across the room. It hit the yellow vase and chipped its lip. Then Wesley realised his anger was pointless and childish, and he forced himself to sit quietly and let it pass from him. A minute later he felt quite calm.

Paul had brought the fire into the living-room but the air was still cold so Wesley dragged it as near to the sofa as the flex would let him. He looked at the broken record player. Tomorrow I'll get my tape deck, he thought. It was quite portable; the speakers could clip onto the sides, and they had a good system in the front room so it wouldn't be like he would be taking it to wind Sharon up. He also wanted to pick up some clean clothes that he could fit into.

He decided to go during the day when she was out. It wasn't

that he was afraid of her, it was just he had nothing to say to her yet, and if they met they would have to talk, and if you have nothing to say you just end up lying and blaming and being bitter, and he didn't want to do that. He wondered what was in her mind but he couldn't think. It reminded him what a stranger she had become; someone he only went back a long way with, like so many schoolfriends he'd had where eventually he'd realised that for all that experience shared, they had nothing in common now. Like he had known a lot of white kids at school and they had all been good mates then but he didn't see any of them anymore. They'd stopped thinking the same way. And if he saw any of them in the street he wouldn't even bother to say hello, there wasn't any point. He knew it and they knew it. But still it seemed a shame that they had all just stopped being friends and stopped even being people who knew each other. Like him and Sharon.

He stood up and went over to the window, feeling a little lonely. The towerblocks glittered like upright fish catching the sunlight. The city looked empty beneath him, like an empty glass. He turned round just as Paul closed the door behind him, a large, flame-red towel wrapped round his waist, soapbox and shampoo in his hands. He smelt clean and radiated warmth. They stood facing each other, eyes meeting uncertainly.

"Sorry I pissed you around, Wes," Paul said.

"It's alright, man, it's alright," Wesley replied, taking Paul gently in his arms and hugging him to him. Then he started rubbing Paul's smooth back, unable to resist touching his hot skin. He kissed Paul's neck and Paul shivered. Wesley moved his hand down Paul's torso, gently biting his tensed stomach, and sank to his knees in front of him. Paul ran his fingers through Wesley's hair as he knelt there, and moaned as Wesley ran his hands firmly up his thighs inside the towel and slid it off, moaned like he hadn't been touched for months. And he gasped as Wesley took him into his mouth and slid his foreskin back, and fluttered like a butterfly on a pin as Wesley moved his head backwards and forwards, his soft woolly hair touching Paul's stomach in regular rhythm. Paul felt a sheen of perspiration breaking out on his clean new skin. He put his hands on Wesley's head and pulled him back so he could kneel down opposite him. They kissed and Paul could taste his cock in Wesley's mouth. He ran his hand towards Wesley's crotch but Wesley caught it.

"Uh-uh," he said, shaking his head. "Just let *me* do it, man."

He eased Paul onto his back on the towel on the faded yellow rug and looked down at his smooth, taut, stretched-out body.

"You know what?" he said, kneading Paul's trembling belly firmly with both hands, making him writhe.

"What?" he whispered.

"You're the most beautiful guy." Paul closed his eyes and Wesley worked his hands up Paul's sides, reducing him to a quivering jelly.

"Let me rub your back." He lifted Paul and turned him over, rubbing his neck and broad shoulders and moving down to his waist. Then he began to knead Paul's backside.

"You got a nice ass, man," he declared, running his hand between Paul's buttocks. Then he spread them and bent over and tickled Paul's asshole with his tongue. It smelt clean and perfumed. Opening his mouth wide, he pushed his muscular tongue against the sphincter and past it. Paul gasped and Wesley forced his tongue in as far as it would go, until its roots ached, until Paul began to move his hips back against his face. He put his hands on Paul's hips, stopping their movement, and reached over to his jacket for the bottle of baby oil. Paul lay beneath him on the red towel, still radiating warmth. Wesley knelt down between his legs, slowly pushing his thighs open with his own. Fumblingly he unzipped his boiler suit and let it fall to his knees. He stripped off his tee-shirt and threw it onto the sofa. Then he pulled his briefs down, letting Paul hear the sound of the fabric sliding over skin, not freeing his erection but allowing it to spring up and softly slap against his belly. He unscrewed the lid of the oil and poured a spot of the cool liquid between Paul's shoulderblades. Paul sighed as Wesley worked the oil outwards over his back and down his spine. He picked up the bottle again and poured a stream of clear oil between Paul's buttocks. Paul flexed them and relaxed them, lifting his ass up slightly, offering himself to Wesley, who was now slowly moving his oily fist on his heavy erection, watching the oil drip over Paul's loose, vulnerable balls. He looked down at his glistening hard-on and saw in its light-brown, mushroom-shaped head and curving veined shaft a beauty he had never seen before. His pubic hair glittered as if woven with diamonds. He reached a hand round inside Paul's crotch and gripped his dick, which had softened with the slow sensuality of the massage. He held it tight and began rapidly pumping his fist on it. The sudden movement changed the tempo of their lovemaking. Paul cried out as his heart skipped a beat and his dick stiffened painfully. He rotated his hips to ease the frenzy with which Wesley's moving fist was hitting his belly. When Wesley could feel the veins on Paul's dick against his palm he slowed down and released it. Then he gathered a fold of the soft red towel to stroke the oil away from Paul's asshole and reached over for the KY. Wesley slipped one glittering finger inside Paul. Paul tensed, then relaxed. Wesley worked the finger back and forth, feeling the ring of Paul's muscle gradually soften, accepting him. He slid in a second shiny finger and Paul exhaled, but he kept his ass where it was, and a few moments later began to push it back onto Wesley's hand, taking the fingers down to the palm. Wesley was more turned on than he had ever been in his life, watching Paul work his ass like that. He slowly slipped the fingers out of Paul's hot body.

"No," Paul whispered, half-looking round at him.

"Stay cool, baby," Wesley said, fumbling momentarily with the packet of condoms. "I just gotta — " the foil tore and he slid the latex disc out and rolled it down over the length of his aching dick, " — do it right for you, man."

He climbed up behind Paul and gripped his shoulders, sliding his slick hard-on between Paul's chocolate-peach buttocks. He reached down with one hand and held his crown firmly against Paul's sphincter before pushing smoothly inside.

"Say if it hurts, man."

Paul moaned as Wesley pushed past the muscle, kicking for a moment, but then Wesley was inside, sliding in as far as he could go. Wesley began to move his hips slowly back and forth against Paul's butt. He groaned as Paul clenched his ass, and began to move more rhythmically, kneading Paul's back as he did so. After a few minutes, worried for Paul's comfort, he reached over for the KY again and squeezed more around the base of his dick where it was inserted into Paul's trembling body. Then he resumed pumping. Soon they were both gasping with every movement and wet with sweat. Wesley's erection was hot and humming as it moved inside Paul's body, so full and pregnant and large and deep inside Paul where it belonged, black and hard and as full of mystery and life-giving as the African sun and sky and so heavy, humming, humming and too heavy to hold on any longer. He came with a shout, his heart too exploding inside Paul.

He had never shouted coming before in his life.

He left his still-erect dick pushed firmly up Paul's backside and reached round between his legs. To his astonishment Paul's dick was limp and the towel was sodden with come beneath his belly. *I didn't think guys could do that*, he thought. Something else new. He started to gently pull out.

"No," Paul said. "Stay inside me a bit longer."

"Sure, man. I like being there. But ain't it hurtin' you?"

Paul had turned his head sideways and Wesley could see a white line of tears along his eyelashes. He didn't answer.

"Guess I can only know by you giving me some of the same, right, man?"

Paul swallowed. "How do you understand that, man? I mean, *I* can't even explain." He faltered, stopped.

"Cos I was made for this, man. I was made to be here doing this with you. That's how I understand. I never done it before

183

just like you never done it before but you understand, you know what I'm sayin'? I'm gettin' cramp, man. I'll have to pull out, okay?"

Paul nodded. He breathed in sharply as Wesley withdrew. Wesley turned and cradled him in his arms.

"It's alright, baby," he said. "If you don't want me to do it again I don't mind. I'm not into you being like the man or the woman. I don't do that shit. I want it to be just you and just me, doing what we want and being ourselves, being natural about it, you know what I mean?"

"Yeah, I know what you mean, but." He paused. Wesley looked at his face, concerned. "But what you did, what we just did, I feel better than I ever felt before. We can do that anytime you want, man. Because I've never felt anything like that good. Ever."

"Yeah?" Wesley grinned. "For real?" He laughed, hugging Paul. "Well, look, right? I was married for three years and what we just did was the best sex I ever had. Fuck it, man, it was the best *thing* that happened to me for four years." He looked into Paul's eyes. "For ever." Paul looked down.

"So are you happy?"

But he didn't have to ask.

They slept in front of the fire like spoons, hands knotted together, Wesley burying his face in Paul's perfumed hair.

After they had eaten breakfast, Paul started on the stack of dirty washing-up, chiselling hard spaghetti and burnt-on fried egg off the pans. Warm yellow sunlight filled the room and the foam in the sink sparkled. Wesley stood behind Paul dressed only in a grey jumper and a pair of yellow underpants, hugging his waist and kissing him on the back of his neck in between desultorily drying things with a red-and-white dishcloth. He had left his overalls off because it seemed stupid to wear them now he was sacked. Paul didn't seem to be complaining.

"What's in here?" Wesley asked, peering into a dusty carrie

bag that hung on a nail in the wall. Paul looked round.

"Fruit and stuff. It's probably gone off by now."

Wesley rummaged around and pulled out a smooth, glossy, yellowy-orange apple-sized fruit. It was slightly speckled and its stalk looked like a dry flower opening.

"What's this?" he asked.

"Pomegranate," Paul replied.

"Yeah? I've eaten them when I was a kid. One a me uncles worked on a stall. He used to bring us them when they were in season. I never knew what they was called though. You got a knife, man?"

Paul pulled one out of the sink tidy and handed it to him. The water on it made the blade sparkle in the sunshine.

As it bit into the flesh with a crisp rasp, Wesley struggled to remember a bit of the Bible his mum had liked and he had learnt off by heart. He began uncertainly, but once he had started it quickly came back to him:

"Let us go out early to the vineyards and see whether the vines are budded, whether the grape blossoms are opened and the pomegranates are in bloom. There shall I give you my love."

The pomegranate split in half and he put the knife down on the table. The seeds were red and perfect.

"It's in the Bible," he said, in reply to Paul's unspoken question. "I heard a lot of it when me mum got religious. She ain't now, though." He handed one half to Paul and slowly forced the shell of his half inside-out, pushing the seeds up. Paul watched him and imitated the movement. The seeds were sweet and on the verge of going rotten. They left the skins sitting on the little blue table.

Paul had to go to college that afternoon because he had a tutorial at two, which decided Wesley to go back to his flat for the stereo and some clean clothes. Paul gave him the keys and said, out of the blue and in an anxious voice,

"You will come back, won't you?"

Wesley started and replied angrily, "Look man, of course

I'm comin' back. For fuck's sake man, I love you. Okay?" He grabbed Paul's chin and kissed him, not moving his lips, forcing Paul to break the kiss by gasping for air. He touched Paul on the cheek.

"Okay?"

Paul nodded and put his arms round Wesley's waist.

Just as they were about to kiss again there was a loud knock at the front door of the flat. Paul let his hands slip over Wesley's buttocks and his cool bare thighs. He wrinkled his brow.

"I wonder who that is?" he said.

"There's only one way to find out, man," Wesley replied, grasping Paul's hands in his own. The knocking came again, more loudly this time, and they heard a male voice shouting,

"Paul! Are you okay?"

"It's Steve," Paul said, relaxing slightly. Seeing Wesley's blank look he added, "he helped me get you back here."

"Well, you gonna let him in, man?" Wesley asked, gazing deeply into Paul's eyes. "Or are we just gonna stand here?"

Paul slipped his hands out of Wesley's and crossed the room, opened the door.

"Hi, Steve," he said. "I was just getting ready to go in. This is my friend Wesley. Wesley, this is Steve."

They shook hands. "Paul told me you helped me out the other day, man. So thanks, yeah? I owe you one."

"Na, it's alright, mate. I couldn't've not helped, could I?"

"Thanks anyway, man."

Steve turned to Paul. "So you're going into college now?"

Paul nodded. "I'll just get my coat."

While they were waiting for Paul, Wesley realised he wasn't wearing any trousers. He shrugged to himself and hoped his legs were muscley enough to seem covered by being bare. Paul flapped out of the bedroom in his greatcoat, sketch-pad pinned under one arm.

"You've got the keys, haven't you?" Wesley nodded. "See you later," he said.

"See you around," Steve replied. "Nice meeting you."

"Later, man."

The door banged shut behind them and Wesley was on his own. He wandered back to the kitchen and munched on a chewy slice of cold toast left over from breakfast. He felt loose and relaxed in the empty flat. He thought back to the night, when he and Paul had woken in the small hours and talked for hours or what seemed like hours in a room that was silvered by the moonlight, lying there in the dark together, sharing their private thoughts and dreams, each unafraid for once of exposing himself to another, each beginning something new. If it wasn't love, it was something so close as to be indistinguishable.

They had talked about the fathers they had never known. "He had style, man," Wesley said, thinking of the one photograph of his father that was kept turned face-down in his mother's dressing-table. "Like — a hat. A fedora. And a wide tie and lapels and checked flares from when it was cool to dress that way, yeah? And gold on his fingers. Maybe he was a shit, man, but me mum never said anything much to me against him. She never said much about him at all. When I was younger I used to think of him travelling round the world in boxcars, ragging the pianos like in all them blues records."

" Was he like a musician, then?" Paul asked.

"Oh, man, I don't know. I'd like it if he had been one though, you know?" He paused. "I'd like to think that I'd know him, like, if I met him on the street — I'd know him cos he was me dad. But I don't think so. I don't think I'd know." He felt a sense of loss and looked across at Paul, who was staring at the ceiling. "What about you, man? Did you ever get told anything about your real parents?" Paul shook his head. "Man, that must be bad. D'you wonder what they were like?"

"I used to hate them," he replied. "But then I thought, what if they were dead? So I sort of forgave them. I don't think I want to know what they're like. Not really. I used to make up stories about them when I was a kid, all the time." He stopped talking and looked puzzled. Then: "I never used to have them both in the same story. I suppose if I'd thought they were happy together without me it would have made me feel worse."

"What were the stories like, man?" Wesley rubbed Paul's upper arm and ran his fingers over his collar-bone, finally letting them come to rest cupped over Paul's breast. He could feel the beat of a heart under his fingertips but he didn't know if it was Paul's or his own.

"I don't know. They were always on the run, though. That's why they had to leave me behind. Maybe they were always going to save the world."

Wesley turned to face Paul in the bed and wrapped his arms and legs round him, kissing his soft, hot lips. Paul put his arms around Wesley's broad back and held him close. They shared each others' breath.

"What do you think he'd think, your dad, if he could see you now?" Wesley asked, running his hands down Paul's spine and over the curve of his buttocks, pressing gently on the sensitive spot just behind his balls.

"I don't know. I hope he'd be happy because I'm happy. He owes me it, you know what I mean? You know, he doesn't have the right — *I* don't think he has the right — to tell me he likes it or not. I don't think anyone does."

Wesley slipped out of Paul's clasp and lay beside him on his back. Paul rested his head on Wesley's chest. He could hear the words buzzing inside Wesley before he spoke.

"I remember there was this kid at school. Everyone used to say he was queer. Man, *everyone!* I don't know he ever did anything but they always called him a queer. I don't think no-one ever thought about, like, what it meant. It was just he didn't have any friends and he picked his nose and scratched his ass in front of you. He had like, blond curly hair and womany hands and he was like really thick, you know? I mean, he got a grade five in Home Economics. And I didn't like him either. I don't think I ever even spoke to him. Now I wonder what that kid was, cos he was ugly and stupid but he weren't queer. If that means what we got, he weren't queer."

And Paul understood that beneath what Wesley was saying he was afraid of being laughed at and spat on, of being locked outside and locked in, of finding that what he thought had made him free was only another trap.

"Look, man." Paul's voice was urgent. "What we did tonight and last night, did it make you feel less of a man? Did you feel like a woman?"

Wesley stared into space. "No, man. What we did was all man. There was no woman in it."

"Then are you ashamed of it?"

"No, man. No, I ain't."

He kissed Paul deeply and began to pump his lips on Paul's extended tongue. They both felt a need for closeness after so many confessions. And that night Wesley stroked Paul's hot erection until it dripped, the precum a libation, and sat astride Paul and moved his butt up and down on its glistening latex-covered length a little pain at first as Paul pushed his hips up and slid past Wesley's entrance but then a sense of fullness and excitement as he pushed his ass down onto Paul's crotch and his own dick was watering and always and only a second away from coming as he started to move. And he knew how Paul had felt the night before, riding the storm and the storm inside him too. Paul spread his legs like a butterfly warming its wings and slowly pushed Wesley over until he was lying on his back with his ankles at Paul's shoulders, more than ever where he wanted to be and excited still because Paul stayed deep inside him all the while. Paul moved his hips slightly and Wesley groaned.

"Are you alright, baby?" Paul asked, stroking Wesley's face. "Do you want me to stop?"

Wesley drew a breath and shuddered, shaking his head. "Feel me dick, man," he gasped. It was hard and heavy and corded with veins, and his balls hung loose against Paul's pubic hair.

"Don't stop."

And the sweat fell like diamonds from Paul's hair as he

pumped his hips against Wesley's ass sliding his tingling wet erection right up inside him and they moaned and shouted as the heat grew between their legs, their hoarse voices a chant and a song. And for Wesley Paul thrusting deep inside him completed a circle, filling and fulfilling him, making his manhood complete, and the rhythm of their bodies around a single point in the circle's centre the point where Paul's hard-on was sliding in and out of Wesley's asshole was a dance that took him back to Africa and in the grey and cold and rain with Paul he opened up that blue sky and that black earth that was buried there within them both. And they thrashed and screamed and shuddered as they came.

* * * * *

There was a long queue for the bus into the city centre. He must have spent months of his life queuing; every morning and evening to and from work, eighteen months signing on the dole after school, even on Saturday nights to get into the clubs, standing in line, waiting.

After quarter of an hour the bus came and in just over an hour Wesley was there, standing in front of the entrance lobby of the towerblock where he and Sharon lived. He felt nervous because he didn't want to meet her. He could press the intercom and find out if anyone was in, but he didn't want to do that either. An unreasonable suspicion that she might be in there waiting for him crept over Wesley, though he hadn't said he'd be coming. On the other hand it wouldn't take a genius to work out that he would need some clean clothes.

But she had a job to go to.

He didn't press the intercom.

The lobby was empty and for once both the lifts had been repaired. He pressed both buttons and listened to the faint pneumatic whine of lift-doors closing somewhere above him. A moment later one of the lifts arrived. The doors slid open smoothly like it never broke down. It didn't even stink of piss.

There was just the faint odour of stale tobacco. He stepped inside and pressed the 14. It had been silent in the lobby and now as the lift glided upwards Wesley could hear no human sounds — no babies crying, no rows, not even the pulse of music or the hum of a vacuum cleaner. It felt like he was dreaming.

A small bell chimed and he was on the fourteenth floor. He felt as if he hadn't lived here for a long time, and that everyone he knew would be long time gone. He didn't belong here any more anyway. The man who lived here was gone forever.

He fumbled with the keys and the door handle felt quite unfamiliar as he pushed it down. But it was the door leading into his own flat. He still felt like a burglar as he closed it quietly behind him.

"Anyone in?" Pause. "Sharon?"

There was no reply of course and the sound of his voice only emphasised the stillness. He went into the living-room. All was calm and ordered there. The settee cover was smoothed, the cushions plumped up, the ashtrays empty and sparkling. It seemed like a stately home after Paul's flat, but he felt alienated from its orderliness because all traces of his having been there had been erased from it. He lay hidden in drawers.

Looking around made him realise that although it was him who had painted the ceiling and walls cream, it was she who had chosen the carpet and the suite covers. And she had chosen the colours of everything else in the flat too, even the cream he had painted. He'd had a say of course, but he hadn't had anything to say when she had asked him if it was okay, so it had all been her choice really. He looked in on the spotless red-and-white kitchen. Sitting on the dining-table was an empty Silk Cut packet, a wedding-present plate with a few crumbs of Ryvita on it and a cup with a little sickle of black coffee in the bottom. One big plate sat draining in the rack along with a knife and fork, (also wedding presents). The pedal-bin lid was slightly open. He lifted the lid and saw a litre bottle of white wine caught in the billows of the clean white binliner. He let the lid fall and went through the living-room, down the passage and into the bathroom. Already his Bics and shaving-foam had got pushed behind Sharon's nail-varnish remover and a wad of pink cotton-wool. He slid them out carefully, leaving the other things where they were. Then he glanced around the room for anything else. His large, pale-blue towel was hanging over the electric towel-rail. He pulled it off and flicked it over his shoulder.

The bedroom was hotel-tidy. Thinking what to take, Wesley was struck by how few possessions he really had. Most of his things, like the clock-radio, were really his and Sharon's. He opened the chest-of-drawers and pulled out all his socks and underpants. Most of his sports gear was at the gym. He started getting out all his most fancy clothes, wanting to show Paul how *safe* he was, and wanting to feel as good outside as he felt inside. He had bought a new suit only a month ago, double-breasted and cut like a gangster's, the material grey and shiny and all sharp angles, and a shirt and tie to go with it. The clothes he was wearing felt very shapeless and stale and he was eager to get out of them. He decided he would change into his black denim jacket, white trousers, socks, and low-cut black Italian shoes he had picked up cheap in the summer and hadn't worn much. The trousers would hug his ass but they were full at the front and had three pleats which made a nice curve from his waist to his ankles.

He unlaced the heavy boots and pulled them off, throwing each one carelessly towards the built-in wardrobe. Just being without their weight made him feel lighter and fresher. Work-boots. He wondered whether to throw them down the rubbish chute as he left, but then decided to leave them at the back of the wardrobe. He remembered forty-five pounds of his first wage-packet going on them and the overalls, and it seemed too abrupt as well as too wasteful to just throw them away. Maybe he would next week. If he came back. He deliberately avoided thinking about whether he was going to come back here at all.

He laid the jacket and trousers at right angles on the light yellow duvet cover and slowly began to undress. The overalls fell to his ankles and he stepped out of them. He started watching himself in Sharon's dressing-table mirror, admiring his stomach muscles. He pushed his chest out. The mirror cut him off at the neck so he was just body. He stepped forward and tilted it so his head was in view as well and smiled at himself. He flexed his biceps and admired their size, and the shape and line of his triceps. Then he slowly went through the posing routine he had done for the competition, only more animal this time, more graceful, because he already knew what his body was worth, what he was worth. He had seen it in Paul's eyes. And that was better than prizes and applause because when Paul had said he was beautiful he meant it in his laziness as well as in his strength. Paul had seen all of Wesley and found only beauty there.

He rubbed his eyes. They were bleary with too much sleep. He stretched and relaxed, and as he did so he realised that he had a hard-on. He looked at the outline it made under the tight fabric of his briefs and he was tempted to jerk off standing there in front of the mirror. He wondered who he would fantasise about, Sharon or Paul. But as he stared at the reflection of his own crotch he knew he wasn't even fooling himself.

Suddenly he thought that he wanted a photograph of Floyd, to keep for himself, and maybe show to Paul. He remembered there was one of him and Floyd all dressed up to go out somewhere, leaning against each other like drunks. Sharon had taken it. He pulled on a fresh tee-shirt and self-consciously looked through Sharon's bedside chest of drawers for where she kept a red plastic photograph album full of their loose snaps. It only took a moment to find. He lifted it out carefully from under some blouses and searched through it quickly, not allowing himself to get seduced by nostalgia.

He soon found what he was looking for. One corner was creased into white wrinkles but that didn't really matter. He slid the photograph out and dropped it on the bed. Looking into the drawer he saw that underneath where the album had been there was a thin gold chain he had forgotten ever owning. He fastened it around his neck and put the album back where he had found it. He could have taken a photograph of Sharon to show Paul but he didn't want to. He didn't want to threaten him.

He looked at the photograph of him and Floyd. They were both wearing tuxedos and black bow-ties. Floyd's eyes looked slightly red from the flash. It had been someone's wedding reception, Floyd's sister Gabriella maybe. Wesley had only met her a couple of times. She was five years older than Floyd and always studying. She had got a good job and after the marriage she had moved away. He hadn't known her well enough to keep in touch.

Somewhere there would be a photo of Floyd and Sharon that he, Wesley, had taken. Floyd must have kept it. Wesley sighed then, floating for a few moments in a nostalgia that was no longer painful. Then he shook his head and got dressed. Looking at the photograph, it didn't do Floyd justice. Maybe he wouldn't show it to Paul after all.

Now he was dressed up all smart, Wesley felt like he was going out for the evening, and that made him think of music and his portable stereo. He thought about what tapes he could take without pissing Sharon off. It wasn't difficult really as most of her favourites she had on record and he had made tapes of them that were just for himself anyway. His stereo sat on top of the wardrobe along with some old handbags and his blue and red sausage-bag. He lugged the stereo and the sausage-bag down. He had thought of taking the middle-sized cream suitcase, but it was part of a set and again it belonged to him and Sharon, so he left it. He wanted to take nothing that was hers. He wanted it to be a fresh start for him. A man with no past, only a future.

When he had packed all the clothes and tapes he had come for, he straightened the cover on the bed, wanting to leave it all looking untouched, as if he had never been there. Despite that desire he scribbled a note and left it by the telephone where

Sharon would be sure to find it. It read:

Picked up some clothes and my stereo
    See you
      Love,
      Wesley

It was a crappy note, but he couldn't think of anything else to say so he left it anyway.

He closed the door softly behind him. He felt that he ought to put the keys through the letterbox and finish it. But he didn't want to. For as long as he kept the keys he could go back, and that meant that what he did from now on he did because he chose to, not because he had to. And then he left the flat for the last time.

Paul and Steve began to climb the steep hill to the college, their eyes dazzled by the brittle winter sunlight. They hadn't exchanged a word since setting out from Paul's flat. The horizon fled away along perspective lines like loosed arrows and the sky seemed vast and cathedral-like, a bleached infinity after the warm dark closeness of the last few days. And Paul was the invisible centre of it all.

"He seems like a good bloke," Steve said as they climbed. Paul looked around. "Wesley, I mean."

Paul nodded. "I reckon," he replied.

"Is he, like, alright?" He caught Paul's eye. Paul looked away.

"I think so," he said. "All he needed was a break. And some sleep." He might have added, *and some dreams.* "He lost his job," he said, the words the myth that explained why there was no drink, no drugs, no mental illness even. Like Steve's old man, made redundant at forty-five, *just too sodding old* Steve said he had said with his lips wet with lager and his head rolling on his chest, before he had tried to hang himself. But he was a fat man and the washing-line had snapped or the light socket had been pulled out of the ceiling or something because of his weight and now he had a walking-stick and an aluminium hip. He drank too much for his health and his pocket and had empty eyes, and would've beaten his wife if he could have raised the stick without having to sit down. And Paul knew like you know that Steve's father hated Steve painting, would have preferred him to pound tarmac rather than paint, so he could stop mourning his lost manhood.

So Steve knew everything Wesley might feel, how far a sane man might fall while still being sane.

"That's tough," Steve said. "He got any qualifications?"

"CSEs. A couple. That's it."

They walked on in silence, eyes downcast in the white face of the sun. Steve started to laugh softly to himself, shaking his head.

"What is it?" Paul asked.

"He's got great legs," Steve replied.

Paul wanted to say *yeah* and let Steve see Wesley's legs as he saw them, smooth and curving and hard with muscle under Paul's hands and hot against his lips. But instead he said,

"You reckon?"

Steve nodded vigorously. "Is he a bodybuilder or something?" he asked.

"Yeah. Well, not a pro." I could say something about the competition, he thought. But he didn't. He wanted to talk but not to say anything. Steve began to whistle as they walked along, clothes shuffling in time with the rhythm of their feet on the pavement. Paul couldn't recognise the tune. Steve stopped whistling.

"Are you going to paint him, then?" he asked.

Paul shrugged. He hadn't given it a thought. He hadn't given painting a thought for the last few days. All that it had meant to him had unravelled and untwisted in Wesley's arms. All that he had left to paint was straight lines. Only the dry sound of the moving brush like wasps walking on paper, spreading the pigment dry over the dry cotton, the colour drawn out of the hog-bristles into the fabric like a pupil dilating unevenly until the whole canvas-frame is swallowed. Only the sensuality of it. That was all that was left. But thinking of Wesley, his face, his body, shapes carved out of shadow and floating in space, the paint gained a new meaning. *When you do a thing for so long,* he thought, *you can never let go of it. You've always got to bend it to something.*

"There's a party on this evening," Steve said. "You going to go?"

"Whose is it?" Paul asked.

"A friend of Mary's," Steve replied. "I don't know if you know her — Alison. She's an MA student, the one doing the big Rothko rip-offs in Block Two. I'll give you the address anyway. I dunno if she's got a phone, but I don't think she minds who comes. You could bring Wesley too."

Paul nodded. "Give me the address when we get in, yeah?"

And nothing had changed. The sky had been wider, but the bricks and the walls and the streaked grey plastic tiles were all just the same size and shape as they had always been. Being there again just made Paul feel stale. He felt his new-found vision fading away as he hung his greatcoat up and signed himself in on the register. It was 1.35 and his tutorial wasn't until two. He killed time lining up the canvasses and smoking a cigarette. *These are dead now* he thought, looking at the canvasses. *All dead.* But he couldn't start anything fresh until the post-mortem.

"They're great, Paul. Really going somewhere," Mick Reilly said. "I'm not sure I see the driving idea behind it, if you see what I mean — symbolist subject-matter within essentially abstract expressionist technical concerns, is a dichotomy, a philosophy, philosopho-experiential-minimalist duality of decorative dichotomy deep meaningful tongue deep going down (*Paul had stopped listening*) I mean what would you have to say if someone levelled that criticism at you?"

"Well," Paul replied reflexively, "er I think that there is a harmony there, I mean visually at least, and er, in the end that painting is about the visual." *This is crap,* he thought as his mouth flapped up and down. But the old stale words were right for the old stale images and he didn't yet have the new words for the new things he wanted to create.

He spent an hour and a bit stretching and stapling canvasses and left them leaning together like card-houses, stinking of size. Then he bundled a handful of oil-paints, linseed oil and worn brushes into a Boots bag and set off for the flat, his new visions still making a halo round his head, stained-glassing the streets.

After going for a workout, Wesley didn't feel like heading straight back to Paul's — his — flat so he wandered around the shops for a bit, looked at a sale of sports shoes. He was tempted by a pair of basketball boots but since he had no money he managed to resist the temptation. He also looked in the window of the Jobcentre and thought about how he'd be getting fifteen quid a week for the next six months if he didn't get a job. Until then, love would have to be his food. He smiled to himself for thinking that and looked down at his feet, embarrassed in the street. Crumpled by his shoe was a five-pound note. He looked around. No one was particularly coming that way so he bent down and pocketed it. With a bit of money in his pocket he could walk with a sense of purpose.

He wanted to buy Paul a present. But what would be right? Flowers and scents? They were for a woman. He had ordered a bunch of red roses from Interflora for Sharon on their first anniversary, and had them sent to the agency where she was working as a receptionist. She had cried over them, she told him, and that wasn't the sort of thing Sharon would say unless it was true. Red roses. Like the bunch she bought for Floyd the night he died. No. Flowers and scent wouldn't be right.

In the end he decided to give Paul his gold chain. He had bought it himself from a second-hand jewellers' years ago and never worn it much so it didn't have much meaning, but at least it was his to give.

He glanced at his watch. Four o'clock. Time to go home. To

really go home. He got as excited as a kid at Christmas waiting for the bus and tapped his foot restlessly for the whole journey, annoying some nurses in front of him. *She's having it in June and she's got the carrycot and pram and little baby bootees and is it going to be christened people do even if they don't believe I don't think is it will it be Steve or Mary?*

Then finally he was jumping off at the top of Paul's street and running to his building. He raced up the stairs, ran along the corridor and, seeing the padlock was off, burst into the flat. Paul stood up from where he had been bending over the fire. He was wearing skintight jeans, soft black boots that crumpled around his ankles, and a puffy black leather jacket that belted in at the waist. He looked more colourful and striking than Wesley had remembered, larger somehow, like a bud opening into a flower. Wesley dropped his bag and grabbed Paul round the waist. Paul gripped Wesley's ass and ground his crotch against Wesley's. They kissed as if they had been apart for four months, not four hours, like Wesley was a soldier, coming back from battle. He pulled his head back and smiled.

"Pleased to see me, man?"

Wesley tightened his grip and lifted Paul off his feet. Paul wrapped his legs round Wesley's waist and they kissed again. As Wesley put him down, he felt a slight tremor run the length of Paul's body.

"Didn't you think I was coming back, man?"

Paul looked down. "I thought Sharon might have been there and you might have changed your mind."

Christ christ fucking shit. What did he have to do to convince him? Cut his heart out? But he didn't want to be angry with Paul. He knew he had to respect his fear.

"Hey," he said. "That's over, yeah? It was never happening." He ran his fingers through Paul's short nappy hair, looking into his deep brown eyes, eyes trying to conceal their anxiety. "It's you I want." He kissed Paul's lips gently.

"Do you believe me?"

Paul nodded nervously, but now it was Wesley who needed

reassurance.

"Do you, man?"

Paul wanted to believe Wesley with all his heart but he had never found a word so difficult to say, because to say it was to admit that he was worth enough to inspire love in someone; to take a step forward and never look back. He didn't know if he believed in himself enough. No one had ever taken anything beautiful out of him before and even now he wanted to hold himself back from the reality of that. But if he threw his chance away now he knew that would be the end and he would be irredeemable and always live in shadow.

"I believe you," he said, certain the words sounded so fake that Wesley would want more reassurance. But he just smiled softly and said,

"I'm glad to hear it, man."

And his relief made Paul realise that he had meant it, however fake he had sounded, had meant it more than anything he had ever said. And as he realised that, the tension between them dissolved. They touched with a new delicacy now, like butterflies on flower-petals, the slightest movement revealing wings patterned with fresh feelings.

"I bought some food," Paul said. They moved apart but stayed holding hands. "I got pasta, mince, tomatoes, onions, cheese and a pepper," Paul listed. "You eat lasagne?"

Wesley nodded.

"I bought me stereo, man," he said. "I'll get it set up and we can have some music while we eat." He spoke with a little reserve in case Paul didn't really want him to make this his home, but Paul smiled and said,

"There are some screwdrivers just down there by the sofa, Wes. Help yourself."

He disappeared into the kitchen and by the time Wesley had wired the stereo in he could hear and smell onions sizzling. He put a Young Disciples of Freedom tape on and adjusted the balance. The beat flooded the flat and made him feel like dancing. He danced slowly around the room and sang along badly. When he noticed Paul's head peeping round the door, silhouetted by a bare yellow bulb, he began to move robotically, working down his body to his hips and working them more than the rest of him. Then he felt silly and embarrassed and stopped. He looked so embarrassed that Paul laughed and ducked back into the kitchen. Wesley heard him laughing in there. Then he said "Shit" and something clunked on the floor and Wesley laughed too.

About half an hour later they were eating sitting on the sofa. It had just gone six o'clock. After the lasagne was finished, Paul said,

"There's a party on this evening. D'you fancy going? It'll mostly be students, but some of them are okay." *Say yes*, he thought, *I want people to see you I want them to fancy you but you'll be mine.* "We don't have to go, yeah. I'm not that bothered."

"Let's go, man. I could do with a dance."

Paul grinned broadly. He looked at his watch. "What shall we do until then, then?"

"I don't know, man," Wesley said, swinging himself round so he was sitting astride Paul and looking into his eyes. "Maybe you could screw me again."

Chapter Ten

IT HAD BEEN raining earlier and the streets were glistening in the neon light. The air was still gauzy with moisture which they could feel on their faces and see as glitter on each other's hair. They stopped at an off-license to buy some cans of Red Stripe and a bottle of sweet white wine. Wesley was glad he had found the fiver earlier because it meant he didn't have to lean on Paul for money when he knew Paul didn't have any to spread around himself.

The house was one of a row of delapidated terraces sloping down and away from the main road. There weren't lights in many of the buildings and a few of them were boarded up. Wesley could hear the faint pulse of music as they turned down the street. He felt a slight thrill of anticipation and it seemed like a long time since he had been to a party.

The music was pounding from the blue-lit basement of a tall, narrow house about halfway down the street and within its beat Wesley heard the muffled sound of people having a good time. He and Paul climbed the frost-cracked steps to the front door. Paul pressed on the bell and hammered on the blistering wood of the door at the same time. Then he put his ear to it, listening for someone coming to answer it. He was about to hammer again when the door opened. Steve was standing there in a tuxedo, trying to look like a bouncer.

"Hallo Paul, mate," he said. He looked at Wesley and grabbed his hand and shook it. "Good to see ya."

"How're you doin', man?" Wesley asked.

"Could be worse," he replied. "Come on down."

Paul and Wesley pushed past him and went down the narrow hall to the steps to the cellar.

"Mind how you go," Steve called after them as they stumbled into the darkness. "Some burk smashed the bulb on the stairs."

There was more banging at the door behind him and Steve disappeared off to answer it. Paul and Wesley felt their way to the cellar, listening to music pulsing through the walls. It was a Talking Heads track, "Road to Nowhere". Wesley had heard it maybe a hundred times on the radio when it had been a hit, and it made him feel kind of welcome.

The small basement room was close with the heat of bodies pressed together and packed with students trying to look like real, permanent people instead of transients on their way back out to the suburbs. Wesley felt out of place. He had no job and no ace up his sleeve to pull out and transform his life with. He was what they aspired to appear to be and it made him angry. Their scruffy clothes were a masquerade of poverty: Only students dress down to go out. Only the shamefaced rich want to look poorer than they are. His trousers seemed too white for this black-and-grey crowd. He pulled a can of lager and swallowed a mouthful, let the anger pass from him. *It didn't really matter in the end; people can do anything and you can take it all if you understand why*, he thought, and they were only people after all. He turned to look at Paul, who was scanning the crowd for familiar faces. He had five gold studs in his ear and they glittered, glamorous and rich. Wesley offered him the can.

A moon-faced hippy in ripped jeans and sandals shambled past them. He was carrying a bottle of beer which he tried to open by levering the lid against the red tin frame of a fire alarm on the wall. The delicate glass shattered and a siren began to wail. The hippy looked around and, seeing Wesley was staring at him, grinned sheepishly and shambled back into the crowd. Wesley stifled an urge to hit him. He opened another can and began to drink, watching a skinny blonde girl, *perhaps it's Alison* he thought, as she forced the button back into place by jamming bits of broken wood into the frame.

He had been dancing for some time and the Crucial Brew had made him feel loose and light and almost giddy. He was dancing more slowly than the rest of the crowd; they threw themselves around like epileptics under a strobe, panicking in double time. Paul had introduced him to people who were not interested in him, and whose names he forgot the moment he heard them, and then disappeared upstairs, so he had danced. Someone offered him a joint. He drew on it. It was grass thinned out with rosemary but it still gave him a buzz. The beat of the music moved inside his chest as he skanked to a Mad Professor dub. Everyone was beginning to float a long way away from him when he felt a cool sure touch on his bicep. It was Paul, smiling and offering Wesley a swig from a bottle of brown ale. Wesley didn't really want any, but he took the bottle because he knew Paul had been drinking from it. As he lifted it to his lips he looked into Paul's eyes and wondered what he had done to deserve his luck. He was the lucky one here, he thought, not the rest of them.

He lowered the bottle and wiped his mouth with the back of his hand. Then he reached out and gripped Paul round the waist and drew him to him, kissed him on the lips. Paul pulled back sharply out of Wesley's arms, his face a mixture of shock and anger. He looked like he was going to say something, but then he turned and pushed his way through the close-packed dancers, away from Wesley. *No no no no no.* In a moment everything was slipping away from him. *What am I doing? What am I doing?* Too much drinks and drugs and rhythm and drink and he let the bottle fall from his nerveless fingers. It broke without a sound in the silence of the noise. *No no no.* His mouth was dry and stale. *Fuck, fuck* he said in his head perhaps out loud even as he stood there being jostled no longer moving in time with the music, no longer moving at all. He was suddenly afraid that he had thrown Paul away, and he felt broken inside, like Judas felt maybe, but he was his own Judas and there was no silver however stained.

He slid through the crowd, not wanting to touch or be touched or leave any trace of his presence, and ran up the stairs. Paul wouldn't have just gone, he thought, when he saw the hall was empty, so he climbed up to the first floor, steadying himself slightly on the smooth wooden bole of the bannister. All the rooms on that floor were locked and dark. He looked up at the steps to the second floor. Paul was sitting at the top of them, empty beer-can in hand, staring into dim and empty space. The foot of the stairs seemed like a threshold and so Wesley asked,

"Can I come up, man?"

Paul didn't reply. He just lifted the can to his mouth and tipped his head back until he was sure it was empty. Then he put the can down and went back to staring into space. Wesley climbed the stairs towards him as quietly as a cat and as slowly as a kid playing "What time is it please, Mister Wolf?" When he reached the top step he turned and sat down on it, squeezing in next to Paul, who grudgingly made room for him. He looked around at Paul three-quarters on until he was sure that Paul was having to work hard to avoid making eye-contact with him. Then Paul spoke. His voice was thick.

"I didn't go through it all just for more . . . shit. You know?" He looked at Wesley and there was hurt in his eyes.

"All that shit," he continued, "I mean, we're two guys who are lovers, right? You know it and I know it and it's great and we don't need any words for it. But you know what they would call us? I don't need that shit. I don't — " he stopped to catch his breath.

Wesley slowly put his strong, muscular arms around Paul's body which seemed fragile and he seemed as vulnerable as a little kid right now and hugged him. Paul twisted round and held Wesley. Tears ran freely down his face and he started to shake. Wesley held him close until he was still again, and then released him. He reached up and touched Paul's cheek gently with his knuckles, blearing a quicksilver skein.

"Tears," he said, and there was wonder in his voice, his eyes shining and moist too. He looked down shyly and reached up and undid the thin gold chain round his neck and put it around Paul's. Paul swallowed and said, "Thanks, man."

There was a pause. Then: "Look, man," Wesley said. "D'you think they're better'n us?"

"No," Paul whispered.

"And you never been called names for no reason in your life?"

"Course I have."

"But you just carried on, yeah?" Wesley squeezed Paul's shoulders. "Did bein' called a name make you different inside, man?"

"No. Just angry. Sometimes. Sometimes nothing. But, no."

"Exactly, yeah? So it ain't gonna change you now, ennit?"

"I guess not," Paul replied, looking down.

"*Believe* it, man. Cos if I want to kiss you, if I want to hold you, right? I'm not gonna just keep myself to myself just cos a some assholes and their tiny minds, yeah? And if they're going to think worse of you cos you kissed me, then fuck 'em, man, they ain't worth knowing. And me, I ain't gonna be stained by their dirty minds, and if you are then what's the point, man? What's the fuckin' point?"

He stood up then, ready to go, ready to walk out on it all. Paul grabbed his hand. His nails bit into Wesley's palm.

"Don't go." His voice was urgent. "Don't leave me."

"I won't leave you, man, not unless you want to walk in shame."

Because Wesley remembered what Mikey had said, that a man has to be proud of his skin and his life and what he is and never apologise and always say Defiance to Babylon and downpression and there was no Sodom no Gomorrah what he was what Paul was came from Africa with all the brothers in the hold. And he looked in Paul's eyes and knew Paul understood it all, and that he felt no shame.

"You want to go home, baby?" he asked gently.

Paul nodded. They walked down the stairs holding hands,

only letting go when they reached the hall, and left without saying goodbye.

It was gone two o'clock and the sky was very clear, and as crowded with stars as if there was no atmosphere. And in the middle of the blue and orange-lit street Paul kissed Wesley and for a minute they stood there, lost in each other, brought to their senses only by the coldness of the night air, surrounded still by the colour and brightness of the butterfly kiss, their lips the wings, making midsummer in January.

They crossed over to the main road, bumping shoulders as they walked, breathing air that was no longer empty but filled with a thousand intoxicating elements. The neon lights blossomed over Wesley's tired eyes. A police car glided past them as noiselessly as a shark. *Don't stop* Wesley thought. It moved on past them not changing speed and was swept away over a dual carriageway.

Now they were walking behind a row of shops. The smell of burnt fat floated in the air and newspapers collapsed into putrefaction under their feet. Their hands brushed together as they turned the corner into a long alley. The tops of the brick walls were toothed by shards of broken glass that glistened in the starlight. A buzzing, flickering streetlamp twenty feet ahead of them haloed three white youths standing there.

One of them, a punk with blond cropped hair, ripped camouflage jeans and thick crepes, was pissing against the bricks. He rested his forehead on the wall, a cigarette hanging out of his mouth, his eyes closed. The others were leaning there, waiting for him to finish. One wore an expensive blue suit, the other jeans and a black leather jacket. The one in the suit dangled an empty bottle of scotch from one hand. They all looked up when Paul and Wesley came round the corner. The punk, the one who had been pissing, zipped up clumsily and shouted,

"Fuckin' queers, what d'you think you're fuckin' lookin' at? Black bastards!"

He started to move towards them, his mates just behind him, his voice raping the night. The one in the suit scraped the bottle along the wall until it smashed so he was left with a jagged bottleneck in his hand. He was short and stocky.

"Fucking niggers. What're you looking at?" The punk's voice was slurred and he stank of drink.

Wesley said, "Give over mate, we ain't lookin' for any."

The punk's neck was a mass of twisted white cords, his face twisted up too. "Fuckin' niggers," he repeated. "Fuckin' queers."

He reached out as it he was going to touch Wesley's hair. Wesley punched him hard in the face (*like Floyd taught me*) and felt the youth's nose spread out against his fist. The punk fell flat on his back and didn't try to get up, blood pouring out of his nose and onto the ground. It looked good. The kid in the suit dropped the bottleneck. He looked shocked.

"Sorry mate," he said, his voice weak, suddenly sober. "He didn't mean nothin' by it. Honest. Look, come out for a drink with us sometime. Look," his voice was supplicating.

"Yeah," Wesley said, rubbing his knuckles.

The one in the leather jacket was busy propping up his bleeding friend. Paul and Wesley stepped over his legs. The kid in the suit was saying, "See you around, then?" as they turned out of the alley onto a main street. And the city seemed like a movie-set, and they were the stars, Rogers and Astaire spinning across Busby Berkely dual carriageways and before diamond skyscrapers, breathless on love and adrenalin.

"Were you scared?" Paul asked as they looked out over the glittering view. Wesley didn't answer straight away. Then he said,

"Yeah. A bit. But it was more like anger, man. I thought, fuck this, I don't need it. *We* don't need it. I mean, man, I don't like trouble, but sometimes, sometimes you got to fight." Then he stopped talking because the words weren't right. He thought of Mikey again, his mane of dreadlocks bouncing as he spoke, saying how everything is politics, every act is a political act, every oppression something to fight, and, although not yet clearly, he saw that that was true. He couldn't explain it; he didn't have the words yet. But he knew that it was true.

"You think it's gonna work, then, man, me and you?" he asked Paul. And Paul trusted him enough to say,

"I don't know."

"You want me in there with you?" Wesley pushed.

"You got somewhere you'd rather be staying?"

"No."

"I know love doesn't make everything alright," Paul said. "But — "

"Yeah," Wesley said. "It makes it worth tryin', don't it?"

"Yeah."

"Saying 'I love you' to another guy is weird, man," Wesley said. "It feels weird."

"Is it weird?" Paul asked softly.

"No," Wesley said, after thinking about it for a while. "Just different." Then: "We gonna do this one day at a time?" he asked.

"One day at a time," Paul replied, smiling.

They reached the crossroads at the top of Paul's street. Wesley felt full of future possibilities. He could take any road and know he was going somewhere. But right now there was only one road he wanted to take. They stood in silence there for a while, each deep in thought, both a little afraid. Then Wesley broke the silence.

"I'm tired," he said. And put his arm around Paul's shoulders. "What a fuckin' night, man. Let's get home."

They tumbled naked into bed, shivering warmth into the cold, white sheets. Wesley reached over and put the lamp out and they lay in the darkness holding each other, their hearts beating in perfect time.

However it ends now, Paul thought, *I know that I have been loved.*

* * * * *

"You fi tell me or me have to guess?" Sarah asked, after she and Sharon had sat in silence for over a minute over the tea-things.

"I mean, is *you* invite *me* for tea, nuh?" She grinned, showing a gold tooth.

"Yeah, I'm sorry, girl," Sharon said, thinking, *how can I put this into words when everything I want to say is what's oblique, is nuance?* "I met Wesley for lunch today." *You have to start somewhere.* And Sarah'll have guessed that much of it anyway.

"You fight?"

"No. No, we didn't fight or argue or anything."

"Is sometimes better to fight, you know. Finish ting."

"I — " but she still didn't know how to say what she needed to say. "He brought a friend with him."

"A lady friend?"

"No." Sharon didn't want to get into that, into Paul now. She turned back to an earlier train of thought. "There wouldn't have been any point in fighting, I mean, there's nothing to fight over." *Except the dead*, she thought. But she knew, had always known, that that fight was over too. "Maybe a lot of things make sense now."

"So *someting* did actually happen, then?" Sarah asked, patiently but persistently, too good a friend to let Sharon ease herself off the hook.

"Yes. No." Seeing Sarah's expression turning sour, Sharon gripped her hands in hers. "Look, if I try to explain, will you try to understand?"

"Course I will, gal. So tell me, nuh?"

Sharon looked down and tried to put her thoughts in order. "Wesley and me split up because we didn't have anything in common anymore. You know? I mean" — she looked up at Sarah — "he'll always be like family, yeah, but we'd stopped sharing anything. Except the past. And I'm sick of the past." *Floyd and me and Wesley out on the town, with gold on our skins and diamonds in our hair.* "It's dead."

They were drinking tea out of the best bone china, midnight-blue cups with gold lips and flared gold handles floating on flat crimson saucers. Sharon had needed the sense of event and ritual the cups implied. It had only been as she started to pull the crisp, clean balls of crepe paper from the delicate globes that she had managed to sink into the cool, meditative state of mind she felt she needed.

So, Wesley had called her the night before and asked her to meet him for lunch and she'd thought, *okay, why not, there's no reason not to,* even though she'd thought there had been a particular tenseness in his voice too.

They had arranged to meet in a little Mexican restaurant she hadn't been to for maybe six years, not too far away from where she was working. It was cheap and unpretentious, and the food was better than Taco Bell's. It had been raining earlier that day, and now the white November sunlight was turning the wet streets silver, dazzling her eyes.

Wesley was already there, sitting facing the door, looking groomed and shaved and handsome and nervous. Next to him sat a slim young black man with smoky, feline eyes and a pencil stuck through the peak of his hair. He was wearing a voluminous army trenchcoat. Sharon knew she had never met him before.

Wesley stood awkwardly and lent over the table to kiss Sharon lightly on the lips. The young man watched the moment of contact intently.

"This is Paul," Wesley said, squeezing Paul's shoulder. "And this is Sharon." Paul half-rose and they shook hands. He smiled a very slight smile, and Sharon felt the tiniest shiver as their eyes met.

The substance of the meal, their conversation, was non-existent; superficial, easy-going chat. Once she saw Wesley look down at her hand and see that she no longer wore his ring. It was no more than the truth, but still she covered that nakedness with her other hand. And that was the real substance of the meal, the periphery. Something about the way Paul leaned in towards Wesley whenever he spoke to her, and the way Wesley gripped the back of Paul's chair whenever he was nervous. Something about the frequent flicker of looks between them that had made her feel edgy at first, imagining drunken disclosures of sexual positions or humiliating throw-away lines, but when she'd let go of her self-centredness it seemed to signify something else.

And now, funnily, she knew what she thought it was. Funnily, because at the time she hadn't seen it at all. Not consciously, at least.

She gulped in a big breath. "I think they're lovers," she said. Then she held her breath and waited for Sarah's reaction, watching her face bug-eyed.

"Yes," Sarah said, after a pause. Outside the rain was starting to beat on the windows again, although the sky was still bright. Sharon crashed her delicate cup into its saucer.

"Doesn't *anything* ever surprise you, girl?" she said, irritably. She felt disturbed enough, without being told that her life taking a tumble like this was so run-of-the-mill that it wasn't even good enough fi labrish pon.

"Me a surprise as you when Wesley tell me it himself."

"When?" Sharon asked, her face set.

"'Im come by the other day," Sarah said placidly.

"You bitch," Sharon said. "You just sat there and let me make a complete fucking idiot of myself. Plus, you knew what was going on and you didn't even *tell* me. I can't believe you could do that. I mean, Christ, Sarah, I was *married* to the guy, you know?"

"A sorry," Sarah said. "'Im only tell me yesterday, you know? Me na know what to do or say neither. So when you invite me come see you today, me did think, See what Sharon have to say. Hold me tongue till then." She looked at Sharon gently. Sharon looked down into her lap.

"Yeah, I'm sorry too," she said quietly. Then: "So what did he say?"

"That 'im 'ave someone special in 'im life," Sarah said softly.

And she remembered that that was almost all he'd said, that he would have gone without saying anything else except he was so full of words that he hadn't been able to stop them skittering out.

212

"His name's Paul," he had said, almost by mistake. And that was when Sarah had been surprised and, for once, struck dumb.

"The bwai you stayin' with?" she'd finally asked.

"Yeah." He had jumped up out of his chair, too full of energy to stay seated.

"And is workin' out okay?" she asked, stalling while she thought.

"It ain't easy, man. I mean, I'm afraid almost every day, you know? But there weren't nothin' else I could've done. And so far it's workin' out, yeah."

"So when you turn — " she started.

"It ain't *like* that, man," Wesley gestured emphatically. "It ain't like, is you a battyman or shit. It's like, do you love someone. And I do. And I don't reckon it should matter if they're a man or a woman. I love a man, and that's givin' me shit, and it's gonna give me shit. But you can't tell your heart what to do, man. You know?"

And Sarah had known and had nodded. "What about Sharon?" she had asked.

"We both loved someone else, the same guy. I guess we saw that love in each other, yeah? But he was dead, and that made it a fading thing, you know? A fading thing."

He had gone quiet then, looked down at his watch, kissed his teeth and told her he had to be going. She'd called to him at the door,

"What if people don't accept?"

He'd reacted aggressively. "I got no choice, man. It's like the colour a me skin. I ain't gonna bleach meself cos some people don't accept it. And I ain't gonna bleach the rest of me life just cos some people don't accept that." In his voice there had been defiance, fear and, she had really believed, bravery.

And in her heart she had wished him well.

"Well, was that all he said?" Sharon asked, bringing Sarah back abruptly. "And who this person was, yeah?"

Sarah nodded.

Sharon pushed a hand through her hair irritably. "But he loved *me*."

"Yes. And now 'im love someone else."

"It isn't that simple, Sarah."

"Maybe it *is*," Sarah replied. "All a them ideas 'bout 'straight' and 'gay' won't help you, you know, gal. Them just keep you up at night, wonderin' 'im was really *this*, it was really *that*. When the only answer is, 'im someone who did love you, an' now 'im love someone else."

Sharon furrowed her brow. Maybe Sarah was right. Maybe it just didn't matter. Especially since she had left Wesley as much as he had left her. She didn't have to let it touch her at all. Except --

"Sarah," Sharon said thoughtfully and apprehensively. "Did Floyd and Wesley ever — I mean, you know. Did they . . . ?" She knew she wouldn't find the nerve to finish what she was trying to say, so she let the words tail off. They weren't really necessary anyway. For a reason she couldn't explain, her gut clenched painfully with anxiety, and that too made speaking difficult. Then she understood that she couldn't bear to have all her past torn apart and thrown down. Not like that.

"Did they?"

"No," Sarah said, taking Sharon's hands again and squeezing them. "Them did love each other a great deal. But, no."

And Sharon was embarrassed to find herself crying with relief.

* * * * *

Wesley was woken in the morning by birdsong. Flocks of starlings wheeled in the sky and gathered on the roof of the building. It gave him a feeling of being in the country, or what he thought it would be like; he had never been in the country. He stretched his arms out and folded them behind his head. The room was lit with the pale yellow glow of sunlight filtering through the thin curtains. He looked over at the man lying next to him and felt at peace.

He and Paul had been living together for fourteen months now and Wesley was happier than he had ever been. There had been fights of course, but neither of them had thrown in the towel or even come close to it, and the fights were always a step forward, getting them to know each other a little better, making them accept more from each other. And they gave more too:

Like Wesley letting Paul draw him — posing every evening for a week until Paul had filled a pad with colourful sketches. He had enjoyed modelling for them, stripped to his underpants and sprawled across the sofa, sometimes teasing Paul by getting a hard-on when Paul was trying to concentrate. Paul had a lot of self-discipline, though — he only gave in twice in three days. Apart from that, their figure-drawing sessions were very professional, and the work Paul did was strong and sensual and attractive. Wesley took one of the sketches and kept it, and Paul took the rest in to college.

Like Wesley taking Paul to the gym with him and showing him how to use the weights and multigym. And although it would never be the faith for him that it was for Wesley (because his art was that, his faith and his love), Paul did find something new was being expressed in him and carried on going, three times a week, shaping up nicely and growing in understanding.

Like the paintings Paul and Wesley had done together, Wesley starting and saying what was going to be where to start with and painting it as well as he could, and Paul changing bits and finishing it and making things right, pictures of friends, boxers, sex, butterflies and birds of paradise, all caught up in a jungle of dreams, Paul's dreams and Wesley's dreams, riotous and luxuriant. The finished paintings looked strangely African, and they were bright and colourful. Wesley loved painting them, and those times when he was squatting there with Paul stroking the colour onto the canvas or scrubbing or splattering it, those were some of their best, their closest times. Sometimes they painted themselves even, as warriors, dancers or magicians. The new paintings slowly covered the walls of the flat. Steve came around to see them one day just as Paul and Wesley were hanging the most recent of them, fifteen foot by eight, old sheets stretched on stolen wood.

"What you two been doing," Steve said, "it's magic. Real magic."

Wesley and Sharon had separated permanently by then, neither of them giving reasons, neither of them needing to, both understanding that they had to get free of the past, that they were too much of the past to each other to bear each other. He let her keep the flat and furniture, wanting none of it for himself. She had met Paul just that one time, when they had gone for the meal, the three of them, but she didn't guess, he reckoned. Or, more likely, she probably did guess, but he didn't think she did. But he didn't know. Maybe Sarah had told her by now, anyway.

His sister Trish came to the flat and guessed immediately. Seeing her after almost eight months and in a new, smart outfit and with her hair gleaming and tied back, he realised for the first time that she was a woman now, not the child or smart-ass adolescent he had lived with, but a woman, with her own life and her own wisdom. When Paul had left to go into college for the afternoon she put down her mug of coffee and looked at Wesley and said,

"He's nice, Paul."

Wesley nodded.

"You're not using him are you, Wes?"

"I love him, Trish," Wesley said. It was surprisingly easy to say that to her. "I'd rather cut off one of me arms than hurt him, you know?"

She smiled and nodded. "He loves you a lot for sure."

"You can tell, girl?"

"I can tell, boy. It shines out of him. Like the light from a star. You're lucky, you know that, Wesley?"

216

"I know, Trish."

And they who had never been that close were brought closer by that knowledge, that knowledge of love.

Recent fiction from The Gay Men's Press:

Steven Corbin
FRAGMENTS THAT REMAIN

"It's one thing to be called a nigger by a stranger. Quite another when you're sleeping with him."

Skylar Whyte's success doesn't come easy, especially for a black American — a movie actor with a career and a lover. Yet despite all his triumphs he is inwardly tormented, not just by the racism he still encounters in daily life, but by memories of a bullying father himself destroyed by white society.

Steven Corbin shows a strength and conviction in depicting both the horrors and the joys of gay life for black Americans today. He is the author of *No Easy Place to Be*, and his short fiction has appeared in GMP's *More Like Minds*.

" . . . impressively focused and purposeful"
— *Times Literary Supplement*

"Writen with visceral conviction, *Fragments That Remain* is a powerful, assured novel" — *Gay Times*

ISBN 0 85449 186 4
UK £8.95 ex-USA AUS $24.95

Robert Farrar
STATE OF INDEPENDENCE

"The story of how I lost that which can never be regained — my innocence — has amused many a dinner party of bright young same-sexers in the Hammersmith and Shepherds Bush neck of the woods."

Fresh from the reclusion of the Home Counties, the impressionable Lenny relates his own dizzying introduction to London's energetic gay scene, cynically observing the sexual exploits of others while secretly pining away for an unrequited love. Submerged in the hedonistic nightlife and exhausting antics of his flatmates, Lenny finds a place for himself that lies somewhere between the oppression of his parents' religion and the alienation of the discos.

State of Independence captures the humour and chaos of young gay London while subtly evoking an insight into the contemporary scene rarely found in first novels.

"It's zippy, it's fresh, it's now" — *Boyz*

"Farrar writes an extremely funny, and at its end, complex novel"
— *Gay Scotland*

ISBN 0 85449 194 5
UK £6.95   US $12.95   AUS $19.95

Martin Forman
A SENSE OF LOSS

This collection of fifteen short stories displays a counterpoint of different voices, each with a ring of authenticity. Some reflect the shifting kaleidoscope of gay reality in Britain today: the sexual compulsion of "Room With No View", the high-energy rhythm of "Discotheque", or the cynical manipulation of "Simon's Dinner Party". Others take us to wider horizons — to Brazil, and off into landscapes of allegory and myth. Finally, in the masterful title story, we hear the voice of Thomas Mann's silent Tadzio as he relates his encounter in Venice with the writer Aschenbach.

Martin Foreman has created a cast of recognizable characters who are passionately searching for something abstract and ineffable. Their intersecting journeys leave a tapestry that maps the very essence of gay experience.

"Literate and dignified, this is a deeply felt collection"
— *Times Literary Supplement*

"Foreman's prose is finely worked and capable of communicating a bewildering array of emotions" — *HIM*

ISBN 0 85449 185 6
UK £6.95   US $12.95   AUS $19.95

Michael Schmidt
THE COLONIST

In the tropical Mexican town of San Jacinto, an English boy grows u
in an isolated household, on a "Green Island" amid the arid countrsid
His parents are a distant presence, and he is looked after by th
housekeeper Doña Constanza. His only friend is the gardener's sc
Chayo, a boy his own age who becomes a virtual brother. Against th
growing resistance of his parents, he teaches Chayo to read, an
imbibes from him in turn the mysteries of Mexican culture. As the tw
grow into adolescence, their social backgrounds conspire to pull the
apart, and their emotional entanglement spirals towards a devastatin
dénouement.

"Can be ranked with Golding's *Lord of the Flies*" — *Critical Quarterl*

"Will reach legendary and classic status. . . . As near perfection as yo
can get" — *Financial Times*

ISBN 0 85449 187 2
UK £6.95   US $10.95   AUS $17.95

GMP books can be ordered from any bookshop in the UK, and from specialised bookshops overseas. If you prefer to order by mail, please send full retail price plus £2.00 for postage and packing to:

GMP Publishers Ltd (GB),
P O Box 247, London N17 9QR.

For payment by Access/Eurocard/Mastercard/American Express/Visa, please give number and signature.
A comprehensive mail-order catalogue is also available.

In North America order from Alyson Publications Inc.,
40 Plympton St, Boston, MA 02118, USA.
(American Express not accepted)

In Australia order from Bulldog Books,
P O Box 155, Broadway, NSW 2007, Australia.

Name and Address in block letters please:

Name

Address